Visions in Blood

OF BLOOD AND DREAMS
BOOK TWO

KIM ALLRED

STORM COAST PUBLISHING, LLC

VISIONS IN BLOOD
Of Blood and Dreams, Book 2
KIM ALLRED
Published by Storm Coast Publishing, LLC
Copyright © 2022 by Kim Allred

Print edition September 2022
ISBN 978-1-953832-18-4

Three things cannot be long hidden: the sun, the moon, and the truth.

Buddha

To all of us who don't conform to the norm.
No one has power over us.

Chapter One

THE GYM MAT raced toward me, or rather, I hurdled toward it. I curled into a ball just in time to miss planting my face into the floor, then sprang to my feet as I came out of the roll. When I turned to face my adversary, I brought my arms up in a defensive posture, waiting for her next move.

Simone prowled the edges of the mat, and if she'd been a shifter, she would have been a panther. Her full-length leotard accentuated her long, lean legs and toned upper arms. Regal and deadly. She never took her eyes from me, and I refused to lower mine. I caught her grim smile. A predator sizing up its prey. Prey who didn't know it was done for. I never was overly bright.

When her fangs lowered to caress her bottom lip, I sprang. But not in her direction. I wasn't crazy.

I hit the climbing wall a quarter of the way up and clambered to the top like a spider evading a shoe, crossing as I ascended, heading for the rope. As soon as I grabbed it, I pushed off, allowing my body to undulate and pick up momentum. As I swung toward the multi-colored rings painted on the floor, I took a second to glance back to Simone, who waited to see where I'd land.

Grinning, I prepared to release the rope to drop onto my mark and swallowed a scream when I let go. Sergi, who hadn't been there a second ago, was six inches from where I landed. When I hit the floor, he swept my feet out from under me and made a stabbing motion toward my neck, signifying he could have ripped my throat out.

"That's cheating." I rubbed my knee, which had hit at an odd angle and would probably require an ice pack.

"You never take your eyes off your mark. This isn't an amusement park." Sergi shook his head and marched to the only bench in the ballroom-sized gym. He picked up a towel that he threw over his shoulder. "I taught you better than that. Devon taught you better than that."

"Our little Cressa spent too much time grinning like a young bride after her first plucking." Simone's stoic expression was always hard to read. I could usually tell when she was joking, but I wasn't so sure this time.

"My first plucking? I think you're showing your age." I crawled on my hands and knees before getting my legs under me, not confident they'd hold my weight before giving in. Sergi's knockdown had been harder than necessary.

"My age isn't the issue. Your focus is. A typical failing of youth." She picked up a bright red caftan and threw it on. "We'll review the meditation techniques for the next couple of days, then try this exercise again."

I groaned but offered no further complaints. I'd just end up with more days of meditation. Something I was already well-versed with after years of working with a previous mentor. As usual, my education wasn't up to snuff for Simone's standards.

"You have time for a light lunch before your session with Anna?"

I added an eye roll to the groan as I followed her out. "Why did her sessions get moved to right after lunch? You know that's a human's worst time for learning."

"Exactly. Which is why you must practice remaining alert

through all your training sessions. Many assignments will require hours of waiting. You can't become distracted."

"I'm a thief. I'm somewhat familiar with that part of the job role."

"Yet, Anna reports you retain little of what she teaches you."

"Maybe she should teach me mission-critical information instead of how many forks go with a particular place setting or whether a dress would look better with a belt."

"Blood Wards are expected to know these things."

"But I'm only pretending to be a Blood Ward. I need to know enough for light conversations, not some exam."

"You never know when someone will be watching. Questioning."

This argument wouldn't get me out of Anna's lectures, but I couldn't stop whining. There had to be a balance somewhere. "I didn't realize Blood Wards were trained so extensively. How long is the internship before a Blood Ward is ready to be turned?"

"Three years."

I stopped. "You meant months, right?"

Simone turned and gave me one of her intimidating glares. It would have terrified me a week ago, but between training sessions and periods of friendly chats, I usually only worried when she dropped her fangs.

"I always say what I mean." Her tone held an edge that, even without fangs, I took seriously.

"Of course. I didn't mean to doubt you. But if it takes years to train a Blood Ward, why is Anna cramming like I'm taking SATs next week."

Her glare didn't waver. "I don't know what that means, but I see your point. Perhaps you should ask her yourself."

Then she increased her pace, and I took that as my signal that our conversation was over. After the last mission where I'd fallen out the two-story window, everyone had been given a couple of days off. And they had all returned with improved attitudes—

which lasted one day. The tension had increased exponentially since then. That was four days ago.

I hadn't seen Devon since we'd made a new deal. My debt would be cleared by assisting with his mission to remove his censure from the vampire Council. If we succeeded, I'd earn back half of my debt as a bonus. A sweet deal—assuming I survived.

Lucas, the more easygoing of Devon's inner circle, was away on assignment. Simone spent half her time at the mansion. The rest of her time was spent at Oasis, Devon's hidden residence, where she managed the estate and several of his businesses. Besides not being fond of humans, her fluctuating mood stemmed from being away from her domain.

Sergi managed security and intelligence and was, by nature of his job, serious, deadly, and not much of a talker. Out of everybody, he was probably the least affected by the growing tension. Then there was Anna. The sole human of the group. We'd gotten along well initially, but she took her role as an instructor too seriously, and the many times I invited her to shopping trips or quiet time in the pool, she always had an excuse.

If I bothered to analyze my own emotions, I'd have to admit to being more cranky than usual. Ginger's week-long vacation with her mother in Seattle was nearly over, and I worried about my best friend going back to our apartment alone. My stepfather, Christopher, still searched for whatever he thought I'd stolen. He'd been so positive I'd taken something of value from him that he'd harassed Ginger and ransacked our apartment.

The bottom line—I was lonely. Devon hadn't shared what came next in the mission, and the result was days of the same boring routine. The erotic dreams we'd shared had stopped. The last one had been the day of the ball. It had started like the others, intimate moments with Devon until it turned into a nightmare— the premonition of my fall through the second-story window. A fall that should have killed me if Devon hadn't shared some of his blood with me.

I shook my head and closed the bedroom door, stripping as I headed for the shower, dropping clothes on the floor along the way. When I traipsed down to the dining room, I was surprised to find Simone waiting for me.

"I thought you were on your way to Oasis." I sat across from her, our salads already served.

Simone, dressed in a purple bodysuit and caftan that matched her lavender-dyed hair, looked amazing. I fingered the edges of my locks, giving consideration to becoming a redhead.

"I'll head back this afternoon. Sergi wants to review upgraded security measures."

I glanced at the place settings, but only two had been prepared. "He's not joining us?" No one had time for shared meals anymore.

"He had a meeting. Besides, the two of us haven't had time to talk." She dribbled balsamic dressing over her greens and gave me a quick glance. "I imagine this week has been a struggle for you."

"I'm not used to just sitting around waiting for the next job."

"Is Pandora the type of thief to plan them ahead of time?"

I played with the salad, pushed it aside, and tasted the soup. Butternut squash with something spicy added. Her use of my street name made me wonder if she saw me as two individual people—the thief and Devon's instrument of revenge. "Not really. It's too stressful. And it's not easy to get other crews to plan that far ahead, not unless it's a particularly complex job. But I don't wait for someone to ask me to join. Not that it doesn't happen. Harlow called me often with a job, but they weren't always a good fit for my talents. I prefer to search for my own and then determine which crew would be the best fit."

"A woman who takes charge. I should have known." She sat back and grinned. "It's not the spare time on your hands that annoys you. You don't like being left out."

I buttered a roll then dunked it in the soup before taking a bite, refusing to look at her. She knew how much the inactivity was bothering me, but I wasn't going to show any weakness in front of her. It shouldn't have been a surprise that I itched to do something more productive. Anything to avoid routine. I hated routine.

"Finish up. We have time for the target range before your afternoon class with Anna." Her grin seemed at odds with her raised eyebrows, her caftan pushed back, fists planted firmly on her narrow hips. She should be on a catwalk somewhere, dozens of flashes going off as she strode in front of the fashion elitists. It didn't seem right she could wipe the floor with me.

I scowled in response, pushed my bowl away, and faced her, incapable of doing anything other than mimic her pose with hands on hips and chin lifted in acceptance of her challenge. "Are you suggesting I might have some aggression to resolve?"

She released the tips of her fangs. "Sergi procured a supply of silver bullets, but I'm not convinced you're worthy of them. I hear your aim is as appalling as your martial arts moves."

"Those are fighting words."

"As if you'll fare any better with that tactic."

Not able to disagree, I turned and headed for the shooting range located in the basement. Simone, as in everything she did, was far beyond my skill level with a handgun, and after taking a beating in accuracy and distance, I skulked back upstairs.

I made my way to a small room on the first floor that Anna had turned into a quasi-classroom.

Until now, her training had been in the dining room, teaching me how to use the multiple place settings for various vamp events, or in my room, reviewing fashion etiquette with the clothes and accessories Devon had purchased for me. After I survived those mind-numbing lessons, she was finally going to share the secrets of vamps. But when I opened the door and found a table filled with textbooks the size of boulders, I began to back up—right into Anna, who struggled with two more books that had to weigh twenty pounds each.

"There you are." Anna pushed me into the room and kicked

the door shut with her foot. "Letty will be here soon with the coffee service. I know how difficult it is to delve through books in the afternoon. I'm sorry I wasn't able to join you for lunch, but I had a devil of a time locating these." She dropped the books on the desk with a resounding thud. "It's really annoying when people don't return books to the spot where they found them."

She ran a loving hand over them before turning to a gigantic whiteboard mounted on the wall. "If you take a seat, we can get started on the origins of the vampire Houses. We'll have two hours every day, but even with that, it will take some time to get through the material." She continued writing on the board, making columns and writing names in her tiny scrawl.

I stared at the table and the stack of pens, notepads, and folders. Enough supplies for a class of ten people. I cringed. Should I have brought an apple for the teacher? It was one thing to go through etiquette and fashion to blend in with the aristocrats, but I'd left classroom studies in high school and had no desire to return to it. If she was expecting me to write copious notes to fill all those empty pages, I needed to say something now, but the diminutive wannabe vamp was more intimidating than she should be.

I glanced at the title of the book she'd placed on the table next to the notepads. It was written in Latin. I wasn't without some education and had graduated school with a perfect GPA, but college hadn't been for me. I opened the book to the first of what had to be over a thousand pages, thankful they weren't numbered, which somehow would have made it worse. The title from the cover was repeated on the first page, but underneath the fluid script were the barely readable words—Houses of the Vampire. As I flipped through the pages, sweat broke out on my forehead. The type was tinier than Anna's writing.

"We're not going through this entire book, right?" I crossed my fingers in case it helped.

"Of course. The Houses can be confusing, so it helps to start from the beginning."

"This could take months."

Her tinkling laughter sparked involuntary shivers down my spine. I should probably consider myself grateful there wasn't a chalkboard in the room, though her laugh was growing similar to her nails running across one.

Think, Cressa. This had to be stopped now before I was lulled into a coma.

"You know I'm not actually a Blood Ward, right?"

She stopped writing what appeared to be last names across the top of the board. She didn't turn around and only paused for a few seconds. "Of course. We can always speed this up by working three hours a day, but Devon will need to approve that. I know he has additional sessions planned for the afternoon."

I flipped through the pages. The first few chapters discussed vampires from three thousand years ago. Good grief. "I'm here to train for a specific mission. I'm not sure how understanding the Houses before the birth of Jesus will help prepare me for that."

"Are you questioning my ability to know what to teach you?" She'd turned toward me, and I recognized the stubborn set of her jaw.

This required careful treading, and I continued to flip through the tome as I considered a response. I didn't want to ruffle her feathers. We'd already had a rough start, and this could spiral out of control quickly. She was a sensitive person who, for a human, hadn't spent much time among her own species.

I flipped back to the front of the book and ran a finger down a listing of chapters, hoping for inspiration that would get me out of this slow torture. After scrolling through the first page, it was apparent the book was laid out by the names of Houses, but not alphabetically. Perhaps when they were first created? That made sense. My heart rate increased as I searched for the obvious. I found it on the third page. A chapter that covered four Houses: Aramburu, Renaud, Trelane, and Venizi.

I dropped into a chair. Devon and Lorenzo Venizi's Houses

had been created at the same time. Had they been enemies from the beginning or amiable, and the rift began later? If I understood what had made them enemies, maybe I could predict their encounters, weave around them, and best case, find more evidence that Devon needed to restore his Council seat. With that knowledge, I might stumble upon other valuable information when he sent me on an assignment. He couldn't be mad at that.

"I wouldn't think to question your knowledge on vampires." Although I'd mentally done that the previous week. Maybe I could redirect her enthusiasm to match my own. "It's just that I don't think Devon expects this mission to last months."

Her mouth opened, then closed, and her shoulders straightened. "What are you suggesting?"

I turned the pages until I found the chapter where the names of the four Houses were emblazoned across the top. This crazy idea could bring us one step closer to ending Devon's censure or create my own mortal enemy. Lorenzo wouldn't be happy with me digging into his past. I brushed at the hairs rising on the back of my neck and tapped a finger on the page. "I thought we could start here."

She gave me a suspicious look but stepped to the table to see what held my interest. I could see the wheels turning in her faraway stare as the beginning of a smile formed. She leaned over and whispered, "This is one of the more exciting chapters in the book." She glanced at the door as if worried someone might be eavesdropping. "This was a turning point for the Council and the vampire Houses and set the stage for several wars." Her fingers tapped a staccato rhythm on the desk as she nodded, seeming to rethink her training plan. "I'll still need to give you a quick rundown on how the Council was originally created so you understand the importance of this particular time period."

She erased what she'd initially written on the whiteboard and drew a seven-sided figure, rapidly adding names along each side. "Oh, yes, I think this will work. It will take about an hour or two to review, then we'll jump into the actions that changed the entire direction of the Council." She clapped her hands together before giving me a look I couldn't interpret. "This will give you a clear picture of what started the House Wars."

My excitement seemed to be gasoline on her enthusiasm. The start of the House Wars was precisely what I needed to know. Something told me that whatever happened during the wars was at the crux of the hatred between Lorenzo and Devon. And that was definitely something I needed to know.

I grabbed a couple notepads and pens, hardly believing this might end up being my favorite part of the day. But something niggled, like tiny pinpricks on skin. Would Devon get upset if my studies focused on the turmoil between his house and Lorenzo's? I pushed the thought aside. "Let's get started."

Chapter Two

DEVON SIPPED his scotch and shuddered at the cheap burn. He should have ordered an ale rather than expect the club to offer anything more palatable. If only another drink could mask the smell of body odor or the vomit emanating from the floor, but alcohol didn't have that effect on vampires. He couldn't remember the last time he'd been in such a rundown bar, but he had no one but himself to blame. Sergi could have dealt with this, but it had become personal. He shook his head. This was the worst time to get involved. It had been a long time since he'd felt the beast stir with such fervor.

Oh, he'd felt the beast rise in the last couple of weeks, but that had been pure lust, and directed solely at Cressa. He braved another gulp of his drink and convinced himself this evening had nothing to do with revenge for her treatment at the hands of his prey.

"Are you sure this is where he'll be?" Devon rarely questioned his inner circle, especially Sergi, who was the most focused of his guards.

"I could have done this myself." Sergi's tone wasn't accusatory or peevish. Just the facts—as always.

Devon curled his lip. "I need this."

"He'll be here soon. I understand he never misses Taco Tuesday." Sergi's flippant response earned him a grunt.

Devon glanced around the room, which was nothing more than a large square with a bar on one side, pool tables on the other, and a makeshift dance floor in the back. No one danced to the eighties music blaring over the scratchy speakers even though there wasn't a single empty barstool and most of the tables were occupied.

He sensed a handful of shifters, but everyone else was human. The bar was in a district that bordered the Hollows, where most vampires and shifters spent their off-hours. So it wasn't surprising to find magical creatures rubbing elbows with a lesser species. He snorted. At least, that's what many magical creatures considered humans. A prejudice that could one day lead to another great war if balance wasn't restored. One that magical creatures might not win.

Sergi raised a hand to their server before nodding toward the front door.

A beefy man had entered wearing a vest with no shirt, displaying his bulging muscles and thick chest. A tattoo of a cobra covered half his face, which Devon understood hid a twisted scar. This was the man who'd put Cressa in a catch box, something created to hold shifters.

"I can't believe The Wolf didn't rip the man's throat out when he brought Cressa in a box." Sergi voiced his own thoughts.

"I imagine Remus was preoccupied with learning Pandora was the prize."

"I doubt he'll give Sorrento a second pass."

Devon smiled, and the tip of his fangs showed. "No. There will be no more second chances."

Sergi also grinned but kept his fangs in check as his gaze moved back to Sorrento.

"Who's the tall brunette?" Devon finished the scotch and pushed the glass away.

"Patrice. His second, and the only magical creature on his payroll."

"Why would a vampire work for such a man?"

Sergi shrugged. "There isn't much information on her, but the rumor is that she was falsely created by a young blood from House Gresham."

"Ah. So, she was turned out along with her maker."

"The two of them joined together, mostly for survival I would think. But it's been a couple of years since anyone has seen her maker."

Devon nodded with understanding. The most likely scenario was that the child had killed her master. That was why young bloods weren't allowed to turn anyone; they were too immature to understand what being vampire meant and never made wise decisions. They couldn't even begin to fathom their immortality. Knowing Gresham as he did, Devon was surprised the two vampires were turned out rather than eliminated. There had to be more to the story, but it wouldn't matter after tonight.

"Are the other two his bodyguards?"

"Sorrento shifts his personnel around, except for Patrice. I think he likes having the muscle to add to his reputation. Patrice is the only one to worry about. She prefers drugs or poisons to fighting."

Devon snarled. "That probably explains how her maker disappeared." And would also explain how Cressa ended up in a box. The thought of her waking up in one made his beast struggle at its own confinement.

"Most likely."

After the server dropped new drinks at their table, Devon leaned back as Sorrento chatted with two men at the bar before turning to a table with four men. They'd been there when Devon had first strolled in. The men glared at Sorrento's men, who stood over them, clearly wanting the men to vacate the table. The men at the table glared back until Sorrento approached, and the four men almost knocked over their chairs, drinks in hand, as they pushed past people to move to the back of the bar.

Devon waited twenty minutes as various customers wandered by Sorrento, offering homage or whatever it was Sorrento demanded of what he must consider his flock of low-life criminals. He nodded to Sergi and stood, leaving his second drink untouched.

He strolled up to Sorrento's table and kicked the chair of one of the bodyguards. The man scowled and began to rise until he looked up. Devon let the tips of his fangs show, and the man backed down. He glanced at Sorrento, who nodded toward the bar. The two men stood, rolled their shoulders in some demonstrative posture as if they weren't scared shitless, then scurried to the bar, the last of their courage spent.

Sorrento stared at him before he quickly relented and waved his arm toward the vacated chairs. A man of few words.

Devon took a seat, and Sergi settled beside him, neither of them giving Patrice a single glance. He sensed the vampire's rage at being ignored. Did she know who he was or even how old? He doubted it.

"Now, what can I do to help a couple of vamps?" Sorrento thought he had the high ground here. Interesting. How many vampires did the man work with, and was Lorenzo one of them? If so, Sorrento should have more respect for vampires he didn't know. If he'd expected Patrice to understand the nuances of what it meant to be vampire in her adolescence, that would explain the man's reckless behavior. Not that it mattered.

"I've heard a rumor about a certain thief." He'd considered his options on the drive over and decided to test the waters. It would be foolish to make a scene in the bar, and he was curious how much information the man was leaking.

"I have lots of thieves on my payroll." Sorrento scratched his chest with a lazy motion and gave Devon a wide smile. "You'll have to narrow it down for me."

"This one's specialty is personal residences with high-value targets."

Sorrento kept his smile when he leaned closer and softened his tone as if sharing a confidence. "You're looking for Pandora." When Devon didn't respond, he shook his head and sat back. "She's off the market for now. But if you can wait another week or two, I can arrange something."

So, the man planned on picking her up again after she finished her mission with him. But if Sorrento was thinking a week or two, did he even care if she'd paid off her debt to him? The man either had balls the size of coconuts or he was an idiot.

"I hear she's working with a vampire House now. I believe those rumors came from you."

Sorrento shrugged, still undaunted. "It raises her value if her prospective clients know what jobs she's working—" He gave him a slow perusal "And the type of creatures she's willing to work for —albeit temporary."

"So, you determine who she's sold to?" Devon kept his tone even, but the beast rattled its cage, unhappy with how Cressa was being set up. He doubted she had a clue to this man's plans.

"I have the ability to ensure she'll do as she's told." He gave Patrice a side glance, and she actually preened at the attention. She couldn't be more than a decade made.

Devon waited, wanting to hear the man say the words that would guarantee his fate.

Sorrento scooted his chair closer and leaned in for a second time. He was close enough for Devon to make out the fine lines of the inked cobra. "She's working for the Trelane House. Now, I know that doesn't seem like much with the vamp ostracized from his kind, but he's a tough cookie from what I hear." He held up his hands. "I have no doubt Pandora will hold her own against the vamp." He winked. "Although, I imagine this Trelane fellow will probably get a good taste before he sends her packing. If you know what I mean."

Patrice laid a hand on his arm, her gaze showing emotion for the first time. Fear.

At her touch, Sorrento shrugged. "No disrespect to your species."

"Of course." Devon eyed him until the other man lowered his gaze.

"Look, she's excellent at her job, and if she's returned a bit battered, she'll snap out of it. I might need a day or two once I pick her up, but I can deliver her all boxed up wherever you need her."

He held his inner rage from building, not wanting his eyes to flash and give Patrice an early warning. Sergi rose at the same time he did.

"I'll give it some thought." He strode for the door, not hearing nor caring what Sorrento blathered on about. He shoved past people with barely an apology. This man thought he owned Cressa. The thought of someone grabbing her off the street and keeping her locked in a box made his beast howl like a common shifter.

He'd marched a block before Sergi grabbed his elbow. Without a word, he let Sergi direct him back half a block to an alley where a shiny muscle car waited.

"I can put extra protection on her."

He considered his guard's suggestion. "After tonight, she won't require more than Lucas or Simone."

"And Underwood?"

"He's next on my list."

Before he could say more, footsteps came from the direction of the bar. Four people. It could be anyone, but as the group grew closer, he picked up Sorrento's scent. He glanced at Sergi, and a blink confirmed he'd caught it, too.

They backed into the shadows. Sergi placed himself several feet in front of the car while Devon disappeared toward the rear. Time to test what type of vampire Patrice was—a bodyguard with alert senses scanning the area or a foolish, arrogant young blood, dependent on chemicals doing the work for her.

Voices and soft laughter preceded the group as they turned into the alley. The two bodyguards walked behind Sorrento and Priscilla, and after a precursory glimpse beyond the car, approached without any concerns.

Devon waited until one of the bodyguards reached for a door before stepping out of the darkness as Patrice finally became aware of him. When the others turned toward him, Patrice spun around to find Sergi blocking their exit.

The bodyguards surrounded Sorrento, who gave Patrice a chilling stare before turning to face Devon.

"What's this about? If you have a problem with how I conduct business, you should come back during business hours."

Sorrento's strong tone and the way he adjusted his shoulders before stretching his neck and fisting his hands would make one believe he was ready for a fight. But Devon didn't have to reach far with his senses to smell the fear rolling off the man. It stank of old sweat, cheap whiskey, and false bravado.

He stepped closer, choosing a spot within the dim light from nearby windows. "I have a problem with people spreading stories about me and mine."

"What are you talking about?"

"You traded Pandora to The Wolf in exchange for a debt, isn't that correct?"

Sorrento's eyes flashed to Patrice, who backed away, most likely finding a place to spring from.

"You seem to know a lot about my business."

"The Wolf then exchanged Pandora for his own debt." Devon waited for Sorrento to catch on to where this was going.

Sorrento stepped back, his gaze narrowing. He seemed to finally understand his dilemma.

"I don't like people talking about my business or spreading

gossip about my family. Pandora's debt belongs to me, and once paid, she's free to pursue her old trade." Devon took a step closer. "She doesn't belong to anyone for barter." His eyes flashed with the ice blue of the beast. "And she doesn't belong in a box. No one does."

Patrice stepped toward him as one of the bodyguards turned toward the alley entrance. Sergi had moved closer, and the man stumbled backwards, running into his buddy.

"I can be discreet. I give you my word. Just give me a chance." This was a different Sorrento. A submissive part he didn't play often, it appeared.

"If you could be discreet, you wouldn't be telling stories about Pandora. Or the House Trelane."

"Mr. Trelane, I meant no disrespect, a brother just needs to make a living."

"Not anymore."

Sergi attacked first, grabbing the first bodyguard in a blink of an eye as Patrice charged Devon. Her fangs were out, and he caught the glint of something in her hand, Sergi's warning about her preference for drugs and poison made him think syringe, loaded with something that might or might not kill him. At best, it would leave him vulnerable. She was nothing more than a lazy, untrained vamp, not confident in her natural skills. Being a rogue on a human's payroll, she'd probably never tested them.

When she reached him, he used his speed to knock the syringe out of her hand before picking her up and hurling her toward the brick building. The sound of her hitting with a loud grunt along with the snapping of bones made him smile. Cressa was ten times the fighter, and he laughed out loud at the thought as he stalked toward Sorrento. The man had pulled a gun, but his hand shook, and the first shot went wide. It was his only opportunity as Devon leaped. The man had turned to run but only made it a few steps before he stumbled over one of his bodyguards and slipped on the spreading pool of blood. The man's throat had been ripped out.

Sergi was already on the second man, who fought like a wild-cat, though it wouldn't do him any good.

Sorrento scooted backwards on his ass, one arm raised in self-defense. "I didn't know. It wasn't meant to harm anyone. I just needed to drum up some business."

"When you work in the underworld of magical creatures, you play by our rules."

He had to give the man some credit for making it to his feet. Sorrento took a few steps and gulped in a breath of air, probably wondering if he would make it out alive. Devon nodded toward Patrice, and Sergi didn't waste a second as he rounded on the dazed vampire, who struggled to gain her feet, one arm dangling at her side. She stood straight, shoulders back as she waited for Sergi's attack, finally showing what she could have become had she been properly groomed. He'd wanted to save her, but her reputation was too well-known, and he would never be able to trust her. Sergi didn't make her suffer, using his hunter's sword to take her head.

Sorrento ran, but Devon reached him long before he made it to the street. He grabbed him by his collar and the waistband of his jeans, picking him up and tossing him toward his muscle car. Glass shattered as Sorrento slammed into the windshield, spewing a grunt of pain.

He dragged the man out of the broken glass, ignoring his screams as he flung the man faceup on the hood. With one quick movement, Devon pierced the man's throat, grimacing at the toxic taste of his blood before ripping out his jugular.

Chapter Three

"DEVON!"

I sprang up, my heart racing. The sheets were tangled around my legs, and I fought to get free, racing for the bathroom. The light temporarily blinded me, but I had to get away from the darkness. I spit into the sink before turning on the water, splashing my face with the cold spray before cupping my hands to slurp it in, rinsing my mouth from the acrid taste of blood—cheap whiskey, garlic, and meat.

When I realized what I was doing, I stumbled back, smacking into the wall and sliding down until my ass hit the floor.

What the hell?

The dream had started like the earlier ones. I was in the garden at Oasis, Devon's private estate that only his family knew of, and the thick scent of roses clung in the air like an old friend as I raced down the path for the grotto. He had to be there. It had been a week since the last dream, and I hungered for his touch, his warmth, and the strength of his arms wrapped around me, keeping me safe. But when I reached the grotto, he wasn't there.

Then the vision changed.

The dead eyes of Sorrento gazed into the night—his throat

ripped out. Blood covered his chest and pooled under his head, the eye of the cobra tattoo staring at me.

Was this one of those dreams? If so, they'd changed drastically, and I much preferred the erotic ones. I didn't understand why they changed from one vision to the next. I didn't have any control over them, and while I wasn't convinced this was the best idea, I leaned my head back against the wall and closed my eyes, forcing myself to relive the dream.

My body trembled as if fighting my resolve, but I had to know if Devon was all right. It was impossible to believe the dream could have been real. How would Devon know about Sorrento? I shook the thought aside, sucked in a deep breath, and forced all thoughts away except the one.

At first, nothing happened. Then unrelated images flashed by —my mind too busy, too unsettled. I called upon the relaxation techniques I'd learned from an old mentor, but try as I might, her teachings slipped away, leaving me with jumbles of the dream mixed with various bits of images from the last week— training in the gym, my sessions with Anna... Perhaps my subconscious was protecting me from the underlying fear of what I'd see.

If this was about vamps, then I might as well think like one. Simone's long meditation sessions that I constantly complained about might be the answer. I snorted. If this worked, I'd never willingly admit it to her.

I rolled my shoulders, shook out my arms, and settled in. This time, I imagined a single flame surrounded by darkness. I accepted the images as they came at me, and if they weren't part of the dream, they disappeared within the scorching heat of the candle.

Five minutes passed before my body relaxed enough to release my thoughts and accept the entire vision.

I dropped into an alley where the only light streamed from nearby windows. Sorrento's sleek bright-orange muscle car was parked a hundred feet from the quiet street. Everyone knew that car and avoided it whenever possible. Not us. We waited within the shadows, as still as the darkness itself—a standard hunting position. Once they walked past Sergi, the trap would be set.

Adrenaline coursed through my blood, my sense of righteousness eager for the engagement and impassioned to protect one of my own. I sensed them before I heard them. Four people strolled this way, but they were too far away to hear their conversation. Or perhaps I didn't care.

Their laughter stirred something within me, something I couldn't describe but raged to be set free. Then everything sped up as they turned into the alley and approached the car. Sergi stepped behind the guards. Sorrento didn't realize what he'd walked into. Patrice, the bitch who'd drugged me, recognized the danger too late. When I picked her up and threw her against the wall, I heard a gratifying crunch of bone. And I smiled. The vision jumped ahead, and Sorrento ran for the street. I caught his shoulder, picked him up, and flung him toward his precious car.

Amazement pierced the edge of my consciousness when he wasn't killed by the force of hitting the windshield. The speed at which he'd flown through the air was like being thrown from a car traveling at sixty miles per hour, yet he groaned. With a strength I didn't know I possessed, I dragged him from the broken windshield, unmoved by his screams of pain.

When I looked down into his bloody face, only one thing burned in my head. He would never hurt Cressa again. And my fangs sank into flesh, the hot blood gushing into my mouth.

My eyes popped open. I instinctively wiped my mouth before dry heaving from the dream blood. My heart pounded with a combination of satisfaction, anxiety, and doubt. Devon was safe. Sorrento—not so much. And I wasn't sure how I felt about that.

I was Devon's family now. And he protected his family—at all costs.

He'd told me that before, hadn't he? But this feeling, this knowledge, ran deeper. I no longer knew if these were Devon's thoughts and feelings or my own. One moment, I was seeing everything through my eyes, but the next it was through Devon's. His thoughts, his mission, mixing with my own emotions of fear, disgust, and—vindication.

I crawled on my hands and knees to the doorjamb and pulled myself up, leaning against it as I determined my next steps. Up to now, my dreams appeared to be prescient. Had Devon already killed Sorrento, or was this something I could stop, assuming I wanted to?

I limped to the bed and reached for my cell. One a.m. I'd been asleep for a couple of hours. It had been an early night for me. When Devon missed dinner for the fourth night in a row, I'd grown restless, wondering what he was up to and why I hadn't heard from him.

What I'd needed was someone to talk to. No one knew about my dreams except Devon, but it was only a guess on my part that he was aware of what he was doing. At this point, all I'd wanted was a voice other than my own that could keep the remnants of the dream from returning.

Ginger would have been my first choice, but she still had a couple of days with her mom, and I didn't want to bother her. April was always good for cheering me up, but my calls went straight to voice mail. It bothered me that she hadn't returned a single call, but with Christopher's frantic search for me, she was probably lying low. Devon might have assumed he'd backed down, but that wasn't likely. He was like a flea on a hound, and it had to be pissing him off he couldn't find me.

I flopped onto the bed and stared at the ceiling, then turned my head to the large tome sprawled on the far side of the king-sized bed. Each evening progressed as the one before it. No one mentioned the next assignment so, after dinner, I took the opportunity to practice my martial arts using a series of maneuvers I'd developed, blending them with what I'd learned from the vamps. After a good work out and a soak in the hot tub, I'd read until I fell asleep.

Anna's lessons had intrigued me, and after each one, I'd haul the *Houses of Vampire* book to my room. We'd agreed to review the history of vampires starting from a thousand years ago, which was when the House of Trelane had been created, along with Lorenzo's House Venizi. This would have happened five hundred years before Devon. The question was whether the two Houses had been friends or enemies from the start. The fact that the House Wars occurred at the same time only stirred my imagination.

Before I'd fallen asleep that evening, I'd only read a few pages. I sat up and pulled the book to me. It was opened to the last page I'd read and was fortunately in good condition despite my tossing in bed. No pages had been torn from its fragile binding. I flipped through a couple of pages, more to calm myself than anything else, but I wouldn't be able to go to sleep without knowing if my dream had been real.

Unable to stay in my room one minute longer, I slipped on my jeans and a sweater and, with the tome resting on my hip, jogged down to the library. I checked Devon's office and the dining room, just in case. He might already be home, tucked away in his room, but the fire was still lit in the library. I curled up on the sofa in front of the fire and opened the book. I hadn't made much progress when Devon found me.

If he'd killed someone tonight, he didn't look the part. His black shirt and pants were wrinkle-free, his designer loafers polished to a high sheen. Not a hair was out of place. He looked surprised to see me, especially when he noticed the large book in my lap.

"Are you behind on your studies already and find a need to burn the midnight candle?" He sat in a nearby chair. Damn, he looked good.

"No. I just find the topic more interesting than I expected. We spent our first session deciding the proper place to start."

His lips twitched. "And what did the two of you agree on?"

How easy it was for me to fall into his conversation, somewhat starved for it after his absence. Before the ball, I'd grown accustomed to our frequent talks. Now that I was considered part of his family—or seemed to be if my dream could be believed—I might fade into the background until I was needed. The thought irritated me, but I had to stay focused on why I was down here waiting for him.

"Did you see Sorrento this evening?

His expression closed down for an instant, but his eyes narrowed. "Why would you ask that?"

This would be the moment to tell him about my dreams, but I wasn't sure where to start. It made sense to start from the beginning, but the first ones were too erotic. Perhaps the one that foretold my fall through the second-story window. Maybe I hadn't thought this through. My knuckles turned white from gripping the book, and I forced my fingers to relax.

Devon noticed the movement. It was impossible to hide anything from him. I cleared my throat and took a deep breath.

"I had a dream this evening." I shook my head and waved my hand as if erasing my statement. "No. It was more a nightmare." When I glanced at him, he hadn't moved. He was so quiet, he could be a mannequin. The silence continued, and it was obvious he was waiting for me. The man could wait an eternity.

I set the book aside and stood to pace in front of the hearth, already questioning the wisdom of discussing this, but the dreams had taken an ugly turn. Sorrento was dead. I had no illusions of that, not after the dream of my fall coming true. Maybe I wasn't ready to know how brutal Devon could be, yet I already knew how dangerous he was. I'd seen the way his eyes flashed to that icy blue, and my hand touched my throat where he'd held me against the wall after a rather intense training session.

My breath hitched when I turned to him. He hadn't moved an inch. How could he be so patient, so emotionless in my turmoil? But when I was brave enough to look him in the eyes, he wasn't as detached as I thought. They had turned to that cold blue that spoke of danger, but as I watched, they changed to that warmer tone of sapphire. I'd never seen him conflicted before, if that was what I was actually witnessing.

"I saw Sorrento killed."

Now his eyes flashed back to the more dangerous hue, but his tone remained calm and even. "Sit, Cressa. Tell me everything you saw."

Now we were getting somewhere. He wasn't surprised by my revelation. Had it been a mistake to allow me into his thoughts during the...murder? Altercation? I wasn't even sure what to call it. I sat on the edge of the chair, too worked up to settle down.

"It was flashes of images—a dark alley, Sorrento's car. Everyone knows his car. It's like a beacon to run the other way." A strangled laugh slipped out, and I took another deep breath. My gaze must have been unfocused because I was suddenly back in the dream, and I told him everything I saw. Then someone shook me, and the dream vanished.

Devon was there, his hands on my shoulders.

"Sorrento was going to catch me again once my debt was cleared. What an asshole."

Hot tears ran down my face, and he squeezed my shoulders, his fingers soft but firm.

"It's okay, Cressa. It's over. It wasn't you. It was me."

"Why would you share such a horrid thing with me?"

He didn't say anything for several minutes. "That's not what's happening." He pulled away and knelt in front of me. His warm gaze brought comfort, his expression deeply concerned. "We need to talk about all the dreams."

I wasn't able to comprehend what he was saying, though I'd suspected all along he must know about them.

"Devon!"

We both turned when Lucas raced in. I hadn't seen him for days, either.

"What?" Devon's voice turned impatient.

"The apartment. Someone's there."

Devon stood so abruptly, I was left dangling on the edge of my seat before I could get my feet under me. He reached out a hand to steady me.

"Get the car."

Lucas didn't question him as he stormed back the way he'd come.

"Apartment? Are you talking about my place?" The dreams could wait. I wanted to know who was breaking in again.

"Yes." Devon strode toward the door, and I ran after him.

"I'm coming, too."

Chapter Four

DEVON PAUSED to give me a quick scan from head to toe, then back to my face. "The limo." He didn't have to yell it; Lucas and those sensitive vamp ears would have heard from the other side of the house.

The limo was out front by the time Devon helped me into a coat and ushered me out the door. Sergi was in the driver's seat, and Lucas held the door open for us before climbing into the front passenger seat.

I'd lost track of time but, based on the dark, empty streets, it had to be close to morning. Devon sat next to me on the plush bench seat, his hand holding mine.

"Ginger isn't back yet." I didn't make it a question, more of something to break the silence. The dream hovered between us, and I struggled with Devon's earlier actions. Sorrento didn't know where I lived, and with his death so recent, this couldn't be payback.

"No, but she's on her way."

He'd been keeping an eye on her. The heaviness that had tightened around my chest lessened, and he must have sensed it because he squeezed my hand.

"Do you have the video feed?" Devon turned on a small monitor I hadn't noticed before.

"Why would anyone be going there? If it's Christopher, he's already tossed the place, and Ginger and I haven't been back since then."

"I had the apartment cleaned and everything restored."

That surprised me. "But how would they know that? They would monitor the place before going in, wouldn't they?"

He nodded. "I've had someone posing as Ginger staying there off and on."

It didn't take me long to catch up even with my foggy brain. "You were luring Christopher back."

He shrugged. "I wasn't sure it would work, but he's definitely not going to let this go. Whatever he's looking for is important to him—or to someone else."

I was still working through what his last statement meant when Sergi pulled the limo to the curb a block away from the apartment.

Colored images appeared on the screen, displaying the front door of my apartment building. Two people stepped out and hurried away.

"Can you play back from when they entered?" Devon released my hand and moved to the edge of the seat.

The screen went black, then, the front of the apartment building reappeared a few seconds later. Several seconds after that, two beefy men dressed in black entered the building. The front door lock was broken again. It was rare when it worked, and I wasn't sure why the landlord bothered fixing it. We waited for five minutes, and I expected to see the two men exit. Instead, two more people approached. Another man dressed in black and a woman in a black rain duster and knee-length boots. Her head was down, but she lifted it for a split-second as she jogged up the steps.

April.

What the hell?

I tugged at the neckline of my sweater, suddenly too warm in the limo. I didn't dare look at Devon but didn't have to. His gaze was like a spotlight, though he didn't say a word. Then I noticed the time stamp on the bottom corner of the screen. Twenty minutes ago. I watched the digits flip until another five minutes crept by. April and the person I assumed was her bodyguard left the building.

The screen went blank, and then the front door appeared again.

"The screen is back to current time."

"The other two haven't left?" Devon checked his watch as if confirming the clock on the screen.

"No."

"What does that mean?" I asked. "Why would the first two still be there? Maybe they went out the back." I finally glanced at Devon to find him staring at me. His forehead was creased but not in confusion or concern. He was planning something.

"I need to speak to one of them." Devon moved to sit next to the bar, dropping ice cubes into his glass and pouring scotch. Then he poured a chilled vodka neat and handed it to me.

Sergi and Lucas left the limo. When I glanced at the screen, they approached the building and disappeared inside. Devon shut off the screen and turned his attention to me.

"You recognized one of them."

He never missed much. But I couldn't think of any reason not to tell him the truth. Why would April be here with Christopher's henchmen? He could be forcing her. Some threat to see if she could talk me into meeting with him. Or I might have to face the possibility that she was working for him. It was impossible to believe, knowing our history with the man. Yet, a niggling feeling told me something different. Had April changed that much? I never saw it coming if it was true.

"The woman was April."

"Your sister?" He sounded as shocked as me. "I thought the two of you were close."

I snorted. "Yeah. Me too." The vodka went down smooth, and I closed my eyes as it warmed me from the inside. Another thought hit me. "I've been calling her and texting. Can they trace my phone?"

Devon shook his head. "We have other ways of keeping track of the family, but if it makes you feel better, I can supply you another one."

"You keep track of everyone in your family? That's like, what, seventy people?"

"Something like that, but we're only concerned when they're on missions. It's for protection, not monitoring."

I nodded. "And how do you keep track of me?"

He grimaced. "We don't normally track the humans in our family. They're never put in risky situations. Or haven't been."

"Just say it." I closed my eyes, a sick feeling sending shivers over me as to how he might be tracing me. "It's the blood, isn't it? I still have your blood in me."

"My blood shouldn't affect you anymore, but there will always be a trace. More like a ghost image. Just enough to sense you up to a point. If you were vampire, the distance would be much farther."

"I see." I glanced out the window, not sure how to feel about that. "Can other vampires sense me?

"No."

I nodded. I could live with that. Then Sergi appeared in the video, walking someone back to the limo.

Devon opened his door. "Stay here."

"No way. I want to hear what he has to say."

He paused. There wasn't much I could do if he said no. I could jump out, but my door was probably locked. He rolled his window down an inch. "You can sit here and listen." He caught my gaze, his expression stern. "It's imperative he doesn't see you. Sergi will mesmerize him, make this evening fuzzy, but he could still remember pieces, including faces."

"I understand. I'll be quiet as a mouse."

He hesitated again but rolled the window down a couple more inches. Enough for me to see everything going on. Then he exited and met Sergi, who pushed the man against the limo. I couldn't see his face unless he turned my direction, and I doubted Sergi would let that happen.

Devon wasted no time. "Tell me why you're here."

"Looking for Cressa Langtry." He was quick to respond, but spoke in a faraway monotone. Was that how I'd sounded when Margo had mesmerized me at the tea party? I must have appeared like a love-starved teenager when she came on to me. How embarrassing.

"Why are you looking for her?"

"She has something Mr. Underwood needs."

"And what is that?"

"A necklace."

That didn't make sense. That would have been stealing from my mother or April. I would never do such a thing.

When nothing more was asked, I glanced up and found Devon watching me through the narrow gap in the window. Did he expect to see signs of recognition or guilt? He must have sensed that I was as clueless as him.

"What type of necklace?" Devon gently prodded the man, who remained lethargic. There must be different levels of mesmerizing because I'd been more animated when under Margo's temporary thrall.

"Silver."

"That narrows it down," Sergi grumbled.

"Tell me more."

The bodyguard shrugged. "It's some type of medallion with pictures engraved on it. Animals of some kind. Old. Like an heirloom."

My blood ran cold. That couldn't be right. He couldn't be talking about that necklace. It wasn't stolen. My mother had given me that necklace when I was about six. She'd taken it from me a few years later but had given it back when I graduated. I attempted to school my expression, but when I glanced at Devon, I'd been too late. In some vain attempt to pretend I hadn't noticed, I focused my attention on the bodyguard, waiting to see if he'd share something of greater interest. As if what he'd just revealed wasn't already mind-blowing.

"Take him back to the apartment with the other one." Devon got back in the limo.

Sergi led the man away, his head bent low as if he was sharing a secret. Probably some vamp way to ease the man out of the mesmerizing, which appeared to have been deeper than what I'd experienced. That was a scary thought.

Devon didn't speak on the drive back to the estate. I nursed my vodka until we turned into the driveway. Once the limo stopped, I got out without waiting for Lucas to open the door. Devon met me before I took two steps and guided me up the stairs, his hand resting gently on my elbow. When we passed through the foyer, he steered me to his office when I tried for the stairs.

He'd want the whole story on the necklace, and honestly, what did it matter? It was nothing but a trinket from my father. The only connection I had to him. I couldn't see how this had anything to do with his mission, but one thing was a fact. There was no way in hell I was going to hand that necklace over to Christopher.

Chapter Five

I SANK into the leather sofa and stared at the fire in Devon's office. My life used to be normal. A heist here, a heist there. Living job to job. My best friend Ginger and me against the world. Now, our home, albeit a cheap apartment in the worst part of the city, was routinely tossed by Christopher's henchmen. Ginger was living out of a fancy hotel paid for by a vamp, and I worked for said vamp, living in his grand, if not completely dreary estate, stealing stuff by his request, and experiencing the occasional erotic dream of him.

No. Not of him.

I shared those dreams with him. Realistic dreams filled with touches, scents, and tastes. I shook my head and reached for my neck, more accurately for the necklace that wasn't there. The one I hadn't worn in years.

My reverie was interrupted when Devon handed me a brandy snifter and sat on the sofa next to me. Mere inches separated us, but he faced the fire as I did, his glass of brandy braced on his thigh as we stared at the flames.

Before that fateful ball, this was a familiar scene between us, though we'd be in the library. Sometimes we'd read, other times we'd discuss a mission or some family issue he seemed to enjoy talking through with me.

Tonight, tension flowed beneath the casual setting, yet Devon didn't speak or ask any questions. He waited for me. The man had the patience of a saint unless he was truly angry. And, God knew, I'd experienced those times as well. Though if we were alone with his anger, the moments turned sensual, easing his temper, and typically led to those erotic dreams.

I sipped the brandy, the warmth filling my belly, and by the third sip, I was ready.

"I'll make you a deal." Now that we were here, I wasn't sure where to begin, and the confidence I'd felt earlier had been dissolved by his sheer presence, his leg almost touching mine. He was too close to speak of such intimate dreams. I stared at his hand holding the glass of brandy, and memories washed over me like a warm waterfall: that hand running through my hair, caressing my face before his lips followed the same path, grazing my breast and pinching my nipple before his fangs teased them, then the roughness of them as they ran up my thigh, parting my legs... I sat up, sloshing the brandy.

Get a grip, Cressa.

My face burned with the heat of my blush, and I lowered my head so he wouldn't see it. As if he couldn't smell the desire flooding me. I forced the images of less pleasant dreams to resurface and that did the trick. We'd been discussing Sorrento before Lucas interrupted us. He'd said it was time to talk about the dreams. Time for him to come clean. This wasn't about me.

"I'm listening."

Right. I sipped the brandy, both hands gripping the glass as I focused on the fire. "I'll tell you about the necklace if you tell me why you're invading my dreams."

He swirled the brandy before taking a swallow, then glanced at me before nodding. His expression and relaxed posture suggested this discussion had nothing to do with him and everything to do with me.

"That's acceptable."

Those two words were enough to know I'd somehow lost this round. That somehow, both the necklace and the dreams were my burden, not his. Well, half of that was right.

I began with the easy part. "I don't know for sure, but based on the description I heard this evening, I think I know what necklace Christopher is looking for."

I turned away from the fire and pulled my legs underneath me before facing Devon. He shifted his own position, so he didn't have to crane his neck to listen, which added some much-needed space between us. After a heavy sigh, I mentally prepared to walk through the minefield. I never spoke to anyone about my childhood, only sharing snippets with Ginger. Devon had never pushed me on this topic before, so with any luck, we could keep this conversation strictly about the necklace.

"When Christopher told Ginger he was looking for something I stole, I had no idea what he was talking about. I haven't taken anything from that house since I walked away. When the man this evening mentioned a necklace, I was still clueless. I never stole jewelry and would never think to take anything from my mother or April." I snorted. "My beef was with Christopher, and I only stole items that would drive him crazy or were important to him."

"Poking a sleeping bear?"

I gave him a one-shouldered shrug and impish grin. "I suppose." I reached for my neck again then forced my hand back to the brandy snifter. He caught the movement. "When the bodyguard described it, I immediately knew what he was talking about." I held his gaze. "This is the god's honest truth. My mother gave me that necklace when I turned six. She said she'd meant to give it to me sooner, but she wanted to wait until I was old enough to take care of it."

I blinked. Rapidly. What was with the tears? It was so long ago. I swiped at an eye, hoping Devon wouldn't notice.

I cleared my throat. "She said it was something my father had left for me. That it was important. He made her promise to have me wear it at all times, but she insisted it wasn't really necessary. He'd just wanted me to feel him near." My laugh was half-choked. "As if I would remember someone who walked away from us when I was a toddler." I glanced down at the warm color of brandy, the same color of eyes I remembered dreaming of as a child. My father's eyes.

"When I was about twelve, my mother took it from me, saying something about keeping it safe. I had no idea what that meant, other than maybe keeping it away from Christopher. We'd already begun our battles by then. She gave the necklace back the day I graduated, knowing I was leaving."

Devon had turned motionless again. I took a sip of brandy and chanced a glance at him. He was staring into the fire, a slight wrinkle over his brow. Something bothered him about my story, but it was the entire truth. I couldn't begin to guess what he might be thinking. Not this time. My worst fear was that he wouldn't believe me, or that he might question our new deal.

He turned suddenly, and when he looked at me, it was as if he'd forgotten I was there. "Where's the necklace now?"

"Someplace safe."

He nodded. "I'd like to see it."

"I'm not giving it to Christopher." My words came out heated, and I winced when his eyes locked with mine. That icy blue had returned, leaving no warmth in its wake.

In a flash, the warmer blue reappeared, and he gave me a weak smile. "Of course not. I just want to see the medallion. His man said there were engravings on it?"

My shoulders that had bunched since the start of the conversation relaxed. "I don't really remember them all. It's been a while since I've looked at it, and I never paid close attention to the details." I closed my eyes. The medallion had been engraved on both sides. Most of it was border art of some kind, but three images were prominent on the front. "There was some kind of flower, similar to a rose I think, and a stork-like bird." I shook my head. "I'm not sure, but there was at least one other image that doesn't come to mind. Why the interest?"

"If Underwood wants it so badly it must have some value to him or to someone else, and he's being paid to retrieve it. Either way, we need to know why, and perhaps something on the medallion holds the answer."

When I gave him a doubtful look, he squeezed my hand. "And maybe it won't tell us anything at all, and it can remain wherever it is you keep it." He turned my cheek until I was forced to look him in the eyes. "I won't take it from you. It must be dear to you, especially if it was from your father."

A huge breath escaped. "Thank you." It would be simple enough to retrieve the necklace, but with my faithful bodyguards, someone else would know where it was. The emotions that crossed his features were impossible to read, yet I believed him when he said he wouldn't take it from me. Maybe he was mesmerizing me, but after having experienced the sensation with Margo, it didn't feel like it. I'd have to trust him with this, and one way for him to earn that trust was to hold up his end of our bargain.

"Your turn."

Confusion lit his handsome face, those brows dipping low.

"Why are you in my dreams?"

DEVON DIDN'T RESPOND to Cressa's question. His mind was too busy running through what she'd just shared. A necklace her father had given her that he'd wanted worn all the time, yet the information was thirdhand. Did her mother repeat his exact words or was the truth somewhere in between?

He had to see that medallion, curious as to whether it held some magic. It had been taken away when she was around twelve years old. It could be nothing, and considering her troubles with Underwood, perhaps her mother's actions truly were to keep the necklace safe. But twelve was the age of puberty, and that made the story all the more interesting. Maybe it meant nothing, but he had to know for sure. There was more at stake than just Cressa. Although if what he suspected was true, the impact to her life and future would take a dramatic turn. Anything beyond that would be a miracle.

When he sensed her impatience, he picked up their empty glasses and strode to the bar. He considered changing drinks, but this discussion would require delicacy. So, he poured more brandy and handed one to her before taking a seat in one of the side chairs, providing some distance between them. The dreams were too raw, too intimate, and she would be more comfortable with the space.

Her relieved expression when he positioned himself away from her confirmed his thoughts.

"This is going to be difficult to explain and equally difficult to believe." That wasn't the best start, and he considered asking Lucas to join them. Maybe he should wait until Simone returned in the morning.

"You admit you've been invading my dreams." She gulped a generous amount of brandy, waited for it to settle, then looked at him. "They've been so real. Have you been mesmerizing me?"

He chuckled, then let the brandy ease his own growing anxiety. "I've heard tales where two vampires have been able to share parts of their dreams. But this happened after blood sharing and only between mated couples."

"But you gave me your blood."

"Only a couple of swallows, and how many dreams did we share before that happened?"

Her head lowered, but he caught the blush on her cheeks. "All of them except the one tonight." She lifted her head, and though her cheeks were still rosy, her chin held a stubborn angle. She was serious about getting to the bottom of this. Well, so was he.

"I've never experienced anything like what we've shared before. I'd heard stories, but those were long ago, buried under centuries of myths and legends. The very first dream, when I found myself in my private garden at Oasis, somehow I knew I'd find you at the grotto." He shook his head, focusing on his initial impression at the time. "Maybe not you specifically, not by name. I'm not saying this right." He fidgeted, so uncommon for him, and his only explanation was his discomfort at finding the correct words. He drew in a long breath and continued with, "I sensed a presence and knew without a doubt that someone waited for me. When I reached the grotto and saw you waiting for me...with love in your eyes." He paused and gave her a small smile. "It seemed right. Like I'd known all along it would be you."

He braced for her reaction, but other than her rosy cheeks, she only nodded.

"It was a similar experience for me." Her words were so low, he might not have heard them without his vampiric hearing. "I had no idea what was happening or where I was. One moment, I'd been in my bedroom and the next I was in a garden. I was dressed in different clothes." She closed her eyes. "I could smell the roses, feel the prick of its thorns." She rubbed a fingertip, though she never opened her eyes. "I must have been barefoot because I remember the feel of the grass between my toes. But nothing compared to the need growing in me. The desire to..." She stopped, and when she opened her eyes, her blush grew deeper.

"I know."

She appeared relieved to move past the intimate moments. Moments he'd been trying to erase for the last week without much success. And he hated to admit he missed the dreams, the touch of her, the taste of her lips—and other parts. She must have been thinking about their mutual responses because her blush deepened before she turned her head away.

"These dreams, the realistic allure, our senses so entwined, they're simply not possible for a vampire."

When she turned back to him, she'd schooled her expression, similar to the first time he'd met her. Almost bored. What she buried underneath that cool facade was anyone's guess.

"The experience we shared reminded me of the old legends. Myths rarely spoken. In fact, what little I found in my earlier research had been done secretly, with only a handful of my inner circle aware of my activities." He set his glass down and leaned over, his hands clasped between his knees. "I believe you're a dreamwalker."

That broke her quiet reserve. "You're making that up. I've never even heard of a dreamwalker."

"They're illusive—rare and secretive. They can enter dreams and influence them, or so I've been told. I've only found references to them in books. Everything I've dug up has been from short conversations with vampires much older than me."

She shook her head, and that stubborn tilt of her head told him he'd need something more convincing before she'd even consider the notion.

"Think back to your childhood. You probably had strange dreams as a child. Dreams you couldn't explain, that maybe terrified you. They might have created the behavioral issues you experienced."

"You know nothing of my childhood." The calm exterior, stubborn as it might have appeared, crumbled under a torrent of hot rage. She reined it in before falling back against the cushion, but her flinty stare clearly stated that the volatile emotion hadn't gone far.

After a moment to pull herself together, her expression turned triumphant. "If I was controlling the dreams, how would I know about your private garden, or the lake, or the giant oak tree?"

"I never said you were controlling them. You currently have no control, which is why they come through jumbled and out of context. And as far as knowing about Oasis before you saw it? I believe these dreams are prescient."

When she gave him an odd look, he added. "Prophetic."

"I know what the word means. I just think you're nuts if you believe in dreamwalkers." She rubbed her face, then pushed her hands through her hair. "Here's what I think is happening, and you're just unwilling to accept the facts. These dreams are tied to your emotions. Maybe you've never experienced them before. I can't explain that part. But every time you get unhinged because of something I did or didn't do, I end up in one of your dreams."

He considered her explanation. He'd considered it before, but never in all his centuries had he heard of anything similar. And God knew he'd searched for possible answers long before he'd met her.

"Have you considered it's your own emotions creating them?" He kept his tone level in an attempt to keep hers on an even keel.

She stared at him and shook her head. "No. No. You're projecting into mine."

"After five hundred years, I'm to believe I just began seeing the future?"

"One of us is."

He needed a different angle. Perhaps this evening's vision. He had no idea how she could be in his head while he was awake, and the thought was daunting. "Earlier this evening, you said you remembered the taste of the blood, but it wasn't the same as when I gave you mine."

Her eyes widened for an instant. Had she not considered that? "Again, your projections."

He picked up his snifter and took a long sip before sitting back. What was the old saying, you couldn't prove a negative? The best solution would be to let the notion sit and give her time to mull it over.

She surprised him, apparently not finished with the topic. When she set her glass down before standing, he thought she'd walk out, but instead, she paced. "If I'm some dreamwalker, wouldn't that make my mother one?"

"Your father."

"What?" She whipped around so quickly, he thought she'd tumble, but she grabbed his desk for support.

He turned in his seat to face her. "I believe it's your father who is the dreamwalker. Not your mother."

"Why would you think that?"

"Because if it was her, she would have trained you. Instead, she gave you a necklace your father had insisted you wear at all times. I'm not sure why she took it from you at an age where you would have reached puberty, but I believe that necklace is tied to him being a dreamwalker."

"It's a cheap trinket from a deadbeat dad."

"That you keep locked away so no one can find it."

Her face reddened, but this time it was from her returning anger. She wanted to say something; her mouth moved, but nothing came out. He guessed what she really wanted was to erase their entire conversation. Now she did what he'd previously predicted. She stormed out. Her race up the staircase pounded in his ears. He anticipated an attempt to slam her bedroom door. With the heaviness of the door and the thickness of the plush carpet, it was difficult to slam doors in this house. God knows others had tried, yet she somehow managed to do it. He would have smiled if he wasn't at such a loss as to his next step.

A minute later, Sergi entered. "That could have gone better."

He laid his head back. "Maybe. It would be difficult for anyone to hear they're a magical creature, especially when their abilities could be explained away by someone else's."

"How would you like to proceed?"

Devon rubbed his face before running his hands through his hair as Cressa had done minutes ago. Like the way she'd run her hands through his in one of their more intimate dreams. He pushed the memory aside. "I assume you heard that Cressa had another dream. This time of us in the alley with Sorrento."

Sergi grimaced. "She's growing stronger and more out of control."

"I want every tidbit of information you can find about her past. I don't care how small or disconnected it might seem, I want to know about it." He turned toward the dark window, morning still a couple of hours away. "You have the rest of the new day. I want the report before dusk."

Sergi bowed and left the room, closing the door behind him. He, like others of his inner circle, instinctively knew when Devon didn't want company.

He dragged himself from the chair, set his glass on the bar, and picked up the tablet sitting on the edge of his desk, quickly reviewing his latest messages.

A full week had gone by since the ball. He'd spent little time with Cressa, and when he did, he'd made sure others were present. He'd wanted her to have space to settle into the new training regiments and become patient with the slow time between jobs. But that came to an end starting tomorrow. She was going to learn about dreamwalkers if he had to hogtie her. Holy hells, what was he getting them into? He glanced toward the ceiling, his focus on the third floor. And would it stop the other nightmares occurring in this house?

Chapter Six

I RAN at the wall again, leaping to grab a hold a quarter of the way up, then scrambling to cut across its face before reaching the top, pushing to beat my fastest time. When I clutched the rope and pushed off, I paid attention to not only what was behind me but my target as well. My feet landed within the red circle, my breath rushing out in short rasps, and I stopped the timer before bending over to grasp my thighs, sucking in deep breathes.

After stumbling to the bench to wipe the sweat from my forehead and pits, I checked my watch. Five seconds off my best time. I weighed another run against the law of diminishing return. There wasn't anything I could do to get faster unless I turned into a vamp. I snorted. A dreamwalker. What was Devon trying to pull? His mission was more than enough for anyone's plate, though that apparently had stalled for some reason he hadn't felt the need to share.

All I'd been able to do after storming out of his office the previous evening was to toss and turn the last few hours before dawn. If only I'd had a dream, just so I could prove him wrong. My emotions had been more heightened than his, certainly enough to bring one on if I'd been the one influencing them. But I hadn't really slept—not deeply. Was that a requirement? I shook my head to clear the unwanted thoughts, refusing to contemplate his argument. Yet, a niggling seed of doubt swirled in the depths of my gut. If I considered it logically, and if what he said was true, that dream manipulation was beyond the powers of a vamp, maybe I should keep an open mind to other possibilities.

Damn him.

I picked up my water bottle and stood to leave when I noticed Devon at the door in a blue-gray suit that emphasized the electric color of his gaze. His hands were held behind his back, and he'd tamed his hair into a ponytail. How long he'd been there was anyone's guess.

"You're much faster." He stepped closer but left half the room between us, hands still held behind him. All business. His expression was pleasant but guarded, probably waiting to see what the crazy woman would do.

I shrugged. "I think that's as quick as I'm going to get."

"It's enough. And you've become adept at the ropes in a short amount of time."

"You must not have heard about Sergi's surprise visit during training yesterday."

"And you've proved you learned from that experience."

He was being rather amenable this morning. Maybe he was waiting for the next shoe to drop even though he was the one with all the surprises. Although that might not be fair. We'd both been surprised by what Christopher's henchman had revealed.

I took a swig of water, waiting to hear the reason for his visit. He'd been ignoring my morning workouts all week, and he wasn't dressed for a sparring match.

"I know our discussion didn't end well last night, but I wanted to ask if your offer to let me see the necklace was still good."

Good grief, after all the talk about dreamwalkers, I'd spaced the necklace until he'd walked through the door. I shrugged. "I don't see why not."

He seemed to brighten, but I only knew that from watching his eyes and the way they warmed. I cursed under my breath at the slight tremors it evoked. "Excellent. I've called for a cab. You have an hour to shower and eat breakfast before it arrives."

Wait. What?

"A cab? Can't Lucas or Simone take me?"

"They're both on other assignments today. Besides, I had the impression the necklace was with other possessions you'd prefer to keep safe from prying eyes. I didn't want to intrude on that."

Huh. The thought shouldn't have surprised me. He'd never asked anything personal, not unless he thought it might impact his mission. I didn't know why he was so adamant about seeing the necklace or his fascination with all this dreamwalker talk, but this was the first time he'd let me out on my own.

"Thank you." I had no idea what else to say, but I shouldn't have worried. Devon had already left.

Anna was the only one waiting at breakfast, and while I had the morning to run my errands, I would be expected back in the afternoon for her lessons. She was willing to push them back an hour since I'd need time to get where I was going, but her reasonable side only went so far.

The cab showed up on time, and I directed the driver to City Center. It wasn't anywhere close to where I needed to go, and while Devon trusted me on my own, something told me Sergi would somehow trace my route, if they weren't already following me—for my protection, of course.

Santiga Bay was the largest town north of San Francisco and hugged the coast for several miles. City Center had been built closer to the hills that bordered the eastern edge and included a transportation hub with a train and bus station. The large marina five miles from downtown supported small-scale cargo ships, several dozen fishing boats, and even more pleasure crafts. There was a private airport to the northeast, but for commercial flights, the airport in San Francisco was a couple of hours away.

Three different buses and a ten-block walk took me back to my old neighborhood. I had no plans on going by the apartment. After the break-in last night, it was obvious the place was now toxic. My destination was four blocks from the apartment, and I'd bought a baseball cap and shades at the bus station for a disguise. During the morning hours, the neighborhood was quiet, and since this was a weekday, most people had already left for work. The drug trade didn't pick up until the afternoons.

The laundromat was next to Guillermo's mom-and-pop store and across from the Lowdown, the bar Ginger and I frequented when the apartment felt too tiny. The washing machines and dryers were all occupied, not surprising for the morning hours, but the real business was handled in back rooms.

Greco, who ran the neighborhood's illicit drug trade, had his hands in various pots. He was a true capitalist who believed in diversification, and the thought always made me chuckle. In addition to the drugs, he ran an escort business, a sportsbook, and had a private room filled wall to ceiling with lockboxes. The room was as serene and secure as a bank vault. Security cameras were prominently displayed, and I spotted several better hidden ones—just in case someone tried to dismantle the others. If that wasn't enough of a deterrent for theft, there were two guards posted outside the room twenty-four seven. It was good enough for me.

"Hey, Pandora. I figured you'd be laying low after all the activity at your crib."

I smiled and punched Bulldog in the shoulder. He punched back, but his normal greeting didn't push me back a couple of steps like it used to, and his eyes widened.

"Shit, girl. You been working out?"

My grin grew wider. "A bit."

He squeezed my upper arm until tears sprung. "Not enough to go up against those white boys cruising the hood. You start carrying?"

"In a way." I opened my jacket to reveal the bone-handled dagger.

Bulldog whistled. "And I bet you know how to use it."

I held my smile and nodded to the door of the private room. "I need a minute with my box." I passed him some cash, which he immediately put in his pocket.

"Ten minutes enough?"

I nodded. "What's with the time limit?" No one ever stayed long, but I'd never been given a limit before.

"Just today. Special client."

Ah. A new connection. "No worries. I won't need that long."

When he nodded to the guards, one unlocked the door, but before I entered, Bulldog pulled me back and whispered, "I've seen you with some dangerous dudes. Are you okay?"

I was touched. Ginger and I always had a good relationship with Bulldog, and he took care of us as best he could without involving himself with anything that would bring the heat. I didn't blame him for not going up against Christopher's men, they were well-armed, but license plates would have been noted. Bulldog had his own way of payback for disturbing his neighborhood.

I squeezed his arm. "It's all good. Believe it or not, I have my own bodyguards now. At least for a while."

His eyes brightened, and he nodded. "I told you you were too good for running with Harlow."

I laughed. "But you have to admit, he's a laugh a minute."

Bulldog growled. "He thinks so."

"I'm good. So is Ginger. But we have to disappear for a while."

"Take care of yourself, little girl." And he gave me another punch I wasn't expecting that made me take two steps back while rubbing my arm.

I scowled when the guys laughed, but I left them with a grin before walking through the door, closing it behind me. The room was larger than my apartment's living room, and a table with a single chair sat in the center. I glanced at the dozens of various-sized boxes—smaller ones at top and the larger ones at the bottom—before striding to mine and running the combination. All the locks were keyless, and Bulldog loved to share stories about people having to sober up before accessing their box. The guards always had a good laugh watching fools stumble around while trying to remember three numbers.

I opened the door to my cubby and pulled out a tin box I'd heisted from an asshole slumlord. He owned half the buildings in the neighborhood and was miserly on repairs. Twice a year, Harlow and I would hit his place and steal enough cash to help the tenants fix stuff like the heat and plumbing. This particular tin had some street value, but I kept it for what it represented—stealing from the sleazy rich and redistributing their wealth. Our own modern-day version of Robin Hood.

The tin only held two items—a stack of cash I could get to quickly and a key, which I pocketed.

Bulldog wasn't around when I stepped out of the room, but the guards nodded as I shut the door behind me and strode through the caustic smell of bleach and the sounds of tumbling clothes.

I took different bus routes back, knowing any one of them would end up at City Center. Two blocks down from the transportation depot was an expansive indoor-outdoor mall that stretched for two blocks. I slipped through a door to the main building with a group of high schoolers. After walking through several stores just to make sure no one followed me, I stepped out to another street and entered through the side door of a major retail bank. It was probably overkill, but that nagging feeling of someone following me wouldn't go away. Probably my imagination, but it had been two weeks since I'd been on my own, and I'd gotten used to having my own personal protection squad. How sad was that?

After waiting at the counter for several minutes, I was led to the safety-deposit room where the bank teller assisted in retrieving my box. Yeah, the laundromat and the bank. Call me insecure. Once I was alone in the room, I lifted the lid with trembling hands.

I didn't come here often, but when I did, the same emotions always slammed into me. I lifted out the colorfully painted wooden box and ran my hands over it, nostalgia forcing me to blink rapidly. The box was one of those old cigar ones that had been wrapped in white butcher-block paper to provide a blank canvas. Squares the size of baseball cards were glued all over it, leaving little of the white remaining. Each card had been hand-painted with childish drawings of flowers, animals, and landscapes, and my mother had glued them onto the cigar box. She told me the box held special powers and would protect all my cherished items. It was the last project we'd worked on together. The last time we did much of anything together. Before Christopher.

I wiped my eyes, sniffled, then opened the lid to find pieces of ribbons, a seashell, a bead bracelet, and other cheap trinkets from road trips we'd taken up and down the coast. A sharp pain, like a knife through my center, hit me when my hands ran over a short stack of letters. Mother would write small notes and mail them to me. I'd felt like such an adult when I received one, ripping them open to read as soon as I took them from the mailbox before racing up the walk to hug her tight. I swiped at my eyes again. *Good grief and hell's bells, Cressa. Get a grip.* At the bottom of the box, under the letters, was the silver necklace. It laid there forlorn and forgotten, staring up at me as if it called out, "It's about damn time."

I took a moment, not sure the best way to pick it up. "What do you think it's going to do?" I pictured it zapping me, blowing up, then dropping me into some psychedelic dream. My first instinct was to snatch it up, but I ended up lifting it with more care than was necessary. Nothing happened, of course, and I felt silly for thinking something would.

I was going to shove it in my back pocket but fastened it around my neck instead. When the silver medallion fell against my chest, a strange sense of completeness washed over me, startling me with its intensity. Then it was gone. I shook it off and, after brushing my hands across the stack of letters, closed the lid to the painted box. I was stuffing it back in the safety-deposit box when my cell phone rang.

I jumped at the unexpected ringtone then scrambled to find the volume control. For the short time I'd had the phone, the only numbers on it were Devon, his cadre, and Ginger. I didn't recognize the number and waited for the fourth ring before deciding to answer it.

"Hello," I whispered. I'd never taken a call in a bank before. Would that look suspicious on their security cameras?

"Hey, girl." A loud, excited voice pierced my eardrum.

"Ginger?"

Her voice dropped to match my whisper. "Sorry. Are you some place where you can't talk?"

I snorted. "It's not what you think. I'm at the bank."

"Well, that's boring."

"Are you back? You're not at the apartment, are you?" Apprehension filled me, thinking about the break-in at the apartment until my senses returned.

"Oh, yeah, baby. I'm back, but not at the old place."

"I didn't recognize the number."

"Yeah, Lucas gave me a new phone to use."

"Are you back at the hotel?"

"Nope. I totally loved being pampered, but it's not like having our own place."

"Where are you?"

"I texted you the address. Do you have time to stop by?"

The last thing I needed was Anna getting bent about me being late now that we'd reached an understanding on the lessons. "I won't be able to stay long."

"See you soon."

The street name she'd sent didn't look familiar, so I returned to the transportation center and caught a cab. Santiga Bay had several upper middle-class neighborhoods but only two exclusive ones. The one eastside was nestled along the foothills with expansive lots that were dotted with pines and included the hotel where Ginger had been stashed the first time Christopher's men had thrashed our apartment. The area the cabbie drove into was filled with high-end shops, restaurants, and entertainment centers. The same place Lucas had taken us shopping and clubbing. Where the eastside had massive estates, the westside sported tall condominiums filled the luxury units, many with stunning ocean views.

The cab stopped in front of a condo at the end of a short, dead-end street. It was just off the main drag, and I confirmed the address on the phone to the one on the building. There was a doorman, and I don't know why it surprised me. I'd cased several of these high-end buildings in the past, and many had doormen, though I never thought I'd find Ginger in one. Well, not unless she got really lucky with one of her boy toys.

The elevator took me to the fourteenth floor of a twenty-five-story building. When the doors opened, I gaped at the elaborately decorated, floral-scented hall. The condo doors, of which there were only four on this floor, were set back in little alcoves, each with its own settee. I couldn't imagine why that would be necessary and filed it away for some other time. The apartment number Ginger had given me was the last one on the left, and I'd barely knocked when the door flung open.

Ginger jumped out, giving me a huge hug before dragging me inside and slamming the door. She did pirouettes around the exquisite living area. The place was fully furnished, and she gave me a speed tour of the three-bedroom apartment that included a state-of-the-art kitchen, a long counter with a bar, and floor-to-ceiling windows that displayed a stunning view of the coast. A balcony stretched the length of the condo, a divider separating it from the condo next door.

"Can you believe it? Lucas said the lease was good for a year. A whole frickin' year!"

My heart lurched to a stop. Did Devon think the mission would take that long?

"I thought we could make the spare bedroom into part gym, part office. Or, I don't know, I used to knit, so now that we have the extra room, maybe a small craft area."

I could usually keep up with her mile-a-minute rambling, but I was having a hard time this go round. The barstool was the only thing that saved me from tipping over at the unexpected extravagance.

"Maybe you should repeat what Lucas actually said."

She opened the fridge and pulled out two bottles of sparkling water, sliding one to me. I sucked down half of it before calming down enough to listen. She must have misunderstood him somewhere along the way.

"Lucas called before I left Seattle. He kept in touch on my drive down and picked me up at the car rental place. He said our apartment was still being targeted, and Devon didn't think it made sense to live out of a hotel since he didn't know how long it would take to clear up the Christopher problem."

"The Christopher problem?" The spinning sensation dissipated, turning to nausea instead.

"That's what I call it. He didn't actually mention Christopher, but we all know it's his goons."

I nodded and stared at the bottle of water in my hand. A high-end brand. "Did Lucas do the shopping?"

"No. He had another vamp do that, just to get us started. Anyway, the condo has a year's lease, has been sitting empty, and Devon said we might as well use it."

"We?"

"That's what he said."

"Devon told you that?"

She nodded and jumped up when the oven buzzer went off. "I made bruschetta. I know you can't stay long, but you should have something to eat. With this kitchen, I'll be able to make all kinds of cool stuff I wasn't able to do before."

She removed a cookie sheet with little slices of French bread topped with a tomato mixture.

"When did you speak with Devon? I thought Lucas brought you here."

"Devon called while I was racing from room to room squealing." She giggled and sipped her water. "I think it hurt Lucas's ears."

I finally broke down and laughed with her. I didn't have a clue what Devon was up to. Was it possible he was just that nice of a guy? It was so hard to tell with his moods. "Wait. He said we would be living here?"

"That's why it's three bedrooms. A spare room for guests or whatever."

"I thought I was living at the estate?" I wanted to have my own place again, didn't I? Of course. The hole opening in my chest was just fear of living in such a nice place before returning to the old neighborhood.

"You'll still be at the estate until your mission is over. So, I'm going to have this huge place all to myself for a while. And no, he didn't say how long, but I think he was okay with sleepovers."

I snorted. "And should I bring my jammies so we can do each other's hair?"

"I was thinking more of slutty movies, popcorn, and tequila shooters, but if you feel up to jammies and curling my hair, I won't be the party pooper."

God, I'd missed Ginger. And when I left to face the afternoon with Anna, it wasn't lost on me that I owed Devon big time for watching out for her.

Chapter Seven

I DREW IN A SLOW, deep breath. The scent of roses was almost overwhelming as I plucked a bloom from its stem, a thorn pricking my finger like it had the first time we'd shared a dream. This time I laughed while staring at the small drop of blood pooling at the tip of my finger. Without thinking, I sucked it off, and the lightest taste of something sweet yet dangerous shivered through me. I twirled in a circle, my arms stretched wide as I lifted my face to the sky, the sun warming my cheeks.

I felt so alive.

The desire to race to the grotto conflicted with my eagerness to explore every inch of the garden. To revel in the colors and its heady aromas. I picked at the petals of the crimson blossom in my hand and sniffed the dusky scent of each one, remembering other times and other places, the images fleeting and blurry, never fully materializing. They were shadows racing just out of sight.

The sound of trickling water, what I knew to be a fountain, brought forth other images: running through a mountain meadow, drinking from a stream next to a fawn-colored doe, a cabin in the forest, the smoke from the hearth barely visible in the dim moonlight, the flames lighting the windows and removing the dark gloom of the trees.

When the grotto came into view, he waited for me.

Devon.

His indigo shirt was open to his waist, low enough to show off the delicate shadows and contours of his muscled-chest and the lightest dusting of hair as it disappeared into the ridge of his pants. I loved this shirt. It brought out the richness of his gaze, and the warm glow induced tingles along my skin.

He stood quietly at my approach, almost hesitant. I'd never seen him so uncertain, except for the night of the ball when he held my broken body in his arms, deciding whether to give me his blood. The memory excited me. I wanted to taste him again—his skin, his lips, his blood.

For a moment, the thought terrified me, but the unease evaporated before it fully developed. When I reached him, I laughed. A deep, throaty chuckle that made his eyes glow with need. Without hesitation, I pulled his lips to mine.

This time, I was emphatic, plundering what I hadn't tasted in years. A pleasure and craving so intense, so demanding, that I ripped the shirt from his shoulders before clutching him to me. My passion careened out of control.

At first, he drew me tight, matching my hunger with his own, his hands claiming my body. But the more I pushed, the more he pulled away. I scratched my nails across his back and down his arms as he tried to step back. He couldn't leave me. Not now. We were here, and I was desperate to be held, for him to take me to the ground and answer my need. The itch that wouldn't go away. What I'd waited decades to have fulfilled.

A flash of terror raced through me, and I tried to pull back, confused by the depths of my emotions. I wanted this man in front of me, but his face began to morph into one I didn't recognize, and I squeezed my eyes shut, shielding me from the stranger.

"Cressa. Take off the necklace."

Who was Cressa?

My fingers clutched the necklace, refusing the command. I would never relinquish my necklace. Not now, not ever. It was my bridge.

Someone shook me, but I couldn't see anything but that face I didn't know—one of love and desire and rage.

A hand stronger than my own tore my fingers away from the necklace. It was ripped from my neck as everything went black.

DEVON RACED down the hall with nothing on but his sweatpants. He'd barely remembered to grab them before shouting for Lucas and Sergi. Panic overtook him as he raced to the other end of the hall to Cressa's room.

Lucas and Sergi raced down the stairs from the third floor as Devon flew past the landing. When he reached the corner room, he tried the knob, but it was locked. He groaned. After two weeks, she still locked the door. He shouldn't take it personally. It was probably out of habit considering her old neighborhood, but it bothered him for a reason he didn't have time to ponder.

"Cressa!" He pounded on the door, then stopped to listen. Nothing. "Cressa, please open the door."

"What is it?" Sergi glanced at Lucas, who shrugged his shoulders. Of course, neither would know what was happening.

"A dream. A really unpleasant one." He rattled the doorknob again before slamming his fist on the door twice more. "Cressa, please. You need to wake up."

"I'll get the key." Lucas turned toward the stairs.

Devon didn't wait. He took a step back then dove into the door, using his shoulder to take the brunt of the hit. The frame shattered, and the door, hinges ripped out, fell to the floor with a solid thud on the thick carpet.

He was at her bedside in seconds. She appeared to be asleep, her sable hair haloed across the pillow. The sound of busting wood should have brought her into an immediate defensive stance, or at the very least a hand rubbing her head, griping about the noise waking her, yet she didn't stir. He glanced at Lucas, who stood on the other side of the bed, his own concern etched across his face.

No help there. He pushed his hands through his hair, remembering how Cressa had run her own through it just moments ago. But had it been Cressa? In so many ways it had been, but another side of her had surfaced. Maybe he didn't know her well enough, and she'd simply dropped her defenses, yet it hadn't felt right. It wasn't the Cressa he'd come to know.

Then he spotted the necklace on the floor. The thin chain was broken. He'd seen her wearing it in the dream, and when she'd become almost savage in her need for him, it had been a simple reflexive reaction to rip it off her. The medallion wasn't the cool metal he'd expected. It was warm, and something like a spark had run through him before he'd flung it away. How strange to find it on the bedroom floor.

"Do you want me to call a healer?" Sergi's words broke through his muddled thoughts.

Healers worked on vampires and shifters, not humans. But after tonight, it appeared to be a foregone conclusion that Cressa wasn't purely human.

"Yes." A healer wouldn't make it any worse than it was. But how bad was it if they couldn't wake her?

He sat on the bed and nudged her. Nothing.

"Cressa, wake up. I need to know that you're all right." He couldn't remember seeing anything like this before. Holy hells, what was he thinking? He'd never been with a dreamwalker before. How would he know what was normal? Just because this hadn't happened during any of the previous dreams didn't mean this was abnormal.

"Cressa, please." He shook her harder. No response. He glanced at the necklace still lying on the floor. Maybe it had been a mistake to remove it. She could be in shock, or maybe she was stuck in the dream. No. She'd collapsed in the dream before disappearing.

He turned when Sergi picked up the door and leaned it against the doorjamb. "She's on her way. Shall I start a fire?"

He glanced toward the hearth. Cressa had never asked about lighting it. The mansion had other forms of heat, but this seemed like an appropriate moment. He nodded. "Lucas, can you get a tray? Water, a pot of tea..." He ran a hand over his hair again. "Christ, I don't know."

Lucas laid a hand on his shoulder. "I'll take care of it."

Once Lucas had left for the kitchen and Sergi for wood, he picked up the necklace. It was cold to the touch as he'd originally expected it to be. If there was anything magical about it, he couldn't sense it, and it no longer emanated the warmth or energy it had exhibited in the dream. He considered the fact he might have imagined it. It was a dream, after all. Wanting nothing to do with it until after Cressa woke, he placed the necklace on the dresser next to her jewelry box.

He dragged a chair next to her bed so he wouldn't disturb her but would be close enough in case she woke and needed something. His hand trembled as he caressed her hair before running it over her forehead. Like the medallion, it was cool to the touch, not like the warmth he'd felt barely an hour ago.

He'd been breathless when he'd found himself in the garden. It had been over a week since their last grotto dream, and he'd missed the time they spent there. No one but the two of them, exploring their passion in their own place and time, their problems erased— no Council, no Underwood, no doubt. Had they been prescient or simply wishful?

Something had been different when she'd run to him. He'd sensed it immediately, but when her intense gaze held nothing but adoration and hunger, he didn't question his luck. She was always happy to see him in their dreams, and there was never any hesitation in her responses to him. Nothing stood between them.

At first, her eagerness excited him, and he didn't question her assertiveness when she took control. Her passionate kiss rocked him, and all he wanted to do was lose himself in her. Then the kiss changed. If anyone were to ask, he wasn't certain he could explain it, but he didn't believe it was Cressa in his arms, ripping his shirt and demanding more. It was like she was drowning, and then a fierceness took over that was so deep, so ravenous, she couldn't seem to stop herself.

Her kiss no longer tasted the same. Even her scent had been different, and if he hadn't been staring into her face, he would have thought it wasn't her at all. Then he was caught in her gaze, and it wasn't Cressa's eyes boring into his. He barely broke away, her gaze as strong as a vampire's. It might have been some form of repressed energy, leftovers from his blood. Or it wasn't Cressa at all.

That was when he spotted the necklace dangling just above her luscious breasts. All he wanted was to hold her, to run his lips across her breasts and feel her arch into him. It had required all his strength to grasp the necklace, and for a moment he'd felt weak as a kitten, his vampire strengths suppressed. Then he realized there was a barrier between them. Something more powerful than him. When he finally managed to break the necklace free and toss it away, he caught a flicker in her eyes before she collapsed in his arms.

He'd immediately woken, and his only thought was to get to her and make sure she was all right. Nothing else had mattered.

Chapter Eight

A KNOCK STARTLED DEVON, who'd been so deep in thought he hadn't noticed the door had been rehung on a still-damaged frame. Holy hells, he'd been so focused on Cressa, he'd dropped his other senses. He should never allow his thoughts to be so distracted, even in his own home surrounded by his most trusted.

"Sorry, sir. The healer is here." Sergi stepped inside, followed by Madame Saldano, who swept past him and stalked to the bed.

Lucas followed behind them, carrying a tray with cups, a teapot emitting earthy scents, a coffee urn, and a plate of loaf cakes and scones, which he placed on the table near the hearth. Devon hadn't even noticed when Sergi brought in wood and started a fire.

Madame Saldano stared down at her patient. "When Sergi called, I assumed it was about Lyra." She set her bag on the nightstand before performing a quick physical on Cressa. Next, she stepped back, closed her eyes, and began to sway. After five minutes, she shook her head and opened her eyes, a crease forming over her narrow nose. She sat on the bed and laid her hands on Cressa's arms before tilting her head back and falling into a trance.

Nothing she did surprised him. Madame Saldano was a special healer. While she was well-schooled in western and eastern medicine, she'd had limited medical training and never earned a degree. Her specialty focused on magical maladies and cures, and she'd been treating Lyra for years. From what she'd explained to him, the trance connected her to the patient, allowing her to see past the physical and into the mystical realm.

The healer lifted her head then opened her bag, pulling out tiny vials and containers. "Bring me a cup of tea."

He started to get up, but Lucas was already pouring a cup. He wasn't sure how Cressa was supposed to drink anything in her current state, and he snorted at his stupidity when Madame Saldano sipped it before setting it aside.

She mixed herbs and liquids together, prattling to herself the entire time. Sergi, who'd left, once again without Devon noticing, returned with a bottle of scotch and one of vodka. He poured drinks, handing one to Devon before settling in front of the hearth next to Lucas.

"She's in a deep sleep." The healer's words, sharp and definitive, snapped him out of his own trance. "The closest I can compare it to is passing out from too much mental strain. What was she doing before she collapsed?"

Devon hesitated. He trusted the healer—to a point. She was sanctioned by the Council and owed them some fealty. He'd never spoken of dreamwalkers to her, not in all the decades she'd treated Lyra. And while the healers practiced a form of patient confidentiality similar to human doctors, it was too dangerous for anyone outside his inner circle to learn of his suspicions that Cressa was a dreamwalker. If the Council found out, the news would spread like wildfire, and the last thing he wanted anyone to know was that a dreamwalker actually existed. They'd take her away, and he could only hide her for so long. Until he knew for certain and understood what that knowledge meant, their secret had to be kept.

"I heard a scream and found her in bed like this." He didn't glance at Sergi or Lucas. They understood the dangers as well as he.

"I've never seen anything like this happen during one's sleep. Is she a telepath?"

The question surprised Devon, and he didn't bother to mask it. "Why would you ask that?

She continued mixing herbs with familiar liquids, the faded lilac color similar to Lyra's sleeping aid. The old woman shrugged. "I sensed a residual energy. Something I would typically detect in a telepath." She sucked on her teeth before her eyes once more glazed over. "But the essence isn't quite the same." She lifted her face toward the ceiling, her eyes rolling to the back of her head, and she swayed as if buffeted by a light wind. For a split-second, her face pinched before quickly returning to normal.

"Yes. Definitely telepathic tendrils, but not from her. I believe someone, somehow, has linked with her, and the power of this person was just too great. Our minds are fragile, yet very strong. For some, it's a tightrope of balance. Fortunately, the brain protects itself when it can. In this case, I believe the force became too strong, or perhaps she sensed the intrusion and tried to fight it. Either way, the mind shut down to evade whoever was meddling."

She packed up her bag, leaving two vials on the nightstand. "Does she know any telepaths?"

"Not that I know of."

She stood and glanced back down at her patient, sucking her teeth once more, her brows screwed up in thought. "As you know, vampires have the ability to adjust a human's thinking for a limited time. For long term impact, they must physically connect with that person through touch. Through blood exchange, vampires can sometimes share thoughts, though it requires a well-trained mind for all involved. And while these vampire traits are closely linked with telepathy, it's far from the same thing. It's rare to find a telepath with enough power to over-ride another's mind, be it vampire or human, but they are out there." She shrugged. "Most keep their skills secret, and without knowing more, all I can suggest is that this child appears to have an enemy of some sort. Have you seen anything strange while she's awake?"

"No."

She sighed. "It's possible that this attack, if that's truly what this was, only comes when she sleeps, when her subconscious is the most vulnerable. I'm leaving two potions. The pink one is for the headache she'll have when she wakes. I expect it might be quite debilitating. If it is, she should stay in bed for at least a day. Otherwise, just make sure she's stable on her feet before doing anything strenuous. The second is the same drought I give Lyra. It will force her into a deeper sleep that will prevent dreaming. That should block a telepath."

"When will she wake?"

"No idea. But based on the remaining residue I was able to catch, I would think not before noon."

Devon stood and clasped the healer's hand. "Thank you, Madame Saldano. Your assistance was valuable as always."

She squinted up at him. "How's Lyra?"

He smiled. "She's been well."

"Excellent. I worry for that child." She turned to take a last look at Cressa, releasing Devon's hands. "Their maladies aren't the same, yet..." She trailed off, and Devon was thankful the two of them weren't touching anymore. The healer was sure to pick up emotions he could mask from others.

"I'll have Sergi see you out."

The healer's broad smile showed her missing tooth, and she cackled like a witch. "Excellent. I just received a message from the old country I think he'd be interested in hearing."

Sergi gave the woman one of his rare smiles. "I always look forward to your news, Madame Saldano."

"How many times must I ask you to call me Laxana?"

"Many more, Madame Saldano."

Her gruff laugh trailed behind her as Sergi led her down the hall.

Lucas picked up the tray. "Shall I bring you a fresh pot of coffee and your tablet?" He stood next to the bed and looked down at Cressa. "Was it a shared dream?"

"Yes." Devon rubbed his face. He couldn't remember the last time he'd felt so tired. "I knew something was wrong. She didn't seem like herself."

"What could the telepathic residue mean?"

"I don't know."

"You need blood, sir. It's been well over a month."

His inner circle never had to remind him of such matters, but Lucas was only performing his duty as guard, and it had been more than two months since he'd last fed. "I don't want to leave her. Can you have someone brought over from Oasis?"

Lucas's shoulders eased. He'd been expecting a fight. "I'll see to it." Devon reached for his arm as he passed.

"Thank you for watching over me."

Lucas grinned. "If I waited for Sergi to suggest it, you'd look like Nosferatu."

Devon couldn't hold back a laugh, and all the tension he'd been holding released in one burst. "And we can't have Cressa waking up to that."

"No. I'd think not." Then Lucas disappeared.

Devon repositioned himself in the chair, ready for the long wait. Even delegating most of the work to his cadre, he'd been over-taxing himself. It sometimes happened with problematic negotiations, but the stakes were larger now. Between keeping tabs on Lorenzo, Cressa storming into this life, his complex plan to regain his Council seat, and this dreamwalker business—he shouldn't have gone so long between feedings. Now, in order to fully recover, he would need to feed in smaller doses for the next three days, so he didn't injure his blood source.

For the first time that evening, he sensed someone enter the room. Another sign he needed blood. He should have felt them coming down the hall. Expecting to see Sergi, he was surprised when the diminutive form stepped in front of him.

"Lyra. You know you're not supposed to leave your room without permission."

"I know." Her voice was low, but only mildly apologetic.

"Come here." He held out an arm, and she crawled into his lap as a child would with their father rather than the grown woman she was. Her willowy stature made her seem more a pixie than either a woman or child. She turned so she could face the bed. "I know how difficult it's been with our new guest. You've handled it very well."

She leaned her head against his shoulder. "I've been sneaking out in the early morning."

He smiled at her confession and kissed her temple. "I thought so."

"I don't think she sees me do it, but she does like to stay up late."

"You won't have to stay hidden for much longer."

"Is she all right? She'll wake up, won't she?"

Devon considered his answer. Not because he worried what to say, but Lyra had never shown an interest in anyone else.

"She should wake in a few hours."

Lyra played with a button on her nightgown. She was still painfully thin, but it didn't seem to lessen her energy.

"I felt her this time."

Devon stiffened and turned Lyra to face him. He kept his tone even so she wouldn't shut down. "What do you mean?"

Lyra glanced away and shrugged a shoulder.

"This is very important, Lyra. For both of you."

Her fingers moved back to the button before running over the bottom edge of her nightgown. Her head lowered, and her voice was so soft it required a vampire to hear her. "Sometimes I can feel her dreams."

He blanched at the thought of Lyra seeing him with Cressa.

She lifted her head so quickly, she bumped her head on his chin. And her words chilled him at the thought she could read his mind. "I can't see the dreams. But I can sense she's having a special one."

That shocked him. How does one perceive someone else's dreams? If only Lyra would share everything she saw when her nightmares were upon her. Was it possible that Cressa sensed Lyra, most likely without even knowing it?

Lyra trembled, and he hugged her. His next question only a guess on his part. "But something changed tonight?"

She kept her voice low and whispered into his ear as if keeping it from whatever ghost might be lurking. "I don't think it was Cressa."

He could barely breathe. "Who was it?"

She shook her head. "A bad person."

He hugged her tighter, caressing her arm until the tremors faded, and then he kissed her forehead. "Go back to bed, Lyra. I promise I'll figure this out soon."

Her smile was huge when she jumped up, and it almost broke his heart the trust she had in him. She gave Cressa a tentative glance. "I know you will." She kissed his cheek and almost skipped out of the room.

He listened to her footsteps until he heard the door click shut upstairs.

"Simone is driving someone over for you. She'll be here in a couple of hours." Lucas placed a refreshed tray on the table in front of the hearth, then stood over Cressa. "Shall I cancel her sessions for tomorrow?"

"Yes. Thank you for everything, Lucas."

Once the door shut, Devon checked Cressa's forehead, which was the same cool temperature as before. He sat in front of the fire and poured a cup of coffee. If there had been a telepathic residue, that might explain why Lyra sensed Cressa's dreams. Telepathy could be powerful, and if he considered what he'd experienced in the shared dreams, it would explain the connection between telepathic abilities and dreamwalking. It wasn't the first time Madame Saldano had mentioned telepathic tendrils after one of Lyra's episodes. But Lyra had never mentioned being able to discern another's dreams. Was it because Cressa was a dreamwalker? Telepathy alone couldn't explain why the dreams were so realistic.

Maybe the necklace had somehow amplified the properties of a dreamwalker. He was so far out of his depths that all of this was sheer speculation. They needed to learn as much as they could about dreamwalkers as quickly as possible.

He glanced at the dresser as he considered the necklace, then jumped up. After scanning the dresser and the carpet, he opened the jewelry box in case Lucas had put it away.

The necklace was gone.

He rubbed his eyes and cursed his luck.

Lyra and her sticky fingers.

Chapter Nine

A CROAK, followed by a long, low groan reverberated in my head. It took a full minute before I realized the repeating sound was coming from me. My head felt like a battering ram was tearing at its walls, but I couldn't tell if someone was hammering to get in or I was trying to get out. I managed to pry an eye open for a quick peek.

The room was dark except for the glow of firelight. Where was I?

If I kept it to small increments, I could turn my head without increasing the pounding ache. This was my room. I hadn't recognized it at first because the fireplace had never been used, and now I wondered why not. It was pretty.

Good grief, I must be losing it. Whatever happened before waking up was a blur, and if I judged the size of my headache, my first thought would have been an all-night bender. Something told me I wouldn't be that lucky.

"Cressa."

The sound of my name was somewhere between a question and relief. That worried me. Had I fallen through a window again?

"Cressa. Are you awake?"

Devon's concerned tone sent warm shivers through my body. The tingles hit all the right spots, washing all my fears away. How did I let a vamp of all people worm his way past my defenses? It had to be those damn dreams.

A piercing stab breached the walls, shooting past the punishing ache. An involuntary cry erupted before I grabbed my head and curled into a fetal position.

Devon was at my side in a flash, caressing my arm. "I have a potion that will help with the headache. From what I've been told, it acts quickly."

A potion. From the local witch store? I laughed, but it turned into a grimace.

"Can you sit up?"

I tried, but my limbs felt so heavy I couldn't raise an arm more than an inch. If I didn't know better, I'd swear I'd run a marathon overnight—and that worried me. No way in hell would I have done that. Before I knew it, Devon was behind me, gently lifting me to lean against him. I squinted past the increased pain and stared at the shot glass of pinkish liquid he held in front of me.

"Are you sure?" My raspy voice was unrecognizable to my own ears, but he seemed to understand.

"I trust the healer on this. I've seen it used before."

At this point, death seemed better than the repeating drum solo. I sipped it at first, waiting for a nasty kick, but it carried a sweet aftertaste, and I swallowed the rest of it down. If nothing else, the coolness quenched the dryness in my throat.

Devon carefully stacked pillows behind me, and before he laid me on them, the pounding receded to a tapping. I didn't know what the pink stuff was, and I noticed the vial on the nightstand next to a purplish mixture, but someone should be marketing it. Not only had the ache lessened, but my memory was returning, and my arms felt lighter.

"What happened? What time is it?" I pulled the covers tighter, more for comfort than warmth. I wasn't sure I wanted to know, but I'd place all my chips on a dream being involved.

"It's almost noon."

I glanced at the windows. Thick drapes I'd never considered closing before had been pulled together so completely not a drop of light leaked past them. Of course, this was a vamp house.

"I had a dream." I vaguely remembered the grotto and Devon waiting for me, looking devastatingly scrumptious.

"It might have been more of a nightmare. Do you remember any of it?"

"Don't you?"

His eyes glittered. "I'm not the one that collapsed during it. This is about you."

Collapsed? I closed my eyes and focused on the dream. I'd raced to him, and he'd immediately pulled me into his arms. I touched my lips where his kiss had scorched me with his unbridled longing.

No. That wasn't what happened.

I'd been the aggressor, filled with a deep, unsatiated desire. The hunger had raged through me until I'd lost control. My cheeks heated as I reached for my neck.

"I was wearing the necklace. You ripped it off me." I didn't know whether I should be irritated or forever grateful.

"You didn't seem yourself." He didn't sound apologetic, and not having time to fully piece together the dream, I couldn't argue with him.

I had the funny feeling that once I had time to dissect the memory, I'd come to the same conclusion.

A tap sounded at the door.

"Come." Devon stood as Lucas entered the room with a tray.

I smelled the coffee before he breached the doorway and almost salivated.

"Cook wasn't sure if you'd would be ready to eat but insisted on sending something up." Lucas set down the tray and smiled at me. "Too soon for coffee?"

"Never." I gave him an impish grin then gave Devon a larger smile. "The headache is almost gone."

"Excellent. Why don't you eat something and chat with Lucas. I need to take care of a few things, but I'll be back soon."

No doubt to push me for answers. "I'll be ready for my afternoon sessions."

"You're on bed rest for the remainder of the day. You can move about your room and regain your strength, but no farther." When I began to protest, he held up a hand. "The healer's orders, and we follow those to the letter in this house."

"Yes, Dad." I pouted, but both vamps just smiled in that patronizing way they had.

Devon stepped next to the bed. "Try to behave for one day. I'll be back in a couple of hours, and we can finish our talk." He kissed the top of my head before whispering in my ear, "You scared me half to death. Please do this one thing for me."

When he stepped back, it was easy to read his expression. Whatever happened in the dream had frightened him. And if it alarmed Devon Trelane, it should terrify me.

DEVON ENTERED his office thirty minutes later, showered and dressed in chinos and a tailored shirt. Sergi relaxed in front of the desk, studying his tablet.

"Is she all right?" Sergi asked, never taking his gaze from the tablet.

"I think so. I'll speak with her more after she's had a chance to pull her thoughts together." Devon collapsed in his chair and opened the blinds, allowing the afternoon sun to filter through the room. He needed blood and sleep. "Your report is overdue."

"I found something that took me out of town."

"Something worth the trip?"

"I believe so. I forwarded you the file."

Devon searched his tablet and found the document. "Give me the highlights." Excitement revived him, but he reined it in. He'd found promising leads before that had gone nowhere.

"I went back to the apartment where Willa Langtry lived when Cressa was born. We know from my earlier reports that most of the neighbors had moved away, but this time, I went door to door on all five floors. I found an old man who lives on the top floor now, but he'd lived down the hall from Willa back then. He didn't know her other than to say hello, though he admitted he'd had an interest in her, but she was already in a serious relationship. He mentioned a woman who lived across from her. They weren't best friends, but they did spend some time together, or so the old man claims."

"Wasn't this woman in your last report?" Devon's temper was rising, but he pushed it back. His impatience was a sign of low blood levels, and Sergi wouldn't be backtracking over old information unless he was leading up to something. He glanced at his watch. Simone should have been here by now with his blood source.

"Yes. I had four names I've been tracking down from that time period. The woman living in the apartment across from Willa is Veronica LeFay, originally from New Orleans. And that's where I found her, though she's married now. I prefer doing this in person, but she was willing to talk over the phone and remembered Willa quite well. It's like the old man said. They spoke in the hallway mostly, occasionally shared a cup of coffee, until they both got pregnant at the same time."

"She remembers Cressa's father?"

Sergi nodded. "And then some. She couldn't stop talking about the man and gave me a decent description, but nothing that stands out as being unusual. In fact, the man seems to be an average sort except for her comment..." He scrolled through his report until he found the passage he was looking for and shared it with his drollest tone. "He was a looker. And he had an aura of sensuality that made a woman's panties wet."

Devon barked out a laugh. "Veronica sounds like she doesn't hold anything back."

"No, sir. It was difficult to get her back on track after that."

"So, we have a general description. Do we have a name?"

"Just a first name—Rasmussen."

"That's not much to go on. And that's assuming he's truly Cressa's father."

"That's where things got interesting. When I gave the time period of Cressa's birth, Veronica insisted I had my information incorrect. When I told her it was on a birth certificate, she said she didn't care. Maybe Willa had a second child, but she remembered the name Cressa and that she was born the month after her own daughter was born. She was adamant that they'd shared baby clothes and accessories because they were both on a pretty tight budget. When Cressa was about six months old, Willa and Rasmussen had a huge fight, and Veronica never saw him again. A few months later, Willa moved."

"The birth certificate was forged?"

"I'm having that checked now. But this woman has no reason to lie."

"When was Cressa born?"

"Two years to the date earlier than what the birth records show."

"Willa was covering her trail?"

Sergi shrugged. "Maybe."

"Good work."

"It's not enough."

"No. But maybe Cressa can get us closer. Were you able to retrieve the necklace from Lyra?"

"Not without negotiation." Sergi fished the necklace out of his shirt pocket and laid it on the desk.

He snorted. "What did she ask for this time?"

"More time out of her room. If you don't need me, I thought I might take her to Oasis for the day."

Devon considered it. The staff at Oasis knew Lyra and her special needs, though Devon preferred to go with her. But if he was honest about it, chaperoning her was more an opportunity for him to make one of his rare visits to his true home. Until he found a way to remove his censure, it was imperative he kept Oasis a secret from anyone other than his family and a short list of trusted partners.

It was tempting to go, but he trusted Sergi and the rest of his guards to care for Lyra. "The day is half over. See if Marta minds watching her overnight. She can come home tomorrow."

"Is she well enough for that?"

"I think so. I'll speak with her before you leave. I need time with Cressa."

A knock at the door preceded it opening, and Simone peered in, a twitch to her lips. "I'm sorry to disturb you, but I understood this was a rush order." The Somalian beauty didn't appear sorry, and with barely a nod from him, strolled in, her lavender caftan flowing about her legs, a man in his twenties trailing behind her.

UNABLE TO STAY in bed after Devon left, I'd taken a shower, feeling better than I had in days. The pink tonic seemed to have given me a boost as well as diminish the headache. I slipped on my sneakers and ran hands through my damp hair before glancing around for a sweater. When I stepped next to the dresser, my hand went to my neck. My necklace. I'd reached for it as if it was something I'd put on every day, yet it had been years since I'd worn it daily. I remembered putting it on last night.

The hot flash of a headache hit me, then it was gone just as quickly. The dream. I rubbed my forehead. Bits and pieces of the evening returned—my eagerness to see Devon, the exotic smells and textures that felt foreign yet unforgettable, and then the deep, burning, ravenous need to claim him. Even alone in my room, my cheeks burned with shame. The last thing I remembered was the return of impenetrable darkness.

I rubbed my arms to chase the chill away. When I clutched at my chest again, still barren of the necklace, I knew without a doubt, as sure as I knew Christopher was an asshole, that the necklace had somehow affected the dream. And not in a good way. I checked the jewelry box, the pants I'd worn to town the previous day, and every inch of carpet.

No necklace.

From what Lucas said, Devon had been in my room all night until I woke. My irritation flared at his audacity of taking my necklace without asking. I told him I'd let him look at it.

Forgetting the sweater and my promise to stay in my room, I marched down the stairs and stormed through the mansion. This time of day, if he was home, he'd be in his office, but it didn't hurt to check out the other rooms, giving the anger time to cool. Nothing good ever came of confronting him in rage; he tended to toss it right back at me.

When I reached his office, I should have slowed and taken a breath—my irritation still roiling and making me jumpy. His policy about walking in unannounced when his door was closed was a major beef with him. He valued his privacy. Well, so did I, and when he took my necklace, he broke his own privacy rule. So, tit for tat as they say.

I grabbed the handle, ready to shove it open, when an instant of sanity returned, and I inched my way in before I lost my courage along with my outrage.

I stopped cold.

Sergi and Simone stood on either side of Devon, their posture similar, their eyes flashing at me as the bodyguards they were. I was the intruder.

Devon leaned back in his office chair. A man, who appeared to be a couple of years younger than me, had the sleeve of his right arm rolled up, and his eyes held a dreamy cast as he stared blindly past me. His arm was held out as an offering, and Devon's mouth covered his wrist.

I stepped back but couldn't take my eyes off the two of them. I knew Devon drank blood, and that he'd given me some of his own when I'd lay dying after the two-story fall. But other than the hellish dream of him ripping out Sorrento's throat, I'd never seen any of the vamps feed. The stark difference between this intimate scene and the dark horror in that alley was shocking—yet intriguing.

I shook my head and took another step back before turning and running right into Lucas, who must have followed me in. He grabbed my shoulder with one hand while putting a finger over his lips and turning me around to witness the rest.

What had been a foolish act resulting in an embarrassing entrance now became extremely uncomfortable in a voyeuristic way. I wasn't sure I should be seeing this. But he held me fast as Devon finished his—meal? I gulped. He said he didn't drink often. What were the odds I'd be here for this?

He'd appeared tired the last couple of days. I'd thought he just needed more sleep. It never occurred to me, even living with vamps, that he might need more nourishment than an organic salmon salad.

After another minute, Devon stopped, but before he lifted his head, he licked the wound. An unexpected shiver ran through me, and I knew Lucas would have sensed it, if not outright felt it through the hand still resting on my shoulder.

Devon, those deadly fangs still out, turned icy-blue eyes on me. A drop of blood dripped, and all I could think was how amazingly clean he looked after feeding. I must be losing it. Maybe from shock after everything that had happened in the last couple of days.

His fangs receded, and his gaze warmed to a more sedate blue. Simone handed him a napkin, which he pressed against his lips. I guess there was more blood than I thought when he tossed the crimson-stained tissue in the wastebasket.

"We discussed the office door policy. Didn't we?" His voice held a husky note of authority and irritation.

That's what he wanted to chat about now? Okay. We'll forget all about the mobile blood bank that Sergi eased into a chair. I wondered if the young man would be offered orange juice and cookies like they handed out at blood drives. Yep, I was going bonkers.

"I also thought you said privacy was critical in this house." Being snappy wasn't the wisest choice, but now that it was out, I couldn't seem to stop myself.

He raised a single brow before his gaze narrowed and that icy glare sparked.

"My necklace," I all but spit it out, not ready to play his games when he damn well knew what I was talking about.

He blinked, and his harsh expression disappeared as his shoulders relaxed. "Leave us."

I assumed he hadn't been talking to me when Sergi lifted the blood donor by his arm and followed Simone out of the office. She gave me one of her why-can't-you-behave glares but never slowed as she exited. When the door shut with a rather loud click, Devon held out a hand for me to sit.

Once I perched on the edge of the chair in front of his desk, he slid the necklace to me. I grabbed it and studied it as if maybe someone had damaged it. And someone had. I held up the broken chain.

"I'll get you a new one."

When I only glared, he turned toward the window and opened the blinds, the bright afternoon sun banishing the shadows in the office. When he turned back, I noticed how vibrant he looked. The dark shadows under his eyes from just a few hours ago were gone.

He held my stare. "I won't apologize for pulling you out of that dream."

His words shocked me, and I rubbed my forehead. "What the hell happened?"

"Do you remember any of it?"

The earlier flashes in my room returned, but nothing more. "I remember being in the garden. I remember flashes of you." My heated blush returned, and I dropped my gaze, finding my hands clenched around the necklace. "Whenever I attempt to play it back, something seems to block any vision of it."

"I'm not sure it was you. Or the better way to say it might be it wasn't all you."

"What does that mean?"

"Based on our previous shared dreams, I..." Now, he hesitated. Was he as uncomfortable as I was? "You weren't acting yourself," he finished.

Goof grief, what had I done? I rubbed my forehead.

"Do you still have a headache?"

"Not really. It's just frustrating that I can't remember much."

He ran through a quick and embarrassing replay of the event, including seeing the necklace, some instinct that made him rip it off, and the warmth it seemed to exude. He finished with the healer and her mention of telepathic residue.

I dropped the necklace on his desk and pushed it toward him. "Maybe we should keep it someplace safe until we learn more about it." Part of me wanted to grab it back and hide it away myself. No. What I really wanted to do was put it back on, but what if I ended up in another psychic coma, or whatever state I'd been in, and never woke up? It was best if someone else held onto it for now.

"You trust me to do that?"

I snorted, fell back in the chair, and blew out a long sigh. "I'm sorry for getting huffy and interrupting your..." I wasn't really sure what to call it. "Meeting. But with Christopher searching for it and... I don't know, it seems to be calling to me."

"You weren't meant to see the blood transfer."

It seemed we were both ready to make nice. "Is that what vamps call it?"

He chuckled. "I was trying to be polite."

I couldn't help but smile at the sparkle in his gaze. He was rarely in a playful mood, not since the night of the ball. Then his smile disappeared, and his expression turned grave.

Now what?

"You know I had Sergi run a background check on you."

"Right." Well, crap. "What did you find?"

His lips twitched but nothing else changed. He picked up his tablet and tapped a few buttons. "Does the name Rasmussen mean anything to you?"

I was ready to say no, but something stopped me. Now it was my turn to gaze out the window. Had I heard it before? Or perhaps some variation.

"Cressa?"

I glanced up and gave a half-hearted shrug. "I don't know, and I know how that sounds. But I wasn't very old when my father left us. My mother never spoke a word about him, except when she gave me that necklace." I hugged myself as I rocked back and forth. A distant memory lay just out of sight. There was music, but I couldn't quite catch the melody. I couldn't even remember if there had been lyrics.

"Something pokes at me, just like the dream, but it won't solidify. Like I could reach out and touch it, but before I can bring it into focus, it slips away."

I jumped when he brushed my arm, forgetting how quick he could move. He took my hand and pulled me from the chair, his arm going around my shoulder as he steered me toward the door.

"I think every time you force your subconscious into revealing something it isn't ready to share, your memory grows hazy—even blocked. You've barely recovered from a difficult experience that greatly taxed your mind. Telepathic residue is not something to take lightly."

When we stepped into the hall, he let go of me, but not without his hand cupping my cheek for the briefest of moments. "You should try eating something. It will help with the mental healing. And since you seem incapable of remaining in your room, please find something to do that will take your mind off everything we've discussed. There will be time for that later." He lifted my chin. "Can you do that?"

I pushed his hand away but gave him a wink. "What trouble could I possibly get into stuck in this gloomy mansion?"

"That's the spirit." He turned, but hesitated. "I'll see you this evening for dinner."

Then his door shut behind him.

Chapter Ten

By LATE AFTERNOON, I was restless. Whatever had been in that pink vial had not only banished the headache, it left me energized. But with Devon's house restrictions, I had few avenues to expend it. After a long stroll outside and another one through the house, I curled up on one of the overstuffed chairs in the library with the tome *Houses of the Vampire*, my focus on the Houses of Trelane and Venizi. Each of the lengthy House chapters covered four families, but from what I'd read so far, and Anna had confirmed, the other two in this particular section were considered lower Houses, neither having family on the Council, so I'd only skimmed their pages.

These four Houses were created in the same decade, and like the other chapters, each section described their beginnings. From what I'd been able to gather from the tightly written script, the Trelane and Venizi Houses had been very similar in their origins.

Each House leader, referred to as Father, had been born vampire from less distinguished families. Both Trelane and Venizi had fought glorious battles, earning great praise and special recognition from the Council. They'd each been given land and their House names had been added to the nobility and officially recorded. These two men had been friends, fighting side-by-side in many battles, and as their Houses grew stronger, both men were invited to positions on the Council, which lifted them to the highest ranks of aristocracy. This occurred two thousand years ago, and based on the family trees, intricately drawn at the beginning of each section, these two men were the grandfathers of Devon and Lorenzo. That was a hard one to wrap my head around.

Anna had only scratched the surface in our classwork, so when I had time to peruse the tome, I skipped ahead, flipping through pages to see where the two Houses might have broken away from their long friendship.

After an hour of reading, my eyes blurred over the old text, and I nodded off, only waking when my forehead brushed the book. Or maybe it was the scent of coffee that tickled my nose. I turned around, thinking someone must have entered the room. No one was there, but a serving tray had been placed on a table in front of the hearth.

I hefted the tome and dropped it on the couch in front of the slow-burning fire. I took a stroll around the room, stretching my back and neck, working out the kinks. I stopped to stare at a huge portrait of a man I now knew was the man I'd been reading about —Devon's grandfather. Instead of thinking of his family, portions of Devon's words from earlier in the day bounced around in my head.

Rasmussen.

The possibility that this man could be my father felt right, yet I couldn't put my finger on why. I was positive my mother never mentioned the name. Maybe it had been something I read. I rubbed my temples. Everything was still fuzzy from the last dream, and each time I poked at the edges, a headache threatened.

I shook out my arms, rolled my neck, and poured a cup of coffee. I dropped onto the couch, pulled my legs up under me, and heaved the tome back on my lap. I swallowed two more gulps and opened the book to nowhere in particular.

I snorted when the pages flipped to the House Renaud. Of the four Houses, this one appeared the weakest, at least in regard to skill at battle, which seemed to be of great importance back then. Compared to human history, it wasn't much different. This particular House specialized in knowledge, building and preserving mass libraries. While this activity was considered crucial by many on the Council, during these early centuries where battles raged, books were of little note by others.

I'd read through several pages and was ready to move back to the Trelane section when something caught my eye. It wasn't anything special about the sentence, other than the phrase *De første dage*. There were several areas within the tome where other languages cropped up and, from what Anna deciphered when I'd shown them to her, were names of villages, other vamps, and the like. I had no idea what language this was.

I flipped to another page where a sticky note had been used as a bookmark and ripped it in half, using one half for the original page and the other for this new page in the Renaud section. When I read over the passage for the fourth time, nerves tingled as if I were standing under high-voltage wires. My excitement grew, I just couldn't explain why. It was that spark I got, the hairs rising on the back of my neck whenever I found a job.

I was so engrossed in what I'd discovered, I didn't hear anyone enter until Devon stood in front of me, a dark shadow in my periphery. I dragged my gaze from the pages to glance up.

His hair had been pulled back in a ponytail, the firelight playing off the golden strands. Eyes as warm as the Caribbean sea held humor as he studied the book.

"I told Anna not to tax you with homework." He poured a cup of coffee and sat in the chair next to the couch.

"She didn't. I needed something to do, and since the gym was locked..." I let the sentence hang, and while it was obvious it had been his doing, he didn't respond, nor did he appear the least sorry about it. He could be so stubborn. "So, rather than climb the wall or drapes, I decided to do some reading."

My excitement grew when he lifted a brow. I took it as a positive sign and jumped in. "I think I found something, though I'm not sure what to make of it."

"There are probably many things in the House books that would seem odd without a more thorough understanding of our history. It will make more sense as you move farther through the centuries."

"Maybe. I'm still not done reading about the House Trelane and Venizi, but I happened to find this passage in the section on House Renaud." With the weight of the tome on my lap, I struggled to unwrap my legs as I scooted to the edge of the sofa. Once I was close enough for him to see, I stabbed at the paragraph that had caught my eye.

Devon leaned over and fingered my odd selection of bookmarks. "What are these?"

"Oh, just pages where I found items of interest. I still need Anna to decipher some of the words or meanings. See this sentence, these words." I turned the book so he could read them.

After a few moments, he turned to the index of the book and then back to the chapter where all my bookmarks had been placed. "Why are you reviewing this particular chapter? You have dozens of centuries to review before you get to my House."

"Yes, but after chatting with Anna and knowing my purpose for being here, we decided to skip ahead to the good stuff. I'm dying to know what put your House and Lorenzo's at odds." I gave him a wink before pulling the book back to me.

"You can't possibly put context around what you're reading without having a basic understanding..."

"Yeah. Yeah. Anna knows that. She just finished giving me a CliffsNotes version of the Council's origins, then we moved on."

"That isn't the proper way to study this."

I froze, staring at the page until the letters blurred together. He sounded angry. He'd never cared before how Anna went about her lessons. Was he concerned over how I learned about the Houses, or was he just pissed I was digging into his background? I'd truly believed he'd be all right with it. But he probably figured it'd be months before we got to his House, and with luck, my debt would be paid long before then. And the lessons would no longer matter.

"Anna didn't have an issue with it." I lifted my head to meet his gaze, not giving him an inch.

His eyes got that icy glow to them, and I steeled myself for a toss across the room as if we were sparring in the gym.

"The relationship between my House and Lorenzo's is none of your concern." His voice had risen, and if every vamp in the house wasn't already listening to our conversation, they were now, whether they wanted to or not.

"So, I can't learn about your House, but it's perfectly fine for you to run background checks and stick your nose in my life. And while we're on the topic, my history with Christopher is none of your business." My voice was just as steely and equally loud.

"Underwood's involved in businesses that could impact my mission."

"And your war with Lorenzo impacts my job and my life."

That stopped him, and the glow in his eyes vanished. Whether it was uncertainty, concern, or the general realization of the irony of his argument, I couldn't tell. And frankly, I didn't give a damn.

I stood and let the book tumble to the couch, unable, even in my anger, to let it fall haphazardly and damage pages. With as much poise as I could muster, I squared my shoulders, gave him a withering a look, and stalked out.

He didn't say anything. At least, nothing my human ears could pick up. I wasn't sure why I was crying, but the hot tears streamed down my face, and I kept my head down, dreading running into anyone as I hurried down the hall and raced up the stairs, locking myself in my room.

Damn him for taking the joy out of my discovery.

∾

A HAND SLIPPED over Devon's arm and nails scratched along his chest. Her spicy scent floated around him, and he grew hard. He rolled over, gathering her to him, her long legs wrapping around his. Her lips found his, playful and insistent. He returned her inquiry with a stronger one of his own, and her soft moan urged him on.

He ran his hand along her hip, pulling her closer. She arched, exposing her delicate neck. His fangs slipped down, and he traced them along the length of the sensitive skin, the vein pulsing with her life force.

"Devon." Cressa's voice was almost pleading.

He pulled back to gaze down at her. Her eyes were warm pools of desire, but not demanding, not aggressive, not like before. This was his Cressa.

He released her and backed off the bed, rubbing his face, and turning away from her. He would not take advantage of her in a dream.

"Devon, what's wrong?"

He almost laughed. He'd lost track of all the reasons this was wrong—the mission, her debt to him, the dreams, what she was, the questions about her father and the necklace. She hadn't even learned of Lyra yet.

"Why can't you look at me?"

Her voice implored him for an answer. He turned and wished to hell he hadn't. She was on her knees, the sheet wrapped around her waist, her head tilted to one side. Her brows had knit together as she searched his face. Her breasts teased him, as if he wasn't aware of each sensitive spot he'd explored before. Yet, this was the first dream where they'd been naked—fully exposed.

They had to get to the bottom of these dreams before it jeopardized the mission.

"You weren't dreaming about the Magic Poppy again, were you?"

What?

His head jerked up. How did she know about that? He would have remembered telling her.

"That's all behind you. Behind us." She inched toward the edge of the bed, one hand outstretched, fingers curling in a coaxing plea to return to her.

He must have told her about the Poppy earlier in the dream, and they'd argued. That must be what she meant.

"Oh, Devon." She stepped off the bed, the sheet falling away to reveal her entire body.

His breath caught in his throat. Even from this distance he caught her spicy scent, and it weakened his resolve to not touch her.

She moved to him and placed a palm on his cheek. "You know no one blames you for that. Lorenzo will get what's coming to him. It's just a matter of time and patience. Our plan is on track. The trap is closing. You need to let the past go."

Confusion clouded his thoughts. What did Lorenzo have to do with Magic Poppy? Was this a prescient dream or just a fantasy? Up to now, the dreams had been a glimpse into the future. Either a real future or one possibility. The dream before the ball had turned out to be real enough, but none of the others had come true, or perhaps those events simply hadn't happened yet. He shook his head. This was getting confusing.

Her hand slid from his face to his shoulder. She'd gotten closer without him being aware of it. Her lips brushed his, her tongue tracing his lips, and he couldn't stop himself. His arm snaked around her, and he kissed her as he pulled her closer.

The touch of her bare skin, the heat of her breasts pressed against his chest, it was all so familiar. They'd danced this tango before, and he groaned as she ran a hand down his chest, nails sliding over his stomach before she reached for...

He pushed her back.

Icy air raked him, and she was ripped away, leaving him to stare at the ceiling. He was back in his room at the mansion, alone in bed. He focused on the dream and confirmed the bedroom had been his master suite at Oasis. Not a single intimate dream had been in this house, but if that meant something, he couldn't put the pieces together.

Now that he was awake and his head had cleared, no doubt remained that Cressa shouldn't have known anything about Magic Poppy, let alone his addiction to it. An addiction that had almost caused the death of his House. His own personal demon he'd wrestled with and overcame decades ago.

What had triggered her dream? He almost laughed.

Their argument. And she'd been too stubborn to take the potion that would have blocked her dreams. He doubted she did it on purpose. With her necklace safely locked up, she probably didn't even think about the herbal remedy.

He should document each of the dreams while he still remembered them. Something in her subconscious must be directing them, and maybe something linked them all together that wasn't apparent on the surface. Then again, they might not be connected at all. Each dream might be related to something else entirely, and her deep emotions were simply a trigger.

The catalyst for tonight's dream had to have been her excitement over whatever she thought she'd found in the *Houses of Vampire*. Had she stumbled onto something that had evaded him all these decades? He'd read that tome dozens of times. Maybe he'd gotten too close, and he needed another set of eyes. His first instinct had been to yell at her. He was such a fool. These midnight dances between them—what drew them together?

He checked the clock. Another hour before dawn. Cook would be up, but the rest of the house would still be asleep. He dressed quickly then jogged down the steps to the library, releasing a breath when he found the heavy tome where he'd left it after

Cressa had stormed out. He grabbed it and locked himself in his office before making his first cup of espresso.

When he'd settled himself at the desk, he found it difficult to concentrate. Unable to get it off his mind, he walked across the room and opened the safe, removing the necklace. He'd never taken the time to examine it. It was cold to the touch. He would never forget the warmth of it when he'd ripped it from Cressa's neck, as if some energy or magical essence had heated it. But now it lay dormant, and somehow, Cressa was the link.

He turned it around and noticed the images were the same on both sides, but on closer inspection, they were the same images but arranged in a different order. When he focused on the images themselves, his knees almost buckled. The first image was of a poppy. It could have been a rose or any other blossom, but there was no doubt in his mind—it was the Blood Poppy. There was also an ibis and a dagger. The dagger seemed familiar, but he couldn't place the symbol that had been intricately carved within the handle. It was all interesting, but something to worry about later. One problem at a time. He placed the necklace back in the safe and returned to open the *Houses of Vampire*.

He had work to do.

BUTTERFLIES CAREENED around my stomach like skaters at the Friday night roller derby, and they grew frenetic as I trudged down the hall. Barely an hour ago, I'd woken in warm sheets, my body languid, Devon's scent on my skin.

I'd smiled at the memory of his kiss, his fangs on my neck, and his hands stroking my body. Without warning, he'd stepped away, and the loss of his heated flesh left cool air rippling over my skin. Lines had formed across his forehead that I interpreted as confusion and uncertainty, though the spark of icy blue in the depth of his gaze radiated desire. Something had spooked him, and, at the time, I couldn't guess what it could be. Now, fully awake, I still didn't know. I'd been reassuring him about something, but it was hazy, just out of reach as my memory of the previous dream had been.

The only thing I was positive about was that this dream hadn't been like the last one where I wasn't in control. No. This had been like the first ones, which meant the necklace had been the difference. The only question that remained was whether it presented a positive or negative force. Based on my initial reaction in the dream, I would lean toward negative. But the necklace hadn't come with instructions, so the first try might have been simple pilot error.

My other takeaway was that Devon had somehow changed the dream. One moment, he was passionate and fully engaged. I could still feel his erection pressed against my leg. Then it was like someone doused him in ice water. It was possible the dream was supposed to end that way. At first, I was the one in control, but not at the end, otherwise I should have disappeared from the dream first—not him.

My stomach flipped when I entered the dining room. Devon wasn't there. I was chagrined when relief and disappointment clashed, but the butterflies had calmed so I took the small victory. Simone, Sergi, and Anna were the only ones present. Lucas must be away on an assignment. The table was filled with platters of food, and based on the steam rising from the eggs, breakfast had just been served.

When they all greeted me with silent stares, I almost chuckled at how much Anna imitated them—a true vampire in the making. I ignored them and sat, adding nuts and fruit to the oatmeal that waited for me. Before taking a bite, I filled my coffee cup and leaned back to stare at the group who still hadn't moved. I took a long sip, appreciating the excellence of Cook's brew before I let the cup drop and rattle the saucer.

Anna was the only one who jumped, but Simone's tawny gaze flashed a brilliant yellow.

"In case you didn't notice, no screams came from my room last night, nor did I fall into a semi-comatose state. I woke up all on my own, cross my heart." I physically crossed my heart with an expression I was certain mirrored a petulant middle-schooler.

Sergi snickered before he returned to his pile of eggs. Simone kept her cool gaze on me, her flash of vamp eyes now gone.

"You're not taking your episode serious enough." Simone ended her chastisement with a tsk before returning to the fresh fruit and yogurt she preferred. "Psychic residue speaks of dangerous games. I take it you took the healer's potion to stave off any unwanted dreams?"

This seemed like the perfect time for that first bite of oatmeal, and I piled so much onto the spoon, it barely fit in my mouth. I caught her look of disapproval through my peripheral vision.

"Enough, Simone." Sergi spoke between bites of egg and toast. "She'll either do the smart thing or she won't. There's nothing you can do about it."

"We've put a great deal of effort into training her. It would be a shame for her to not wake up one morning." Simone bit into a slice of mango and gave me a sickly sweet smile.

I swallowed the lump of oatmeal and winced as it slithered down my throat, ending with a thud in my stomach, effectively burying any remaining butterflies. "Point taken. But Devon agrees that the episode, as you call it, was most likely created by the medallion, which is now safely locked away."

Simone snorted. "And now everyone is an expert on this questionable necklace."

"No one is an expert here, and I was remiss in ensuring that Cressa took the sleeping potion." Devon strode in, but instead of going to his chair, he stopped next to me. "I'm sorry to interrupt your breakfast, but I could use your opinion on something."

If I expected some hint of what happened in our dream to register with a spark in his gaze or a twitch of his lips, I remained disappointed. His features were cool and practiced, but he'd piqued my curiosity with what I could possibly offer in the way of advice.

I picked up my coffee, but he stayed my arm.

"You can have an espresso in my office."

I slurped the rest of the coffee and followed him out the door, feeling everyone's eyes on me. Even they didn't have a clue.

When we reached his office, he shut the door behind us and held an arm out toward the sofa in front of the hearth where only embers remained. I slowed when I saw the *Houses of Vampire* on the coffee table, the scraps of bookmarks still in place. The book lay open at one of the torn sticky notes.

The sound of the espresso machine startled me before I took a seat in front of the book. He set two cups down then retrieved a plate with blueberry scones, which he pushed toward me.

"My way of apology."

A grin slipped out. "You made these?" This probably wasn't the best time, but I couldn't help teasing him.

"No. I had Cook make them for you." He looked perplexed, then he huffed out a sigh.

I reached for his arm. "I'm sorry. I appreciate the gesture."

"You can be a difficult woman."

I winked at him. He might not have made the scones, but his efforts to make amends touched me.

He didn't return my smile, but the warmth in his gaze was enough. I blinked away the naked image of him from last night's dream. It wasn't easy.

"What you told me yesterday was frustrating." He sat, leaving several inches of space between us as he pulled the book closer. "I've read this entire book a hundred times over through the years, and I reviewed this chapter again this morning. I still don't see what you believe you've found that could have eluded me after all this time."

"You read the entire chapter this morning?" There were hundreds of pages for this chapter alone.

"I'm a fast reader."

That was daunting. "I'm not sure what I found is anything of value, and it's going to be difficult to explain." I sipped the espresso and broke off a piece of scone, mulling over the best approach. "It's this feeling I get when I'm hunting for a new job. More than that, it's when I'm not really looking for a job, but I see something or read something, and this jolt hits me. I get this tingling sensation that calls out to me." I chewed the scone and chased it with the espresso. "I've learned over the years to trust it."

He nodded as I spoke, but whether it was encouragement or something he'd felt before, I couldn't tell. "Show me."

I noted the spot he'd opened to. It was the section that discussed an event that changed the course of history between the Trelanes and Venizis—the start of their first House war. His brows rose when I flipped to another marker.

"The House Renaud?"

I nodded.

"They're the keepers of our history. I've scoured that section too many times to count."

"I admit, there really isn't much here other than how they became the record keepers of vamp history. It seemed surprising the Council would hand such a large responsibility to only one family until I read their process. It leaves little room for bias, assuming they documented the ugly along with the good."

He sat back and sipped his espresso as he stared at the embers. "There have been times when the Council wasn't happy with some of the records. Arguments broke out and loyalties were tested when someone got wind of what had been written."

"Enough to sweep it under the rug?"

"I've heard rumors of shadow books."

I nodded. "Like having a second set of accounting books. One to show the auditors and another with the real numbers. Does everyone have free access to these books?"

"Most are kept in vampire museums and libraries open to all of our species."

"But not everything?"

"No. There is too much inventory. It doesn't happen often, but some Houses fail or die off. Personal items are given to any remaining family, but anything considered important to vampire history is sent to House Renaud for cataloging and storage. There are many written accounts to be stored—memoirs, journals, that sort of thing."

I wiped my hands on my pants and reread the passage that had given me the tingles the day before. No surprise. The familiar sensation shot through me again. I pointed to the paragraph.

After several minutes went by, his forehead creased as he shook his head. "I'm afraid I'm not seeing it."

I pointed to the foreign words. "What does this phrase mean?"

Devon read the words. "*De første dage.* It's Danish and means 'the first days'."

I reread the passage, inserting his translation into the paragraph. Now, my forehead scrunched in confusion. "It reads awkwardly in English, so maybe that's why they switched to Danish in the middle of the sentence."

He gave me a look I couldn't decipher and read the passage again. "To be honest, it doesn't make much sense if the entire sentence had been written in Danish."

"I noticed multiple languages throughout the chapters, but they seemed to reference people and places."

He nodded in agreement.

"But this isn't a person or a place?"

He shook his head, but I could tell the wheels were turning.

"What if this was another book?"

His expression was priceless—one that a kid gets when they discover a toy under the Christmas tree they'd been positive their parents couldn't afford. He slid the tome into his lap, his finger running across the words from the beginning of the page. "All this time it's been right in front of me. Could it be?"

"I'm not sure what the sentence is actually saying, but it just seemed..."

"Tingly?"

I grinned. "I think we need to find this book."

He set the book aside and a flash of ice blue wavered in the depths of his gaze but didn't diminish. "If this is what I think it is, it will be well-hidden, unless it was truly destroyed as we've been led to believe."

"Would this House Renaud destroy books?"

"Never. They are beyond obsessive with their duty. Everything in their collection is considered priceless. But if someone else got their hands on it?" He shrugged.

"Maybe humans weren't the inventors of book burning. What do you think is inside this book? You didn't seem to recognize the name."

Before he could explain it, Sergi burst through the door, his face a mask of anger. "Lucas is under attack."

Chapter Eleven

"WHERE IS LUCAS?" Devon was up and moving to the sideboard, opening a drawer and pulling out two silver daggers.

Sergi glanced at me before saying, "The apartment."

Simone entered behind him. "I've called for backup."

"What apartment?" My throat tightened, the words barely intelligible. I stood on shaky legs, searching each of their faces. Had Lucas been watching Ginger? Devon probably owned dozens of apartments, yet his quick glance told me everything I needed to know. It was my old apartment, and the only reason to attack would be if Ginger was there.

Devon moved quickly. "Sergi, get the car. Cressa, you're to stay here and remain inside. Simone, I need another team here now to watch the house."

They left me standing in the office staring after them. Devon would leave without me. Well, that wasn't going to happen if Ginger was involved. I raced for my bedroom, taking the stairs two at a time. My heart hammered an unsteady staccato as I ripped off the slacks and squeezed into my jeans, hopping around as I slid on my runners while searching for my sweatshirt. I slipped it over my head before grabbing my dagger, then raced down to the front door.

My breath rushed out in spurts, and I mentally crossed my fingers that I hadn't missed my ride. The vamps were way quicker than me. But Sergi was just pulling in front of the house, and Simone was giving orders to three other vamps I'd never seen before. They couldn't have come from Oasis this quickly. Devon must have another house in the neighborhood, close by but not intrusive. Something to remember for another time.

Sergi stepped out of the car, remaining next to the driver's side as he spoke to someone on his cell. Maybe Lucas? I wish I knew what the hell was happening. Simone was still speaking with the vamps, and Devon hadn't come out yet. This was my opportunity. I raced for the passenger door and dove in, shutting it behind me. This was the luxury sedan, all custom leather, plenty of leg room, and more than enough space for the four us. We'd be able to squeeze in Ginger and Lucas, assuming we'd arrive in time.

I scooted to the far side of the vehicle, making myself as small as possible while I texted, praying to any god anywhere for Ginger to respond. Nothing but a blank screen in response, but I continued typing until the doors opened.

All three vamps slid into the vehicle in one fluid motion as if they'd choreographed the move dozens of times. This definitely wasn't their first battle. Sergi put the car in drive, and it sped down the driveway.

"Cressa." Devon's commanding voice filled the interior, but Sergi didn't slow down.

I watched, bug-eyed as the car hurdled toward the large wrought iron gates.

"Stop and let her out." Devon's barked order was ignored.

"There's no time," Sergi yelled over his shoulder.

The gate opened with inches to spare as the sedan slid through. How many times had Sergi practiced that maneuver until the gate opened at just the right moment?

"Bella and Jacques just arrived on scene," Sergi continued to explain his disobedience. "They need more backup, and they need it now. She made her choice. You and Simone need to stop coddling her. She's ready."

Devon swore under his breath before giving me a look that promised we'd settle this later. And while that should have concerned me, I was too busy basking in Sergi's hard-won support. Of course, he probably knew I'd do something stupid and get myself killed. Kind of a win-win for him.

"I know you're mad, but this has something to do with Ginger. I won't sit around and wait while my best friend is in trouble."

He stared out the window as the landscape rushed past. "These are vampires, not street thugs."

I reached for him but pulled back. This wasn't the time.

"I'll keep an eye on her." Simone turned in her seat and gave me a level stare. "And you will do as I say. No questions asked." She held that glare for a solid minute before turning back to check her blades. She carried several. I suddenly realized she scared me ten times more than Devon—and she knew it. But I had to admit, knowing she had my back made me feel bulletproof. And if my incompetence didn't do me in, that misplaced confidence would surely get me killed.

I touched the sheath of my single dagger, suddenly feeling silly. There wasn't anything I could do in the middle of raging vamps other than put the others at risk. "I'll stay in the car and wait for Ginger."

Devon's nod was barely perceptible, and I turned to stare out my own window.

Sergi slowed as we reached my old neighborhood. Devon was on his phone, either texting or using GPS to locate his team. The streets were strangely quiet, but it was a weekday morning when most people would be at work, except for the dealers, and they know to keep their mouths shut. Where would Bulldog be in all of this? Holed up at the laundromat if he had any sense, and he didn't get where he was by being stupid.

I sat up, searching the street and other buildings for anything suspicious. When Sergi pulled in front of the apartment, I assumed we missed the battle. It was peaceful, if not eerily quiet. But the vamps sprang from the car as soon as Sergi put it in park.

Devon bent to peer back into the sedan. "Stay put." It was more of a sneer in combination with the order. He slammed the door shut, and the sound of the locks engaging reminded me how serious this was.

I waited until they were halfway to the apartment before I tested the door, afraid he'd locked me in. The door opened, and I breathed a sigh of relief before reengaging the locks. I kept my eye on the building as the three separated. Devon stormed toward the front door, his long duster, most likely worn to hide his array of weapons, fluttered in his wake. Sergi and Simone broke off, each taking different sides of the building.

They didn't get far before someone, I assumed a vamp, flew through the front door, shattering glass on their way out. It appeared to be male, but it was impossible to tell from this angle, especially without a head. The body landed with a thud on the cement walkway. Devon bent and laid a hand on it, then shook his head as he gave his two guards a quick glance. I didn't think Sergi's expression could get any stonier. Had Devon just lost one of his family? I closed my eyes, hoping like hell it wasn't Lucas.

I scraped my fingers along the door handle. My anxiety moved from high alert to all out terror, imagining Ginger being the next one to fly out the smashed door. By the time I pulled my attention from the dead vamp, the other three were gone—quick as a flash.

I scooted across the bench seat, my knee bouncing as I stroked my dagger, waiting for whatever was happening inside the apartment. I couldn't roll down the window, so I inched the door open.

The sounds of demolition, or maybe war, made me jump, and I slammed the door closed, pressing the lock button a couple of times—just to be sure. I pictured Lucas and Ginger barricaded inside the apartment or at the end of the hall as vamps pulled the place down around them. How many vamps were there? I should have demanded Devon give me specifics during the drive over. Slim chance he would have told me, but he might have.

Minutes ticked by, and try as I might, I couldn't sit still. I gave the neighborhood a more thorough scan, focusing on doorways and the handful of cars on the street. If there were any vamps out there, they would have attacked Devon on his way in. Vamps weren't the skittish type.

After one last check, I slipped out of the sedan, making sure to unlock all the doors so I could dive back in if I had to, and ran across the street, ducking into one of the doorways where drug deals went down. It was a long narrow entryway, perfect for staying out of sight of police cars, which were a rare occurrence, or other gangs. I paced in the shadows, keeping an eye on my surroundings. While it was a private spot against prying eyes, it was also a dead end, so I'd have to run before anyone got close.

The sounds of breaking walls and windows had slowed but weren't completely silenced. I had a view of the front door and the single side door that led to an inside staircase where Simone would have entered. The only other door on the ground floor was the one in the back that I assumed Sergi had used. The building had been through a partial upgrade back in the seventies, adding the inside staircase on the west side of the building. External fire escapes were the only emergency exits on the other side, leaving a twelve-foot drop between ladder and the ground—child's play for a vamp.

After what seemed like forever, but was more likely mere minutes of pacing, the side door burst open, and Ginger ran out. Instead of heading toward the street, she ran for the alley behind the building. What the hell? Why was she alone? Seconds later, someone raced after her, and it didn't take a genius to recognize the speed and grace of a vamp.

I didn't hesitate and barely checked the street before bolting after them. I'd expected one of Devon's vamps to storm out next, but I couldn't take the chance, already running at top speed and grateful I'd switched shoes. Ginger must be terrified and not thinking clearly because she knew the alley was a dead end except for a short stretch of chain-link fencing a person could either jump over or crawl through the jagged section that had been cut away.

She wouldn't have the time to try either choice.

I pumped my arms and legs faster when Ginger turned around, her back against the fence, and faced down the vamp, who shifted from foot to foot as if deciding the best way to grab her. It seemed odd since he could pounce on her before she even decided which way to dodge. He was playing with his food—or his orders had been to retrieve.

Why was she out here by herself?

I was too far away so I did the only thing I could think of to create a distraction.

"Hey, vamp. Want to play with someone a bit more challenging?" I sucked for air. I needed shorter taunts. And after all that, the asshole didn't turn around. I dragged in another ragged breath and shouted, "Are you one of those pussy vamps?"

That did the trick.

His movement was a blur as he spun around then hesitated to determine the threat. He sniffed the air then threw his head back to laugh.

Let's see if he'd still be laughing after a few moves from my training sessions. I hoped to god this vamp didn't have the mad skills of Devon's cadre. The element of surprise and his underestimating my skills would be the only thing to save Ginger before his supernatural endurance gained the advantage.

He was still laughing when I reached him and only quieted when he noticed I wasn't slowing. I grinned with great satisfaction when he stood and stared while I leaped. My feet him square in the chest, and I rode him like a surfboard as he fell back under my unexpected weight.

I didn't land right and planted a hand on his face to keep me from falling flat on mine. After regaining my footing, I spun with my dagger out and kicked the vamp in the stomach while he fought to get to his feet. Guess he was more surprised than I anticipated, and I took full advantage, stomping on his back when he went down.

I glanced at Ginger; her doe-sized eyes were glassy. "Run out front to the black sedan." When she only stared, I kicked the vamp in the head and yelled, "Ginger. Black sedan. Lock yourself in. Now. Ginger."

The second use of her name seemed to do the trick, and she edged around us as I kept striking the vamp to prevent him from getting up, but that wouldn't last forever. Once she passed us, she raced down the alley, glancing over her shoulder as she ran.

I refocused on the vamp, who grabbed for my leg as I prepared to give him another kick. I managed to avoid his grasp, but the move knocked me off my center, and I stumbled. He was up in a blink of an eye. I swiped my dagger, and he jumped back.

That damn smile was back, but after facing an even deadlier smile each time I sparred with Sergi, I ignored his game. He was proficient with martial arts, but I was better. I'd built stamina over the last couple of weeks, working with two vamps in most of my training sessions, and could last fifteen minutes without losing a step. I had no delusions after that but didn't think I'd need that much time. Maybe another couple of minutes for Ginger to make it to the car or before help arrived. I refused to entertain the possibility this guy's buddy might show up before the calvary.

We circled, and I watched his footing as Devon's training pounded in my head, and that was the single lesson that saved me. When he put his weight on his right foot, I moved. His attack was quick, and his intentions clear—take me out. I used a roundhouse kick that clocked him in the jaw, following it up with a slash of my dagger, and was surprised when I felt the knife slice skin.

He didn't scream, but I heard the soft intake of surprise, and could only imagine the burn he must be feeling from the silver. That was when I made a mistake. I thought I'd gotten away clean, but he grabbed my free arm and swung me around, attempting to roll me into his grasp for what I knew would be a neck-snapping move.

He grabbed the wrong arm, and that was his mistake. I rolled with him, getting closer than I wanted, closer than I should, but when he had my waist in his grip, reaching for my neck, I rammed the blade into his gut and twisted. He released me, taking two steps back to glance down at the blood dampening his shirt.

Before I could take advantage of the moment to run away, a sword swept out of nowhere.

One minute my adversary faced me with a look that said he'd kill me before I took another step. The next, his head bounced off the asphalt.

Simone stood behind the still-standing body like some sweet avenger, her fangs bared, and her lavender hair bleached to white in the stark sunshine. Blood streaked her sunflower-yellow bodysuit. I think I could have kissed her at that moment.

"Where's Ginger?"

A dead vamp in the street, my breath struggling to get out, and that was all she asked?

"Don't worry. I'll be fine." I held my side, just now feeling the punishing blows the vamp had been able to land.

"Obviously. Where's Ginger?"

Worry crept in. "I sent her to the car. Didn't she make it there?" I glanced past her, already moving to jog down the alley, until I saw Devon stalking toward us.

"Where's Ginger?" I yelled, taking up Simone's mantra.

"She's safe." He stopped to take in the scene.

"This was only a young blood." Simone responded to Devon, but her hard stare was on me.

I don't know why I'd expected something more positive in regard to my performance, but her words held a lesson. Point taken. This vamp wasn't more than ten years made. His new abilities were still being honed. I'd been lucky.

I simply nodded in acknowledgment of message received.

Devon said nothing. If Simone's dress down was enough of a reprimand, time would tell. He grabbed my arm to hustle me down the alley.

I limped to keep up, and he stopped. "You're injured?"

"Just some bruises."

He swept me into his arms before I could stop him, and he jogged the rest of the way to the sedan where Sergi, on the phone again, and Lucas waited. Bella and Jacques stood with them. They were all bloody.

"I can walk." I tried to get out of his grip, but it was like pushing against iron bars.

"We need to get you out of here before police arrive. Our cleanup crew is on the way."

I snorted, then grimaced. "It will be an hour before police arrive, and that's assuming anyone called it in. Most people wait for Bulldog to handle any problems."

He set me down and took the time to look me over more thoroughly, taking liberties to test my ribs which induced an involuntary groan.

"How many did we lose?" I wasn't sure I wanted to know.

A glimmer of a smile passed over him before his expression shut down. "One. Justin."

"I'm sorry."

"We could have lost more without your quick thinking, even though I would never have approved your participation."

His mixed compliment meant we'd have words once we were back at the mansion, but it was his acknowledgment that we would have lost Ginger without my interference that caused the shakes that rattled my body. It was shock. And I knew it wasn't from the fight or seeing the vamp's head removed, but that Ginger could have been taken from me.

I barely had a chance to slide into the back seat before she was in my arms, crying against my shoulder. Everything until this moment had been about paying back a debt. A debt I'd created by saving Ginger. Now that debt had put her at even greater risk. All I was supposed to do was steal stuff. But what good was being debt free if I lost my best friend? I glanced at Devon over Ginger's head. What new hell had I created?

～

"It was all my fault." Ginger leaned back into six-inch tall bubbles that covered the entire tub. Her head rested on a fluffy towel as she stretched her body, a glass of wine gripped firmly in her left hand.

"Devon's team should have protected you better." I sat on the toilet seat, clenching my own glass, the half-empty bottle within easy reach on the counter.

She shook her head while managing to keep the towel in place. "I begged Lucas to take me, even though he said it was a bad idea. We waited twenty minutes at a coffee house for two more vamps to join us. Even then, we were outnumbered."

"Wait. What?"

Sergi had driven us home with a second car of vamps following. Devon had called for a meeting, but I'd brought Ginger up to my room so she could shower the blood spatter off before settling into a bubble bath. With how quick everything had happened, I'd never heard how this nightmare started. "I thought Devon had people watching the apartment."

She nodded. "Lucas said they monitor the security cameras. The two vamps that met us, God, I can't even remember their names." Her breath hitched. "They walked us to the apartment. There were three of them waiting for us when we got to our floor. Two went down quickly, and we were able to set up a barricade when we reached the apartment. We were going to wait for reinforcements, but then Bella and Jacques— Whew, at least I remembered their names. The wine must be working." She sipped more and released a small grin before it slipped away. "Bella contacted Lucas and warned him that four vamps got by them. He didn't want us to get trapped with that many coming, and we managed to get by the one in the hallway, but the others arrived before we made it to the stairs."

She brushed away a tear. "Somehow, we made it to the stairs, and he told me to stay with him, but I freaked halfway down when the other vamps came after us. When Lucas had to engage one of them, he still told me to stay, but I ran. One of the vamps got by Lucas and blocked my path back to him."

She dropped her head. "I messed up and someone died because I had to go back for some trinket."

"I'm the one who messed up getting us involved with vamps. I should have made a deal with The Wolf."

Ginger snorted. "Like hanging with shifters is any safer? Besides, I'm the one who messed up by putting you in debt in the first place."

"This is an old argument."

That ended our recap of the morning, and we turned our attention to our wine and seventies rock-and-roll that bled in from the bedroom. It was Ginger's favorite music.

"How did this change from Christopher's goons harassing us to vamps? Does it have something to do with what Christopher thinks you stole?" It seemed Ginger wasn't done with the previous subject matter after all. She held out her glass, and I refilled it.

She posed an excellent question. I had no idea why the necklace was of any interest after all these years. Devon only made an assumption, albeit a seemingly accurate one, that the necklace had interfered with our shared dream and kicked me into some kind of psychic coma. I had no idea if Devon considered it significant to anyone else.

"I don't know if the vamps and Christopher are working

together, but I'm sure that's one of the first things Devon will investigate. Until we know more, you're staying here."

She shook her head. "I'll stay overnight, but only because we haven't had a movie night in forever. Lucas assured me the new apartment was safe because the ownership is buried under tons of false corporations. And I'll probably get more bodyguards."

I had a whole line of arguments for why she should stay, but it wouldn't do me any good. We'd always joked about which of us was the most stubborn. In the end, it would be up to Devon, and he wouldn't decide until he'd had time to review everything that had happened tonight. I lifted my glass. "To movie night. I'll make sure we have popcorn and plenty of ice cream."

Her smile was addictive as she raised her glass to meet mine, but her eyes couldn't hide the worry that lurked just below the surface.

Chapter Twelve

AFTER GINGER FINISHED HER BATH, I left her tucked in a fluffy robe with a stack of women's magazines Anna had left for me and hustled downstairs with three specific tasks in mind. My first stop was a seldom used entertainment room tucked away down a side hall. Anna said it was used more frequently when the mansion was filled with vamps, but Lucas and Sergi occasionally watched old movies. I checked out the channel selection, discovered several that would do, then headed for the kitchen.

Cook was ecstatic about a movie night and lamented that no one in the house appreciated his special varieties of popcorn. After leaving him with an order for three flavors—buttery, kettle corn, and caramel-coated—in addition to a promise of chocolate chip and brownie fudge ice cream, I headed for Devon's office.

I meandered through several rooms on the off chance Devon might be relaxing somewhere, but the truth was I was dragging my feet. My first emotion on the way home, besides bits of shock as Ginger cried into my shoulder, was anger at Lucas and Devon for putting her in that dangerous situation. But as I sat on the toilet seat and listened to Ginger recap the events, my temper cooled.

Lucas had contacted Devon, who'd approved taking Ginger to

the old apartment. No one had any reason to believe vamps were staking out the place. They'd stayed well out of sight of the cameras. Now I was as curious as anyone why the vamps had been there. Had they been waiting for Ginger—or for me?

By the time I reached Devon's office, all my questions were buried under worry that he'd be mad at me for leaving the car. He'd disapproved of me going in the first place, but then, who would have saved Ginger? Maybe it would have played out differently if Devon hadn't been worried about keeping me safe.

I rubbed my face and mentally prepared for the lecture before knocking on the door.

"Come."

I opened the door slowly and peered around the edge. Devon was by himself, writing something on a slip of paper. "Do you have a minute?"

He glanced up, his brows rising for an instant before he set the pen down and leaned back, studying my face. "I always have time for you."

I wasn't convinced that was true, but his warm voice sent a pleasant tingle down my spine. Had he added just a touch of mesmerizing? He'd once told me a vamp had to be touching a person, but I wouldn't be surprised if that wasn't the entire truth. And if it settled the rattlesnakes in my gut, I decided not to be a hypocrite and accept it as a gift. Though I'd probably imagined the whole thing.

I took a seat facing him from across his desk. "Could you tell me what happened at the apartment? Ginger told me what she knew, but I think there's more going on than Christopher looking for a necklace."

He tsked. "You think?"

His snark surprised me. He tapped on the armrest then reached for the white crystal but stopped, resisting one of his habits. Instead, he shifted it a few inches to the right. "I have to admit, I assumed you'd storm in here, raising holy hell."

My lips twitched involuntarily. "That had been the plan."

"Thank you for your restraint." He picked up his pen, an old-style fountain type, which seemed appropriate for the fine linen stationary he wrote on. It suited him better than the tablet that sat mere inches from him. "If you don't mind, I need to finish this." He continued writing as he spoke. "Would you mind making me a cup of espresso? And feel free to get one for yourself."

Since he asked nicely, I didn't see a reason to object, though I hadn't used an espresso machine before. I tested a few knobs, and it didn't appear too daunting. God knew I'd seen enough of them made. When I set two cups on his desk, he set the letter and its accompanying envelope aside, and went back to staring at me. It was unfortunate I couldn't read his handwriting upside down. Where exactly did the line between curiosity and nosiness cross?

I sipped the drink and was pleasantly surprised by my first attempt. "Do you think Lorenzo sent those vamps?"

"Yes." After several seconds, he dropped his gaze and tasted his drink. "But I have no proof at this time."

A knock at the door, and with a quick nod from Devon, Sergi sauntered in and dropped into the chair next to me. He glanced at the cups of espresso but didn't say anything. I knew he wanted one, but he'd have to make his own.

"We have it now." Sergi took out his tablet, and after swiping and punching out something on his keyboard, he continued, "The headless vamp in the alley was a rogue from a small house in the New Orleans area. However, word on the street said he'd been seen with a group of vamps known to be part of Lorenzo's family. It's not a solid connection for retaliation, but enough to know who we're dealing with."

"How would he know about the necklace?" Devon had turned to stare out his window, the partially opened blinds providing the only light in the room. I wasn't sure if he was expecting an answer.

Sergi didn't hesitate to respond. "Did he know Underwood

had it at one time, or did Underwood offer it to him for some reason but then couldn't get his hands on it?"

"Or was it mentioned in a book that Lorenzo has access to?" I couldn't help but chime in.

The men swiveled their heads toward me in a synchronous movement.

"Why would you ask that?" Sergi stood and moved to the espresso machine.

I glanced at Devon, and he nodded, remembering our conversation from earlier. A discussion that seemed days away after the way the morning had finished. "I found mention of what might be an ancient text in the *Houses of the Vampire*. It was mentioned in the section about the House Renaud, and the time period is close to the break between the Trelane and Venizi houses."

Sergi almost spilled his espresso on his way back to the desk. He shot a look at Devon. "Is this true?"

"I wasn't sure at first, but now that I've had time to study the entry, it seems likely."

"Where is this book?"

"At one time, it was part of the Renaud collection, but that entry was eight centuries ago. If Cressa is correct, and Lorenzo knows about it, it's possible he either has the book or recently saw it."

Sergi shook his head, but his expression turned thoughtful. "If Lorenzo learned about it from a book written hundreds of centuries earlier, and this is nothing but conjecture, how would he connect it to Underwood?"

Devon fiddled with his cup. I'd never seen him perplexed, but I'd never seen him strategize before. He'd always had a plan when he'd asked something from me. "I don't know. Our first problem is that we don't know what Underwood is doing with Lorenzo. It could be nothing more than a business venture, or maybe Underwood has access to places Lorenzo doesn't."

"It might be as simple as Underwood seeing a picture of the

necklace, if there is one, then remembering he'd seen it before. I'll dig deeper on their connection." Sergi scowled at his own supposition, clearly not happy at not having all the answers.

Devon spun back to the window, his cup of espresso in his hands. After several moments of contemplation, he turned back to the room. "Excellent espresso, Cressa. Thank you."

The change of subject threw me for a second before I considered this might be his gentle way of dismissing me. Concerned I was going to be asked to leave, I threw out an idea that had poked at me since they'd mentioned Christopher. It wasn't anything I was keen on, but it seemed an obvious avenue we couldn't ignore.

"I want to see my mother."

Their heads turned as one, and I couldn't help smiling. I'd never seen such a tight-knit group that could mimic their moves with such elegance.

"No." Sergi folded his arms across his chest.

I'd expected that answer from a security guy, but I focused on Devon. He was the only one that mattered.

"Why?" Devon gave me an opening.

"Isn't it obvious? She was the one my father gave the necklace to. If Christopher knows about the necklace, it had to have been from my mother, and he probably assumed she still had it tucked away somewhere. He wasn't there when she gave it back to me, which was the day before I left, and I'd already packed it away with my other stuff. Besides, she's the only one that can give us a lead on my father. So, two birds."

Devon had that look—that crease along his forehead and his gaze unfocused—that told me he was considering it. "He might have remembered it, searched for it on his own, and when he couldn't find it, assumed you'd stolen it."

That possibility hadn't crossed my mind. "Wouldn't he have just asked my mother?"

Devon shrugged, his gaze returning to normal. He pushed the cup aside and pulled his tablet to him. "Maybe he's keeping her out of his dealings with Lorenzo. A naïve attempt to keep his family safe."

Sergi grunted, and a chill crept up my back. I didn't need anyone to explain that comment. Christopher, through what might have been nothing more than a simple business partnership, had marked his entire family. I might not get along with my mother. Hells bells, she all but abandoned me to her new lifestyle, but I didn't want to see her or April hurt. April. I wasn't even sure where we stood anymore after seeing her at the apartment. Had she been forced to go so she could talk some sense into me, or had she joined the family business?

"It's not a good idea for her to go to that house. It's well fortified." Sergi might be holding firm on his security concerns, but I'd piqued his interest.

"I have no intention of going back in that house. Not unless I have no other choice." I'd scooted up on my seat, my idea taking shape.

"What's your plan?" Devon was on board, but that protective shield was going up.

"My mother is a very exacting woman. Everything is scheduled and organized to the last detail, and she's a creature of habit." I shrugged and scooted back, a slight grin on my lips. "I suppose in some ways we all are. But she takes it to new heights. She has an appointment at the spa every Thursday at two o'clock. There's a tiny coffeehouse down a side alley half a block from the spa. All I need is fifteen minutes with her."

"Will she have a driver and bodyguards?" Sergi was back on his tablet.

"A driver for certain. I don't know about bodyguards."

"Does she have any other scheduled meetings during the week?"

I'd been surprised I remembered her spa day, but that had been the only day April was always at home and had become our day to meet at the pool house. "I think she gets her hair done on Wednesdays, about the same time I think." I nodded as my mother's busy schedule came back to me. "Yeah, that's the day she meets with her garden club for lunch. She goes to the hairdresser after that."

"She's a gardener?" Devon asked. His warm gaze ran over me with a sense of encouragement and what seemed like approval.

I snorted, and my cheeks warmed when he smiled. "Hardly. She has people for that. Her garden club is about planning events to be held in the garden. Everything is about parties, networking, and gathering rumors about other people in their circle of influence."

"I need the names and locations of where she'll be on both days." Sergi had quickly changed his tune. "The timing couldn't be better with today being Tuesday. I'll have a team follow her to the luncheon and then the salon afterwards. That should give me enough to prepare something for the following day."

"The distraction can't be traced to us." Devon had finally picked up the crystal and was tossing it back and forth. "Use different teams each day. I want Bella and Jacques on Thursday."

Sergi nodded, drained the last of his espresso, and deposited the empty cup on the bar before he left.

"What can I do?" My nerves were already prickling at the thought of a face-to-face with my mother.

"Provide Sergi what information you can, then return to your normal routine. Enjoy your time with Ginger. I'll have Lucas take you both out for breakfast before returning Ginger to her new apartment, then have you back in time for your session with Anna."

"What about my training with Simone?"

"The break will give her time to catch up on business at Oasis. I'll arrange for a special session before dinner. We'll decide Thursday morning whether the mission is a go."

My leg bounced. A special session of training didn't seem ominous at all. Devon was a patient man, and this could be payback for my earlier disobedience.

"Is there anything else?"

"What? Oh, no." I stood, now being officially dismissed. I met his gaze and gave him an earnest, "Thank you."

I was almost to the door when he said, "Perhaps I should thank you."

I turned, waiting for him to explain, but his head was already down, the fountain pen scratching out another letter.

It wasn't until I reached the door to my room that I smiled. I'd helped. It might not go anywhere, but between the elusive book, if it was a book, and a meeting with my mother, we might garner critical information to assist Devon in completing his mission. And maybe discover something about my missing father and my dreams. I was becoming part of the team.

I WALKED into my room without knocking and was surprised to see Lucas and Ginger huddled knee to knee in front of a low-burning fire.

Ginger jumped back and brushed off the robe she was still in, a light blush on her cheeks. I couldn't remember a single time I'd ever seen her embarrassed. When she flicked her gaze to the fire, I reconsidered my word choice. It was more like she'd been caught pilfering my snickerdoodles. A small act that someone shouldn't feel guilty about unless they understood my undying adoration and gratitude for the best cookie in the world. A treat that saved me in so many ways.

Lucas turned and gave me his slow grin. His California beachboy looks gave him a half innocent, half all-knowing persona. I doubted I'd ever see guilt on that gorgeous face.

"Hello, Cressa." His voice held a lilt of mischief, and when I glanced at Ginger, she seemed to have recovered, a glint of merriment in her own twinkling gaze. "I wanted to make sure Ginger was all right and to apologize for not being able to keep her safe."

"I told him it wasn't his fault. I'm the one that ran off after he told me not to. And then when that other vamp showed up, I just freaked. I thought I'd be braver than that but, I guess you just don't really know until you find yourself face to face with a vamp." She blushed again when she glanced at Lucas. "Well, not any vamp, but a really, really pissed-off vamp, who obviously doesn't like you."

I've known my best friend for over five years, and she had an amazing ability to ramble on for minutes without really saying anything. She was a professional babbler. It was one of her charms. Yet, something was different this time, and I reconsidered what assignment Lucas might have been on that had kept him away from the mansion for almost the same length of time Ginger had been in Seattle.

"As I told her, it was a frightening situation, and anyone not familiar with vampires would certainly have handled the situation far worse than she did."

"Huh-huh. Well, you were outnumbered." I inched into my room, feeling like the intruder. "I thought Ginger might like to hang out in the pool for a bit. Our movie night is all set."

Ginger leaped up, the robe slipping open to reveal her bra and undies, which would have been difficult for any man, including a vamp, not to notice. And Lucas stared for longer than what was considered acceptable. In this case, I wasn't sure if it was the vamp stare they all did beyond the point of politeness, or something more intimate.

Ginger sashayed to a dresser where she kept a few of her clothes and didn't bother closing the robe. Since she'd be changing into a bikini, there really wasn't anything Lucas wasn't about to see anyway, unless he'd already seen more skin than that.

I'd never judged Ginger on her hookups, but wasn't this different? When my erotic dreams with Devon came to mind, I didn't have much room to criticize. And I'd be lying to myself if I claimed I had no attraction to him outside of those visions.

Lucas strode to the door, pausing when he reached me. "I understood you did well keeping the enemy busy while Ginger escaped."

I lifted a shoulder and a grin slipped out. I did do well. "I have good teachers."

"Even if it was foolish to go running after her by yourself."

My smile faded. "And there it is. Always a back-handed compliment. You vamps sure know how to make a person feel good."

His smile showed a bit of fang. "Training to overcome an enemy is to save your life, not make you feel good." His gaze roamed over Ginger, almost possessively. "Making a person feel good requires other measures." He bowed his head and left.

When I turned to Ginger, she had her bathing suit in her hand and was dodging into the bathroom, the door slamming shut behind her.

Good grief. Those two were getting chummy under the sheets. I rubbed my face. It wasn't any of my business. If she wanted me to know something, she'd tell me. Though I was curious. Ginger had a system for tracking her hookups. If a man interested her enough to punch his number in her phone, she'd add a rating from her "would I fuck them" scale. If anything, I was tempted to search for her phone and see what she put next to Lucas's name. If he was playing bodyguard—and didn't that word have a whole new connotation—then his number would definitely be on speed dial.

I gathered my own bathing suit and changed, then wandered into the closet to pull my dirty clothes together. Greta, the housekeeper, took care of the laundry, but I never liked someone else doing what I could do myself, even when I lived at Christopher's. When I strolled out and dumped the clothes basket by the door, I noticed Ginger sitting by the windows, the robe back on to cover up the bikini.

"Are those the gravestones where you saw that woman?"

I tugged on my own robe and sat next to her. "Yeah. But I

119

haven't seen the mystery woman since before the ball. Maybe she's from the house next door and occasionally wanders over."

"How would she get past the gate?"

"Having your backyard edge the coastline leaves some weaknesses. Walls can only go so far. There's a small-game trail that skirts the edge of the wall on both sides of the property. It's a pretty scary drop, but a person could clear it."

Ginger glanced toward the ceiling. "No weird sounds or moving of curtains from the third floor?"

I nibbled a nail, my focus on the grave markers. "No. I haven't paid much attention lately. It would have been the best time with Devon gone most days, but I've had my mind on other things. At this point, I could probably be talked into it being nothing more than my imagination."

She squeezed my arm. "I didn't properly thank you for earlier."

Words stuck in my throat and tears pricked my eyes. We weren't going to rehash that near-death experience. "Which part? The saving your life or the shoulder I lent you for all the blubbering."

She snorted. "The last part, of course. I look horrid when my mascara smears."

I laughed. "Don't we all. Let's grab another bottle of wine and hit the pool. We'll need a good buzz before movie night."

Chapter Thirteen

THE LANDSCAPE RUSHED BY, turning from coastal views into suburban homes then city streets. The car was quiet except for the soft purr of the motor and the fan blowing warm air to dispel a chilly coastal day as Sergi drove to my mother's spa. The stoic security guard didn't play the soft jazz he enjoyed, but maybe that was for me. He probably sensed the trepidation beating drum solos in my head. I had no doubt he smelled the sweat reeking from my pores.

Earlier that morning, Devon had reviewed the plan several times with the team that consisted of me and five vamps. It was solid. I'd been on sketchier jobs that hadn't created this much anxiety. But it wasn't my mother's bodyguards that had me cranked up. It was what to say to her after all these years of stubborn silence on both our parts. I should have been the bigger person to reach out, but didn't she have a responsibility to her daughter? She was the one who abandoned me in our own home when I was barely tall enough to ride the Ferris wheel at the summer carnivals.

A cellphone vibrated in the center console, and Sergi tapped his headset. "Teams one and two in place. Understood." He gave me a side glance but said nothing more.

I sucked in a deep breath and refocused on the job. The quick call meant the mission was a go. I played each step over in my mind. Four vamps had already found their mark. Two had trailed the sedan that drove my mother to town and the black SUV that followed her. Bella and Jacques waited near the spa where they'd create the distraction that would keep the bodyguards busy while I did my thing.

Sergi pulled the car to the curb on a side street a block from the spa and two blocks from the coffeehouse. He would remain behind and wait for me, available for backup if needed. This part of town was filled with luxury stores I could never afford to shop in, but I knew it well. Ginger and I enjoyed window shopping here on sunny, warm days while we fantasized of better times. I'd been to the tiny coffeehouse a handful of times to splurge on their over-priced lattes and rich, sinful desserts. I knew it well enough to know the layout and exits but not enough for anyone to recognize me.

Once parked, Sergi sent a text to the teams. We waited two minutes while they checked in.

"You ready?" His gaze was cool, all business.

I checked my watch, noting that I'd have ten minutes to make my way to the spa. Then I confirmed my phone was in vibrate mode. "Yeah. I'm good."

I opened the door, and Sergi caught my arm before I could exit. "Stick with the plan. We can always try again. You can't be seen."

If this was Harlow, the crew leader I usually ran with, reminding me of the obvious, I would have given a snappy retort. But Sergi was the lead today, and with Devon remaining behind at the mansion, he was under pressure to ensure I returned safely.

"I know. I'll be careful." I slipped out of the car, turned the collar up on my Dior jacket, and fiddled with the tweed beret. No one would recognize me as Pandora or Cressa, not with the designer labels Devon dressed me in. Nor would anyone think twice about me shopping in such a high-end store. Any other day, I'd feel at home, pretending to fit in with the upper crust.

I'd surveyed my surroundings before exiting the car, but I took another casual sweep before stopping halfway down the block in front of a small art gallery. No one would question my hovering as I peered at the colorful displays of paintings and sculptures, which gave me time to use the window's reflection to see if anyone followed me. I checked my cell—all clear—then scurried to my target, not wanting to miss Mother.

The spa's front lobby was huge, featuring a comfortable waiting area as well as an extensive retail section where customers could purchase their outrageously priced goops, which meant I wouldn't look odd if I went in and just browsed. The building was also conveniently located on a corner, which meant more than one door. I went in the main door, keeping my head down, but not before I easily identified what was most likely the sedan waiting for my mother. There were dozens of expensive cars on this street, but not many would have a driver. While I didn't spot the SUV, it would be close. I did notice Bella, who leaned against a lamppost on the opposite corner.

She gave me the tiniest of nods. Game on.

I pulled open the door to a blast of warm air and over-whelming scents. Several customers circled the lobby, staring at the shelves with perfectly organized products or trying the myriad samples offered at various displays. A receptionist was speaking with a client while another waited behind her holding a glass of something bubbly. Only on Castle Street, the Rodeo Drive of Santiga Bay, could one find clients being primed with sparkling wine while they waited.

There were two hallways that led to the back rooms. One was directly to the left of the receptionist along the far wall. The other was on the right side of the store, near the checkout station and second door. The floor plan Sergi had provided was spot on.

I positioned myself next to a large, circular display closest to the side exit and checked the time. Almost three o'clock. Mother should step out any minute. Without warning, a loud, metallic crunch followed by yelling and screaming penetrated the glass windows of the store. I turned with the rest of the customers, almost forgetting that the destructive sound announced the start of the planned diversion.

I stuck near the display as others ran toward the front window. Whatever was going on outside would be highly abnormal for this quiet upscale neighborhood. Not thirty seconds later, as if on cue, my mother strolled out of the hallway, her head down as she studied her phone, probably checking for messages while she'd been at her appointment. She'd barely lifted her head to register the commotion when I swept next to her, sliding my arm through hers, and turning her toward the side exit.

"Hi, Mom. I was hoping we could have a little chat. It's been a long time."

She'd taken a few steps before realizing I was directing her out a different door, at first probably assuming her bodyguard had grabbed her. Her surprisingly strong struggle subsided when she registered my voice.

"Cressa?" Her shocked response stirred memories from long ago. I didn't think the sound of her voice would carry such an impact.

"Surprised to see me?" I hurried her through the door, but when I turned left away from the main street, her resistance returned.

"Where are you taking me? Stop right now and explain."

I gave her a quick look as I continued to drag her along. She'd aged since I'd last seen her, though she was still a beauty, and the spa treatment gave her a youthful glow.

"I just need a few minutes, and there's a nice coffeehouse just a few doors down. Have you been to it? It's been a while for me, but they used to have the most divine chocolate and raspberry truffles."

"We can stop right here and talk." Her voice trembled as if she were scared of me.

I stopped short, and she almost tripped with the suddenness. "I'm not going to hurt you, and it kind of bothers me you'd think me capable of that. But we're not having a conversation with your bodyguards hovering, or worse, give them the chance to drag me off to Christopher. Can't you spend five minutes with me?"

Her gaze changed from concern to that hawk-like glare I was more used to. Whatever anxiety had filled me earlier dissipated like water on hot desert sand. I might have tugged her along a little harder than necessary, but she no longer resisted.

When we entered the coffeeshop, I worried there wouldn't be any seating, but there were two places, and I picked the one closest to the back. Just in case I had to make a quick escape.

She sat and adjusted her designer coat after I released her arm. "Five minutes is all I have before my driver will be concerned. I have another appointment."

"Of course." I sat back and watched her set her purse on the table then touch her hair to make sure every strand was still in place.

She checked the table to ensure it was clean before resting her folded hands on it. "What's so important that you couldn't call me?"

"So, no hello, it's been a long time, we really should get together more often?" I tamped down the snipe from my tone, but based on a single raised brow from her, I gathered I wasn't successful.

"I think that came to an end the day you graduated and ran away."

I snorted. It seemed more conducive for this meeting than falling into a rage-filled tirade about why I had no choice but to leave that day. "Okay. We'll do this as if I'm not your daughter but the stranger you've raised." I held up my hand when she opened her mouth. "We only have a few minutes, and this isn't about you."

She pushed away from the table, crossed her arms in a huff, then checked her perfectly manicured nails. "Go on."

Now it was my turn to be stymied. I had all my questions prepared, but now that I was here, sitting across from her, none of my practiced speeches came to mind. If I looked past her haughty defensive posture and the coldness in her gaze, I remembered the mother she used to be. The one with the loving gazes, the warm embraces, and soft murmurs of comfort. I shoved it all aside as I straightened and held her glare.

"Is Rasmussen my father?"

I shouldn't have relished her widening gaze or open-mouthed stare, but the childish part of me jumped enthusiastically. Then I waited as she flapped her red-painted lips while her eyes darted around, most likely trying to come up with some lame response. Maybe she didn't think she'd ever hear that name again. Any question as to the validity of what Devon and Sergi had dug up vanished. I waited her out.

Once she had a minute to pull herself together, I could tell she was going with a lie. I don't know when I'd gotten so good at reading people. It might have been my career as a thief, but it probably began years before that when I needed to sense people's moods before crawling out of a hiding spot. And though it hurt, her lies were the easiest to catch, even though she'd become so practiced with them.

"I would rethink what you're about to say. It's obvious you hadn't expected to hear that name again, especially from me. But you owe it to me to tell me the truth."

She lifted her chin and gave me her best chilly smile. "Yes, that was your father."

"Was? Like he might be dead now?" I couldn't remember the last time my emotions hit such a high before they were crushed. I held my breath, waiting for the news that I'd never have a chance to meet him and caught a glimmer of her old self before she turned her head away.

She stared out a nearby window. "I honestly don't know. I haven't seen or heard from him since he left us."

The clamp around my chest eased a bit. I wanted to know so much more, but our time was short. Maybe there would be another time we could take this stroll down memory lane. "Do you know where he would have gone? Where his family came from?"

"He never mentioned his family. He didn't like to talk about it." Her tone had softened. "He never mentioned a town, but he had a quirky Southern accent. He spoke of New Orleans a couple of times, but that might have been just another place he passed through." Her voice changed, becoming sharper. "He didn't like to talk about his background, not until you were born."

When she stopped talking, I wanted to reach out and shake her. No one ended a conversation with a statement like that. I took a chance and asked, "What did he tell you after I was born?"

She bit her lip, which meant she was sorry she'd let that piece slip. I'd learned all of her facial expressions. Most of the time, they mattered more than her words.

"Mother?"

She turned on me so fast, her intensity forced me back against my chair, and I did a quick scan of the place, grateful no one else seemed to notice.

"He made up some sordid tale in a ruse to cover up his medical condition, telling me you'd inherited the same thing. Nothing but mythological crap, but by then, I already knew there was something wrong with him." She made that circle motion with her finger and pointed to her head—the symbol for a crazy person.

That helped absolutely no one.

While that was my first sarcastic thought, the information was of some benefit. Whatever was happening to me was linked to my father. Maybe I was just a mental case, but Devon didn't think so.

A complete stranger, who'd known me for little more than two weeks, had more faith in me than my own mother.

When I didn't move on to the next topic, she did me the favor.

"Do you have the necklace Christopher is looking for?"

My look of surprise caught her off guard. And it had nothing to do with her admission that Christopher was searching for it. No. For some reason, I thought maybe she wouldn't take his side in this. A misguided wish at best. Now the only question was whether she'd told him it belonged to me in the first place or that I'd stole it. The end result was the same, yet that wasn't the point.

The rage boiled, and it was all I could do to keep it bottled up, though a slice of it slipped out.

"Why would you tell him I had it?" I bit my lip, wanting to say so much more. Instead, I kept the personal hurt tucked away, stuffing it back in its corner and slamming the door.

She leaned into the table, her voice low but fierce. "A very dangerous man is looking for that necklace. It would mean the world to..." She searched my eyes, but it wasn't with understanding or regret. It was pure calculation. "It's important to me that we find it."

She was going to say it was important to Christopher, but she knew how I'd take that. It was what I'd expected all along—she put him before me. And instead of being the mature one of the two of us, I gave her one of my well-known flippant responses. "If I'd known the trinket had any value, I would have sold it by now."

Her eyes went wide. "So, you know where it is?"

Everyone was so concerned about this necklace. If I attempted some rationality, there were plenty of dangerous men in the city. Case in point were the handful of vamps outside creating chaos for my fifteen minutes with her. But I didn't need a mind reader to know she was talking about Lorenzo. Or was it a crazy coincidence that Christopher was meeting with another dangerous man? Yet, it had been vamps that were at my old apartment, not Christopher's bodyguards. Unless he was working with more than one vamp, and if that was the case, the man was all kinds of stupid.

"I don't know where it is, Mother." Since Devon now had it, I didn't have a clue where he'd put it. So not a complete lie. "Christopher's henchmen have tossed my apartment so many times, maybe he should ask them." I should have walked away right then. I wouldn't get anything else from her; we were both too keyed up.

It would have been the perfect exit. But I couldn't help myself. I needed her to stick the dagger in a little more, then feel it twist in my heart.

"Why do treat me like you do? I'm your first daughter, but you don't treat me any better than Christopher does. I can understand why he's like that. I'm just a nasty reminder there was someone in your life before him. But why did my own mother turn her back on me?"

For a second, her shoulders dropped, and I readied myself for the second truth of our little chat. To this point, her confirmation of my father's name was the only other fact I could be sure of. But the moment passed, and her chin took on that stubborn tilt.

"Never mind." I pushed way from the table so fast, it shook, jarring her as she fell back.

I stormed past the other tables on my way out, barely paying attention to my surroundings as I shoved open the door to the cool air beyond. I didn't want to hear the answer—afraid of her truth.

Chapter Fourteen

DEVON KNOCKED on Cressa's bedroom door for the second time when Greta walked by carrying her dusting kit.

"She left her room an hour ago, sir. I think she's in one of the rooms downstairs."

"Thank you, Greta." He was halfway down the hall when she called after him.

"She's in a mood."

He paused but shook his head and mumbled, "I'm aware."

He started with the gym. Cressa was like him in that regard. Physical punishment eased the pain of working through personal issues—or with hiding from them. But if she'd been there, she was long gone now. He searched the library, the hot tub, pool, and even Anna's classroom. Nothing.

She might be outside. There was a path she seemed to enjoy that wound through the garden, and the blooms were especially beautiful this time of year. He stopped by the kitchen on his way out.

Cook chopped vegetables while Lucas hovered.

"I just need one recipe for her to try." Lucas's tone was pleading. "I wanted to give it to her as a gift along with the ingredients. She's never had a decent-sized kitchen to work with before."

Cook shook his head but smiled at the younger vampire. He stopped dicing tomatoes and gave Lucas a long look. "You know I don't like giving out my recipes." He ran an arm across his forehead, his expression serious. "But it's been some time since I've had an apprentice."

"She's not going to work here." Lucas appeared offended for his ward.

"Of course not. I'll give you one recipe, but in exchange, I want a serving of whatever she creates with it. If I approve of her skill, I'll consider something more unique."

Lucas's smile couldn't have stretched any wider, and he slapped Cook on the shoulder. "Deal."

Devon shook his head as he strolled in. The two of them were constantly bartering over something. "I didn't know you were back." He took a seat next to his bodyguard, easily drawn into Cook's impossibly fast dissection of carrots and sweet potatoes.

"Bella took over for me. She likes Ginger."

Devon smiled. "It's difficult not to. That woman has no inhibitions."

Lucas's smile took on a dreamier appearance, and Devon could only return a smile for his smitten friend. He didn't care what the two of them did. There weren't any rules about it as long as Lucas performed his job, and Devon had no reason to think he didn't. In fact, he'd handled himself with calm professionalism when he and Ginger had been attacked at the apartment.

Lucas turned serious as he eyed Devon. "Sergi gave me a quick rundown of Cressa's meeting this afternoon. I couldn't tell if it was considered a success other than hearing one of the most prominent intersections in the area was blocked for over an hour."

Cook shook his head with a grin, not missing a beat with his dicing.

Devon chuckled. "Bella does have an evil streak when it comes to creating distractions."

"That explains her good mood when she relieved me. Did you get the answers you needed?"

Devon stole a carrot from Cook, narrowly missing the knife that shooed his fingers away. "Partially. We've confirmed the name of Cressa's biological father, but whether he's alive, where he's from, or anything else about him is still a mystery."

"And the necklace?"

Devon grimaced. It had been a good decision to remain at the manor while Sergi ran the operation. He might have done something regretful to Willa Underwood. The woman was cold-hearted. Or appeared that way on paper. Sergi had been thorough in his report of the events, having interviewed Cressa as soon as she'd returned to the car.

Her anger was easy to read between the lines of her statement. She hadn't recorded the conversation, nor given specifics, but she'd provided enough to form a conclusion. Her mother knew Christopher was looking for the necklace and had all but directed him straight to Cressa. The woman was also being tight-lipped about Cressa's father. She knew more than she was telling, but he wasn't sure what to do about that. For now, nothing. But if he ran out of other leads, he'd have to reconsider how to deal with her.

Devon focused on Cook's knife as garlic was diced then minced. He knew Lucas waited for an answer, but his family had grown accustomed to his occasional propensity for lengthy deliberations. It was a quirk he couldn't seem to stop.

"Nothing has changed. Lorenzo is looking for the necklace, though we haven't found a direct link. How he discovered its existence, or what he knows of it, remains elusive."

"And our next step?"

"I have an idea but need to do a bit more research. I'll call a meeting in the next day or two."

"Status quo until then?"

Devon stole another carrot and turned for the door. "Say hello to Ginger for me."

"She's in the theater."

Devon stopped and turned to Cook.

"I just sent popcorn."

He nodded then strode to the back of the manor and down the short hall that led to the theater. It had been installed decades ago, a special request from Lyra, and he'd been surprised to learn Cressa and Ginger had spent an entire evening playing movie after movie. Lucas said the two women had talked and laughed for hours. He'd never cared for films, preferring books and the quietness of a room, but most of his family enjoyed them, so he'd had a larger theater built at Oasis. He'd have to show Cressa the next time they visited.

At first, he didn't see her in the dark room where an old black-and-white movie filled the screen. Each of the eight rows consisted of six high-backed recliners. He found her in the middle of the second row from the front, slumped with legs pulled up and arms hugging her knees. The tub of untouched popcorn shared the seat next to her.

The light from the screen reflected off her face, which was pinned to the movie, though he didn't think she was watching. Her gaze appeared unfocused, and he considered leaving her to whatever demons haunted her, yet he stayed. Vampires experienced loss differently than humans. Each loss was felt deeply, but the sorrow didn't last as long as it did with humans. It had to do with being nearly immortal. One would think each loss would be more difficult the longer one lived, but even within this modern world, vampires had developed within a war-like culture, living for the moment, where many humans lived in the past. And while Cressa hadn't lost anyone today, the bond between mother and daughter was strong, and it must hurt her deeply to not have that with hers.

He advanced slowly and waited until he caught a flicker in her periphery vision. When she blinked, he picked up the bowl of popcorn and sat in the seat next to her, noting for the first time what movie continued to play.

"Bela Lugosi?"

Her snort gave him some relief that she wasn't as morose as he'd expected, though she was good at hiding her emotions. He sensed her sadness but also a slow-burning anger buried deep, the type that, from his experience, could be difficult to extinguish. Was this what fed her strength and resolve? He'd seen it in others, and for those who never released it, the darkness eventually ate at them, leaving nothing but an emotionless husk. He didn't want that for Cressa, and though she'd have to find her own way to reconcile those emotions, there was one thing he could do for her.

"I wasn't expecting such a large array of vamp movies in your collection." She took the popcorn from him. "You shouldn't be eating that."

"It's organic."

This time her laughter was honest if short-lived. She munched a few bites.

He leaned back and watched the movie. "Why did you turn down the sound?"

She gave him a one-shouldered shrug. "I wasn't interested in the dialogue."

He suspected it was more that she didn't want to be alone yet didn't want to talk. "These are Sergi's favorites."

Her shock wasn't a surprise, but then her brows pinched together.

"I'm not lying. He prefers black and white films, but everyone has their favorite. His is *Nosferatu*."

"And Lucas?"

"He has several, but the one he plays the most is something called *The Lost Boys*."

"Oh, that's a good one. A lot of humor mixed with the horror."

He cringed. "Horror. It's no wonder we're considered such monsters."

"It might be the drinking blood thing, but at the end of the day, humans aren't comfortable with anything that might be more powerful than them. More alien."

He sighed. "I don't think humans are the only ones that have that problem."

She gave him an odd stare then nodded. "You're talking about the shifters."

He smiled. "Yes."

"I'm sorry I wasn't able to find out more about Lorenzo."

"You gathered what you could. Let's hope your mother is as reticent about your father with Underwood and Lorenzo as she is with you."

Her focus shifted again, and she rubbed her forehead on her knees. "I hadn't considered Lorenzo might be looking for him."

"We don't know that he is, only that he's interested in the necklace. And before you get ahead of yourself, we still don't know how Lorenzo learned of the necklace."

"We need that book. I know it's wild speculation that a connection might exist between it and the necklace..." She rubbed at a spot between her breasts. "But you know when you get this deep feeling, this tug that just clicks and won't go away?"

"I do. Which is why Sergi is tracking down the book."

"Is that possible after all this time?"

"The Renaud family is as obsessed with their libraries as they were eight hundred years ago. There will be a record somewhere, and while the trail might be hidden, one does exist." He took her hand. "But enough about work. I came to show you something." He pulled her up and took the popcorn from her, dropping the barely touched tub on the vacated seat.

He led her out of the room and toward the solarium, turning down another short hall that ended at a door one would expect to be a hall closet. This particular one led to a set of stairs. When he turned on a light, he felt her resistance, but it dissipated as her curiosity grew. Once they'd passed the second-floor landing, her reticence returned.

"I thought the third floor was off-limits."

"It is. We're not going to the third floor."

"There's an attic?"

He chuckled. "All old manors have an attic, but we're not going there, either." When they reached another door, he paused. "We're on the north side of the manor." He knocked on the wall to their left. "The attic is behind there."

A cool breeze tasting of the sea greeted them, and he pulled her onto a widow's walk.

"I didn't know this was here." Her voice was filled with awe, and she pushed past him.

He followed her and stopped at the end of the ten-foot-long walk that opened to a deck with two lawn chairs. "It's only visible from the north side of the manor, but it sits far enough out that you can see a good portion of the coastline." He pointed south. "And in the evenings, you can catch the lights of South Rim."

South Rim was an artist community just south of Santiga Bay filled with galleries and quirky restaurants. One in particular catered to vampires, and Devon often hosted small family gatherings there. He should take Cressa there, and the sudden impulse unnerved him. He'd sworn to keep her at a distance. It seemed the shared dreams were bleeding into their reality.

She climbed onto the bottom rung of the railing and leaned over. He was next to her in a flash, but didn't reach out. Her foot was hooked around the post, and she had a solid grip on the top post. She stretched out as if she had no idea how far up she was. He chuckled, thankful the coastal breeze was strong enough to disguise it as nothing more than a clearing of his throat. She was a cat burglar who spent a good portion of her time scaling multi-storied residences to steal valuable items. Did he think she'd simply forget her surroundings? She most likely thrived on heights.

"I come up here on occasion when I need solitude to think."

She glanced down at the chairs then back to him. "Not always alone."

He shoved his hands into his pockets and looked out to sea. "Not always. Sometimes you need a second party to offer an alternative view."

She laughed but nodded her head. "Ginger has always been that person for me. She sees things from a very different perspective."

"The two of you seem to be an odd pairing."

She stepped down from the railing to lean against it. "We met at a time when we were both at our lowest. I think our differences were what we each needed."

"Opposites attract."

She laughed. "I think that was meant for lovers."

He took a step closer and drew in her scent. Memories from the dreams cascaded—her lusty moan when they kissed, the taste of her silky skin, and the feel of her fingers as they traced a path over his chest and down the length of him. He pushed a lock of hair behind her ear and kissed the tip of the delicate lobe. She shivered at his touch, or maybe it was the chill of the ocean breeze, but her head tipped back, exposing her delicate neck and the vein that pulsed with a light tremor in the waning light.

He trailed a kiss to that spot, unable to stop, knowing he should. More flashes of her from their dreams rushed his senses, as vivid as if they were in one now. Some place where the world didn't matter, where nothing mattered but the heat growing between them.

At some point, she'd turned into him with her head thrown back. She pulled him closer until she cradled his head, her fingers roaming through his hair, and when he claimed her lips, she met his passion with her own. He wrapped an arm around her waist, lost in the moment, and unable to step away. He'd never felt this way with any female, especially a human. But he was drawn to her as surely as a moth to a flame. Their shared dreams meant something—foretold future events that confirmed this woman belonged in his life. The dreams could just as easily be nothing more than a reflection of her attraction to him, but in this moment, with her in his arms, he couldn't muster the concern. She'd smothered all his reasoning except the deep knowledge that this was right. His decades-long journey in search of the truth had led him to this moment.

Her hands had found a way under his shirt. Her fingers were light as butterfly wings as they explored. His kiss became urgent, needy, and assertive, and she didn't fight it. Her need was as great as his own, but he broke away. Her soft protest urged him on as he moved back to her neck, his own hands just as curious as they roamed beneath her sweater, knowing exactly how to elicit a cry from her when his fingers found a nipple.

Her knee pressed against his thigh, slowly rubbing its way higher while her hand drifted lower, searching for his zipper. He pushed her arms away and lifted her sweater to kiss the underside of her breasts, the chill of the air forming goosebumps over her flesh. She arched back when his tongue flicked over a tip.

He'd gone too far now to stop. Didn't want to stop. Needed more. So much more.

An obnoxious beep sounded from far away, growing louder until it broke through his erotic haze. He wanted to ignore it, still under Cressa's enchantment, but a different urgency broke in as the beeping increased. He stepped away, his forehead falling on her chest as he tugged her sweater down.

"Just turn it off." She kissed the top of his head, and tried to pull him back, but he took another step back, reaching for his phone.

He didn't need to look at the message to know who'd texted, but he did anyway. She wouldn't like something else taking priority over what had almost just happened. Though maybe this was the metaphorical cold shower he needed to prevent whatever was between them from going further. At least until after she was no longer indebted to him.

"I have to go."

He cupped her face, and her disappointment was plain to see. He wanted to explain, but this wasn't the time. Not yet. They had a mission to complete and couldn't afford to be distracted.

"I wanted you to know about this spot."

"Is there news? Something about Ginger?"

"Nothing like that. I'll see you in the morning." He wanted to give her a last kiss, but she'd taken a couple steps back, her earlier desired-filled gaze tamped down.

He turned and raced down the stairs, undecided whether he should be grateful to Decker or knock him on his ass for the interruption.

Chapter Fifteen

SIMONE DROVE into the valet line at the Emporium Tea House, which was rumored to be the most popular among the aristocrats. This would be quite different than the first tea house she'd taken me, or so she promised. I wasn't convinced Devon would approve of me hobnobbing with the upper crust, but if anything went sideways, I'd let her explain it to him.

"Are you sure this is a good idea?" I glanced at the vehicles in the lot—all high-end models and several limos. It wasn't that I didn't trust her. It was all the other vamps, who might take a dislike to me. We could easily be outnumbered.

"No one would dare take advantage at a tea house. I assure you the Council would take immediate action with the severest of penalties."

"Comforting words for my family," I muttered, but my nerves took a breather with the conviction of her words. Anna had mentioned, during one of her etiquette lessons I typically napped through, that the tea houses were sacrosanct among the vamps and all animosities were left at the door. Never hurt to have a vamp confirm it.

"Is it the tea house you're worried about or not knowing where Devon went?"

The valet attendant opened my door, saving me from having to answer. It was a ridiculous question. What did I care where he went? Even if it seemed more important than the wild, crazy, passionate whatever that had been happening on the roof. I followed Simone as she led us through the door that opened as we approached. Besides, I might be mildly curious about where he went, but who wouldn't want to know what a vamp was up to in the middle of the night?

Once we were seated in a private booth with a view of the dark ocean, she continued her assertions. "You're the first human I've seen so closely involved with his business, but you need to remember your place."

I glanced down at my hands. My place. An employee. I inwardly snorted. Not even that. More an indentured hireling.

"Don't pout. I didn't say that to demean you. Your role in Devon's household is a Blood Ward. While we both know what that truly means in your case, it will be more believable to others if you truly acted the part—in both public and private settings. Even at home you should act as a Blood Ward would."

"I'm still not sure what a Blood Ward should be doing. I mean, he's taken me to parties, and I assumed I'd acted well enough since he didn't say otherwise."

Simone nodded. "I agree. From what I saw the evening of the ball, your actions before the theft were acceptable. Although, Devon mentioned he found you drinking and placing bets on a billiards game with two male vampires at Gruber's tea party. That is unacceptable."

"So, okay as long as I'm hanging on Devon's arm. Not okay to be on my own unless I'm in the process of stealing something." Funny that Devon hadn't mentioned he'd left me alone for an hour at the tea party.

Her brows narrowed. "You're not making fun of me, are you?"

I glanced around then swallowed my smile along with a piece of antipasto. The last thing I wanted to see were fangs at a restaurant. "Of course not. Like I said, no one gave me a handbook."

"Which is why your training with Anna is essential and should not be curtailed."

I rubbed my forehead. There was so much to learn, most of it having nothing to do with the mission. Good grief, I didn't even know how long it would take to work off my debt—weeks or months. God forbid not years.

She took my hand, startling me. Other than during my defense training, she'd never touched me. "Relax, Cressa. It's easy to see you've been on your own a long time, making your own decisions. This will be difficult for you, but you must let part of that go."

When I tensed, not at all happy with her words, she rubbed her thumb over my skin in slow imperceptible circles. "Only long enough to get through this mission. I thought little human girls wanted to grow up to be actresses."

She released my hand when our first course was removed and a second placed in front of us. I performed a quick sanity check, assuring myself she hadn't just mesmerized me into submission.

"Princesses." I tasted what looked like calamari and relaxed when my guess proved correct. And it was scrumptious. So far, the food here was more palatable than the first tea house. I wasn't into experimental entrées.

"What?"

"Little human girls want to be princesses not actresses."

"Ah. An even more unachievable goal."

I snorted. "Didn't you have dreams of being something when you were a kid? Like an astronaut or runway model?"

She took a tiny bite and washed it down with what I considered a rather earthy and nasty tasting tea. "I dreamed of being free and not whipped every day."

Okay, I'd stepped into that one. Suddenly, the calamari didn't taste so good. "I'm sorry."

She waved a hand as if to dismiss what had to have been the world's worst childhood. "It was centuries ago."

"Still, I had no business prying."

She set down her fork and stared at me. "That is one thing I've never understood about humans. And I wasn't one long enough to learn."

"What's that?"

"Why some humans are so compassionate to others while many are cruel and uncaring."

I snorted again. "As soon as I figure that one out, I'll be sure to tell you." When she gave me a disappointed frown, I decided to cut the cheeky responses, and not suggest it didn't appear much different in the vamp world.

I tasted the tea being served, thankful it was a new blend with a light mint flavor. "There are so many influences that shape a human. I suppose I thought it was the same for the magical. Genetics, environment, experiences, but I think for some it's hard-wired in our brain." I pointed a fork to my head before trying something rolled in rice like a piece of sushi.

She nodded. "That would explain many things."

I wasn't sure what she meant and wondered if she'd been thinking of herself. Before I could decide whether to ask, her head shot up and her gaze narrowed, a bit of fang showing. I tensed, rubbing my left boot against my right, confirming my dagger was in my boot.

"Simone, what a surprise to see you here, especially without your Father."

The voice came from behind me, and I inwardly groaned. I'd recognize that oily, salesman-pitched tone anywhere. Lorenzo. And here we were without Devon.

"You need to remember what century this is, Lorenzo. Women don't require escorts anymore."

He stood close, hovering over us like some lord of the manor. "And more's the pity."

Simone glanced behind him. "I don't think I've seen you at a tea house before."

"It's not my usual haunt, but it does provide an intimate setting for private meetings."

I kept my head down, not wanting to invite his attention, but I kept an eye on the other vamps that had trailed behind him. Most passed our table, striding for the exit, but one caught my eye. He kept his head down, as if he didn't want to be seen, and skirted the tables on the far side of the room. I couldn't say for sure he was with Lorenzo. It was possible his departure was coincidental. He was a big man with brown hair, and other than his size, was similar to half the men in Santiga Bay. Yet a memory poked that I'd seen him before.

Simone must not have had anything else to say because she returned to her meal as if dismissing him.

"It would do you good to remember you're speaking to a Council member. One who has a say over who is capable of leading a House."

I expected Simone to rise up and show this asshole how capable she was of running a House, but she set down her fork, took a sip of tea, and gave him her full attention. The tip of her fangs brushed her lips. "I know how the Council works, Lorenzo. You have no extra sway when not in Chambers. I owe you no more or less respect than any other vampire, and the Council has no say on who rises to lead a House."

"Not currently." Then I felt his gaze fall on me, and it was all I could do to not shudder in disgust and fear. I really needed to grow a pair around this guy. "And I see you're with Trelane's Blood Ward. How are you, my dear?"

"I'm fine. Thank you for asking." Not a tremor to be heard. Maybe I should have been an actress. Something told me not to cower in front of this man, but I also knew I shouldn't poke a feral animal.

He lifted my chin with his finger and glared into my eyes. I swatted his hand away the same time Simone grabbed his wrist.

"You know better than to touch a Blood Ward." Simone's fangs had fully dropped, and there was murderous intent in her flashing amber eyes. I was captivated by the array of colors in a vamp's glowing eyes, though now probably wasn't the best time for reflection on the topic.

"Is there a problem here, Simone?" A muscle-bound man appeared out of nowhere and positioned himself between Simone and Lorenzo.

Simone simply stared at Lorenzo, still holding onto the wrist he was trying to extricate. I was aware that everyone was staring, but the only thing running through my mind was that Simone was stronger than him. It was possible he simply didn't want to escalate the confrontation, but for an instant, I could have sworn I'd caught a flash of fear. Could it be that he was the weaker of the two?

Simone released his wrist, and Lorenzo stepped back.

"My mistake." He cleared his throat and turned to the man, who must be security. "A mere misunderstanding."

"Then perhaps we should let the women return to their meal. There's been enough disruption." The man wasn't cowed by Lorenzo, and I was grateful tea houses were neutral territory.

"Quite right." Lorenzo bowed his head to Simone, ignored me, and strolled out as if nothing had happened.

"My apologies, Simone." The security man received a nod from Simone then hurried to ensure Lorenzo left without any further trouble.

Simone sat back as another course was delivered, and the other vamps went back to their meals. When the server left, she carved off a slice of what looked like brie. "You must try this with the rosemary cracker and just a touch of the apricot jam. It's divine."

I leaned in and lowered my voice. "So, we're going to forget that just happened."

"No. But now isn't the time. I'll speak to Devon about this. Lorenzo grows bold with his plans."

"Which are?"

"He wants control over the Council to put stricter rules in place and remove the shifters from it. He wants the old ways restored."

Devon had told me as much, and it explained why Lorenzo wanted to keep Devon's censure in place. He would be a formidable opponent in the battle for control. A tingle shivered through me as I considered the House Wars. Normally I wouldn't care, but what happened to humans when vamps went to war?

We were walking to the car when I suddenly remembered where I'd recognized the large man sneaking out of the tea house. Gruber's tea party.

Once we'd driven a couple blocks from the tea house, I turned in my seat to face Simone.

"When Lorenzo's vamps were leaving, did you notice the one on the other side of the room?"

"Of course."

How silly of me to ask. "I'm not a hundred percent positive, but I think I've seen him before."

She gave me a side-glance. "You've been to a tea party and a ball. You could have seen someone like him at either of them."

"Exactly. I saw someone who looked like his double at Gruber's tea party."

"As I said."

Sometimes I just wanted to shake that exactness out of her. She really needed to learn to loosen up. I sucked in a deep breath and tried again. "As you well know, I took it upon myself at that party to steal something that discredited Devon's reputation with the Council."

I took a double take when Simone snorted. Maybe she could loosen up. "I'd overheard Gruber talking about a file they didn't want Devon to know about. The man Gruber was talking to was the one sneaking out of the tea house tonight."

I braced—feet smashing into the floorboard as if I had both of them on the brakes, and my hands pushed against the dashboard so my head wouldn't slam into it as the car curved and screeched to a stop in a strip mall parking lot.

"What the hell?"

Simone turned to me, her hands gripping my wrists so tight, tears erupted. "Are you positive?"

"Ow!" I had no doubt my howl could be heard all the way back to the tea house. While she didn't release her hold, the pain receded as her fingers loosened. "No. I'm not positive." I shook my head and focused on that evening. "He didn't want Devon to see him, so they must know each other, but I never saw the man's face."

"Then why would you think it was the same man?" She didn't appear to doubt me, only wanted to understand my reasoning.

I tugged on my arms. She released me, and I instinctively rubbed them, though they didn't hurt anymore. "I'm not sure I can explain, but I think it was how he moved. The man at the party had that same skulking movement, like he didn't want to be seen. The second I saw him tonight, I immediately thought of the tea party. I know it's crazy." I hung my head, sorry I'd brought any of it up.

"I wish I'd paid more attention."

My head popped up. She believed me?

"I agree it could be a coincidence, but I've had better luck with much less. It's still not enough for retaliation, but..." She tapped a fingernail against her teeth. "...if he's snooping around, we might be able to catch him at his own game." She glared at me. "Not a word of this to Devon." When I opened my mouth, her fangs slipped out.

"Not a word. But what are you planning?"

"I want to see if any of this has merit before adding to Devon's agenda. I have several people I can put on this."

"And you'll need me."

She gave me a long look. At least she didn't laugh. "Not yet. But when I have a suspect, I'll call for you." Without another word, she threw the car into drive and raced out of the lot, debris flying behind us.

I glanced out the side window, hiding a smile she wouldn't approve of. Bit by bit, I was becoming an integral part of the team. Then my grin faded. What the hell was I thinking?

Chapter Sixteen

DEVON HUNCHED in a corner seat with his collar turned up, hair left untamed, and his focus on the bar that stretched along the far wall. The place was similar to The Den, the fight club Decker owned, but instead of nightly fights, this club held them on weekends. From what Decker told him, the rest of the week was reserved for customers to make underground connections and enjoy the more pleasurable aspects of sexual pursuits. While Decker's club would never entice high-end customers, this club thrived on the Hollows' underbelly.

"Here he comes." Decker kicked out a chair as a man and a woman headed in their direction. They both took a seat, but the dark-haired woman shifted hers to take in the whole room, while the man had merely given the room a single scan before facing Decker and Devon.

"Elijah. Thanks for coming." Decker pushed the open bottle of whiskey toward the man, but he shook his head.

"I prefer tequila." Elijah lifted an arm to flag down a server.

"When did that happen?" Decker swallowed a shot and poured another. "Never mind, don't tell me. Boobs as big as inflatable rafts and legs up to here." He lifted a hand up to his chest to reflect an exaggerated motion of long legs.

The woman snorted, but Elijah grinned. "Something like that."

"I think you know Devon."

Devon didn't wait for the man to reply. "We met briefly at Remus's gala about a year ago. I was expecting Mateo."

If the shifter was annoyed by Devon's reference to The Wolf's beta and second in command, he didn't show anything other than another broad smile. "Mateo is back east on a territory dispute. This is my beta, Raquel."

Raquel gave them a curt nod before returning to her hawk-eyed study of the room.

"Elijah is the alpha of the Humboldt pack," Decker interceded, playing the negotiator.

Devon sat back and considered the shifter. The Humboldt pack controlled the territory north of Santiga Bay and east to Redding. From what he understood, they were one of the strongest packs in the US, and since it ran along the border of Remus's personal territory, it made sense for The Wolf to call upon Elijah when his beta was called away.

"I remember. Apologies. I've been too focused on internal matters lately."

Elijah shrugged. "That's one of the items Remus asked me to discuss with you."

Devon finished his shot and pushed the glass to Decker, who refilled it. "I wasn't aware my internal matters were a concern of The Wolf's."

"It does when it appears to interfere with our longterm partnership."

Devon picked up his shot and flashed a glance to Decker, who held his gaze, and he caught the look of a man walking a fence. Decker was a rogue shifter, and while he didn't belong to a pack, he'd given his allegiance to The Wolf. At the same time, Decker had saved Devon's life, and though they hadn't spoken in years, their decades-long friendship was as strong as ever. It would take a great deal more than Decker siding with the shifters to break what they had.

He sipped the whiskey as he turned his attention back to Elijah. "I understand his concern and remember our timetable. My current internal affairs are part of that plan, but I need time to nurture those before we can complete our endgame. It won't be much longer." He sat back and gave the alpha a slow grin. "In fact, it was Remus who gave me the key to unlock the information we need."

Elijah didn't hold back his surprise, then he grinned and showed off his wolfie bite. "I'll be interested in hearing that story someday."

Decker cleared his throat. "There was a specific reason Devon asked for this meeting, but I recently uncovered something you both need to hear." He glanced around before pulling his chair closer to lean in. "One of my regular fighters went crazy yesterday. Almost beat a guy to death. It took four of my vampire security to pull this guy off. He's another vampire, who's been working at the club for over a year now. Not once in all that time has he lost it like that." He downed a shot and looked directly at Devon.

It wasn't difficult to see the dread in his friend's stare, and Devon pushed his own growing anxiety down. "Magic Poppy."

Decker nodded while Elijah released a small, troubled whistle. "I called off the fights for a couple of days and have him drying out in one of the cages. He swears he didn't buy it. He thinks somebody slipped it to him. I made some calls but couldn't get anyone to talk to me. Most were clueless, but some seemed...I don't know...not exactly afraid." He shook his head. "Hell, maybe they were scared shitless and hid it beneath that vampire facade. But I found one guy who finally opened up. He's not one to scare easily, but I didn't think the others were, either." He wiped his forehead and glanced around the club. "He said there's been a spike of the

Poppy in SoCal, mostly in the smaller towns, but it's been moving closer to L.A."

"This has happened in the past." A cold chill swept Devon. "The Council will send in the Sentinels and shut down the dealers." The Council had exterminated the major suppliers of the addictive drug that made vampires go mad, or so he'd thought. The drug had almost doomed him to a similar demise, and while they weren't the suppliers, any infected vampire unable to recover had been put down for everyone's safety.

Decker shook his head and mopped his forehead again. "No one knows who's supplying it, and nobody's buying it. They just get slipped some and go nuts. Most come out of it after a day or two, but some seem to stay hyped-up longer, like maybe someone keeps dosing them."

"That actually matches with something Remus heard from the southern packs. They're also seeing similar instances of vampires raging out, but no one knows why," Elijah said.

"And now we have our first incident in the north." The thought of someone slipping the drug to unsuspecting vampires was terrifying, and Devon recentered his aura to douse the growing shakes. "They're not selling it, so profit isn't a motive. And why give what appears to be a single dose to some but more to others? It sounds like some type of experiment."

"Or someone's sick joke." Elijah's brows drew down, either in concern or concentration, Devon couldn't be sure. "Maybe whoever's slipping the stuff has access to certain vampires while others are simply chance encounters. This could impact our timeline."

What the shifter didn't want to say was that this could be the tip of a larger push toward war between the factions. With the Council waffling over their future, vampires hopped up on Magic Poppy could incite fights and territory disputes, forcing a war with the shifters. He and Remus both believed the shifters would be the ultimate losers. If that happened, the shifters wouldn't just disappear, they'd be subjugated—forced to survive under complete and total vampire domination.

Decker sat back, hands folded over a stomach that had grown too lean since the two of them had reconnected. "This could create chaos for decades, if not centuries."

Elijah typed a text then stuffed the phone back in his pocket. "The shifters won't be tamed. You know this."

He knew they were only voicing their worries, but his anxiety nipped at him, and he snapped his response. "I understand what's at risk. We know there are members of the Council and a handful of dominant Houses who believe things should return to the days before the House Wars. This is what our partnership is meant to prevent."

"If we're not successful, there will be bloodshed on both sides." Decker's hand shook as he reached for his drink.

"But this time, the humans will be caught in the middle." Devon's first thought was of Cressa and whether he could protect her if that eventuality happened. He might be vampire, but the Council knew his thoughts on this matter quite well. For those who forced the change in the paradigm, he might not be considered on the same level as the shifters, but any new Council would likely take his House and family from him. While he didn't have the numbers of other Houses, and though censored by the Council, no one today would dare threaten the Trelane House. But if Lorenzo had his way, that would no longer be the case. They wouldn't want him to have his own army. And though this issue alone should be enough to find a way to break his censure, it wasn't the only reason. "In the days of the House Wars, there were far fewer humans. They were superstitious, unorganized, and had little in the way of weapons that could harm us."

"This time—" Elijah leaned in to finish Devon's train of thought, "—the humans are more advanced, with organized armies and fearsome allies. They won't go down easily and could possibly destroy us all."

"With the Council's long-ago decision to allow the making of vampires, humans could be turned and used against their own. That was why my father was against the Council's decision." What he didn't bother sharing, though Decker knew part of it, was that his father's opposition to that vote occurred the same time his family's troubles had begun. Something he'd originally assumed were coincidental—a string of bad luck. He'd been naïve.

"We need more intel on this situation." He turned to Elijah. "With my history with the Poppy, I'll need to assign this to one of my personal guards."

"I'd like to work with Sergi if possible," Elijah said. "I know him from a mutual issue we had over in Hayfork."

He remembered the incident. Sergi had been impressed with the shifter. "I'll arrange for him to make contact. Do you think the shifters down south could be of help?"

"I'll speak with Remus. That was who I just texted. He's probably already making calls."

Decker sat back and kicked Devon under the table while pointing his chin toward the entrance. "The main reason for our meeting has just arrived." Decker turned his back, leaving Elijah in the best position to watch the entourage approach. "Based on the description Van, the owner of this club, gave me—" Decker checked his watch, "—and it being close to midnight, I'd say the blond man in the lead is Christopher Underwood."

Devon allowed his hair to dangle in his face so the man wouldn't recognize him should he glance over. Underwood had his arm around a lithe, raven-haired vampire. It had been three years since he'd met Underwood, and it had only been the one time, yet he never forgot a face, especially with humans. He'd always done business with them, even before his censure, but since then, his ventures were split between the humans and shifters.

There was no question as to his identity, but he was surprised when the vampire at his side smiled and her fangs dropped. Not enough to be threatening, but enough for anyone to not mistake her species, or for Devon to mark her as a young blood. Younger vampires dropped their fangs whenever they got excited, and that included when they were enthralled with someone. They simply had no control over their new baser instincts.

Did Underwood realize the danger he put himself in? With a mature vampire, a person didn't have to worry—until they did. But at that point, there was no question as to whether shit was going to go down. With the young bloods, one moment they're excited and happy, and next, someone's throat was mistakenly ripped out. Children, what was one to do? He chuckled to himself.

"It seems Underwood must know Lorenzo is a vampire or at least has connections to them." He couldn't shake the feeling something else was going on, but with everything else he'd heard tonight, his focus had been shattered.

"Maybe Lorenzo picked him because Underwood already had underground connections," Decker suggested.

"Who is this human?" Elijah asked.

"He has some type of partnership with Lorenzo and has recently become a thorn in my side. If Lorenzo dug far enough, he'd find a brief business encounter between our two companies. Underwood's current interest in one of my other ventures is bringing Lorenzo closer than I'd like, considering our arrangement."

Underwood was trailed by two men and two women besides the one hanging on him and pinching his ass. When they kissed, there was no doubt they were more than acquaintances.

"Do either of you recognize the others? Strangely enough, it appears to be a combination of shifters and vampires." None were familiar to him.

"I don't recognize the shifters." Elijah scratched the stubble on his chin.

"I do." The men turned to Raquel. She'd been so quiet, Devon had forgotten she was there. "The two male vampires have been spotted in various cities along the coast, but the majority of their time has been spent in Sonoma." She shook her head. "The women are from the Trinity pack, so I don't understand why they'd be together."

Elijah nodded with a cheeky smile. "Raquel is head of my security. I'd believe what she says. And I do recognize the girlfriend. She's also been seen around Sonoma."

"So, any of the three could belong to Lorenzo," Devon said.

"Well, that would fit with her hanging on Underwood. I wonder if the missus knows?" Decker squinted, his wheels turning.

When Decker turned to him, he didn't have to ask. They might not have seen each other in decades, but the minute he'd walked back into The Den a couple of weeks ago, the years between them had melted away. And maybe that was why Devon had avoided his old friend and the memories they brought back— the dark times. Those days were inconsequential now, and the fact his old camaraderie with Decker had slid into place like a pair of well-used loafers could only benefit their plans.

Devon nodded. "Be discreet."

A hundred years ago, Decker had worked as a private eye before it became a thing, back before his life had been stripped from him. But even after he opened The Den, he'd built a network of connections, keeping tabs on all the magical news. It only made sense he'd be able to track down information on the Poppy.

"Check in with me before doing anything with the photos." He stood and nodded to Elijah and Raquel. "I think we should keep our eyes on this group. If those vamps belong to Lorenzo, their relationship with the shifters won't be what it seems." When they both returned his nod, Devon turned and disappeared before anyone at Underwood's table noticed.

Chapter Seventeen

I FELL INTO BED, unable to stop my mind from racing through images of the long day. First, my mother, as cold as ever. For a moment, I'd thought maybe there'd been a flicker of something when I'd mentioned my father's name. Probably nothing more than a play of light, sunshine hitting the window just right.

Then Devon found me and gave me one of the best gifts—a place of solitude where I could feel the air on my skin. Then he was at my neck, sending shivers of pleasure straight to my core. I touched my lips, and even hours later, I could still feel the heat of his mouth on mine. When his lips blazed a trail under my breast, I thought I'd scream with need. He was such a tease.

I blinked.

Was that something I knew from experience or from my dreams? It had to be the dreams. Great. Now reality was blending with my dreams to where I could barely tell them apart. What could possibly go wrong with that?

I pushed thoughts of Devon aside to replace them with someone much darker. Lorenzo Venizi. Why was he always cropping up, or was I just that lucky? Maybe he was thinking the same thing about me. I shivered. That would not be good. Sooner or later, someone might connect the dots of stolen items and that I'd been at each of the scenes. There would be dozens of names on that list, but if there was one thing I'd learned living with vamps—they were thorough. I'd have to give that possible calamity some thought.

Anna had barely scratched the surface on the House Wars, and I hadn't learned anything of value on what had turned Devon and Lorenzo's Houses against each other. I was still plowing through their section in the chapter, but it was a painstaking effort having to read such archaic language. I'd keep at it, but I couldn't stop thinking about the words *De første dage*. It had to be a book. If I could only put my finger on why I was so adamant about that fact.

The weight of sleep came with images of Devon again, and when I opened my eyes, I stood next to the lake at Oasis. The air was cool and golden leaves blew across the browned grass. The sky was a deep sapphire blue, and the earthy scent of mums filled the air.

Devon paced several feet away. He was mad. More than mad. He clutched a piece of paper in one hand while running his fingers through his tousled hair with the other.

"Don't worry so much." I took a step closer then stopped. "We knew something like this might happen. Simone said you'd prepared for it." Soothing words were all I could provide. Anything else, and he might literally bite me. His beast was close to the surface, and even I was smart enough not to encourage it to the ledge.

"He didn't have to do it." Devon's words were clipped and filled with rage. "He did it for spite and nothing more. A despicable warning that he felt me breathing down his neck and this was his way to get me to back off." He stooped, picked up a rock, and threw it into the lake. Then he repeated it one more time.

I didn't think that was going to do much to cool him off, and being more foolish than I thought possible, I reached for his arm.

He pulled away, but I tried again. This time, he let me pull him close.

"Let me grieve with you. Don't push me away."

His shoulders slumped, and his aura pushed out. His agony and pain rolled off him and crashed over me like waves slamming against a rock-hewn wall. Defeated. For now.

"We'll come back stronger. For now, just be with me."

He fell into my arms, dragging me to the ground where he remained a crumpled heap. All I could do was hold him as he shook.

When I glanced up, the landscape had changed to one of nightmares. The air stank with the coppery smell of blood.

It was everywhere.

I stood in a grand foyer. The gray marbled floor and cream-colored walls were draped in crimson—splashed, spattered, and pooled. Broken bodies, the necks ripped out, littered the floor. Six men in all. I wanted to turn and run away, but my legs moved as if someone else commanded them. The next room, large enough to hold three distinct sitting areas, had been decorated with balloons and streamers that hung from the ceiling, wall hangings, and light fixtures. A champagne bucket had been overturned, and a cake lay crumbled on the floor. More bodies, at least a dozen men and women were strewn across the floor or dropped like broken marionettes over the leather couches—mutilated. Necks had been torn here as well, and in some fit of great rage, arms had been ripped off and a couple of heads had rolled away from their bodies.

A party gone wrong.

A woman lay on top of a table, naked, her body sliced in so many places it was impossible to see the true damage beneath the blood.

My knees went weak, yet my legs held me up, and I continued to move through the house as if on a conveyor belt. I was being given a tour of a horror show.

The worst was in the kitchen. A man had been nailed to the

wall with heavy metal spikes. A message had been carved into his chest.

Had enough?

I recognized the man. I'd met him at a dinner party at Oasis. He was the alpha of the Humboldt pack.

I fell. My knees slammed into the hard stone floor before slipping on the sticky red fluid. I caught myself on my hands, the gelatinous gruel oozing through my fingers. The stench made my stomach clench, and I gagged, wishing I could vomit. Nothing came up but dry heaves. Tears blurred my vision and dripped down my cheeks.

Somehow, I crawled back to the great room, finding the single rug without a drop of blood on it until my hands left prints moving across its surface. My feet trailed gore as I continued my search for a way out.

I didn't want to see anymore, but shutting my eyes wouldn't block out the cruel, barbaric scene. Then a cool wind, blowing in from the windows, swept away the stench of rot and death.

A woman stood in front of a sliding glass door that led to a patio. The door was shut, yet her long golden locks floated around her lithe form. She wore white in a sea of red.

"This doesn't have to happen."

Her voice was childlike. Her blue eyes clear with no sign of sorrow or pain. No. She was smiling, with her arms outstretched —beseeching.

"None of this has to happen."

I didn't understand her repeating words. Did she mean this carnage was preventable? Should they not move forward with their plans, or should they not involve the shifters? Perhaps there was a different plan, or a better plan that could shield them from this. I almost laughed. I didn't even know what the first plan was. None of this made sense. Who could do such a thing in the first place? Then a chortle erupted. Of course, I knew who did this. Didn't everything lead back to Lorenzo?

Then I saw it, hanging from the woman's neck.

My necklace.

I THREW the blankets off and ran to the door, stopping long enough to pull on a pair of sweats and a T-shirt. The images continued to blast me, making me stumble down the hall, each one bloodier than the last.

I'd never been to Devon's room and had only seen him walk from the other end of the second floor the one time. But I didn't stop until I reached the large double doors at the end of the hall. I hesitated for a second before I inched the door open. A rustling came from somewhere to my left.

I raced in. For another brief second, I hoped he didn't have company, then my legs moved faster when a beam of soft moonlight cut a swatch across the floor, lighting half the bed.

Devon struggled in a nightmare. Was he still where I'd left him? On the ground at Oasis, the grip of his agony freezing him in place. The sheets were damp with sweat, and I yanked them off.

"Devon. Devon, wake up."

I grabbed his shoulders, ignoring the feel of hard muscle, the heat of his skin, or the perspiration pouring off him. "Devon, I need you to wake up."

He continued to thrash, his lips moving, but his voice was too low to hear. I kept shaking him, panic seizing me, making it difficult to breathe. Why wouldn't he wake? He was so hot, like his whole body was on fire.

"Devon!" This time my shout filled the room. My vision blurred, not knowing what to do or how to help. He should have woken as soon as I did. Right? God damn my dreams. Why had they become so ugly? What happened to those passionate dreams, the ones that made me blush every time he walked into a room?

Then hands grabbed me and pulled me away. Sergi appeared

on the other side of the bed as he took up the job of shaking Devon. His own voice calling out his name in a steady mantra—over and over.

"What happened?"

Lucas's voice was steady, and though my heart beat faster than a hummingbird's, the anxiety lessened—but not my fear.

"Tell us." Sergi snapped the order.

"It was a dream. No. More like a nightmare. Something horrible had happened, and Devon blamed himself. So many dead."

Sergi glanced past me to Lucas, who'd moved me to a chair while Devon continued to live in whatever nightmare I'd taken him to.

"Was there anything different about the dream?" Sergi pinned his eyes on me, and they glowed a soft red. I'd never seen his vamp side kick in, and something told me the red in his eyes would shine like rubies if I was in real danger. And though he was holding himself back, I knew without a doubt, it was taking every ounce of his strength not to tear a hole through the world.

"Yes, it was all different. There was blood and dead shifters in a house I didn't recognize." I shook my head, trying to get past the gore, shoving it all aside to see it from a distance.

"There had to be more," Sergi insisted.

More what? More blood, more bodies. Wait. I reached for my neck. "There was a woman. Small, thin with golden hair. She wore my necklace, or one just like it."

When Sergi shot a look to Lucas, his lips thinned. "Keep her here. Give me a couple of minutes, and if he doesn't wake by then, slap him until he does." Then he was out the door, his boots pounding down the hall.

I had no idea where he went, but as soon as Lucas's grip lessened, I was at Devon's side, holding his hand. A memory I knew wasn't mine told me I needed to get back inside the dream, find him, and pull him out of it, but I didn't know how to do that. I considered putting the necklace on, but I didn't have it anymore, Devon did, and I had no idea where he kept it.

Maybe I should know where it was kept for moments like this. But would I know what to do with it? It might drop me back to the same dream, but would I have enough control to change what was happening, or would I create a dream worse than the last?

A cold chill swept through me when I recalled the dream when I'd first worn the necklace to bed. I hadn't been me, and whoever I'd been, I didn't like. There was no guarantee that wearing the necklace would help this situation. Not without more knowledge of what it could do.

Devon suddenly stopped struggling and sprang up, grabbing my arms. His gaze was unfocused, his grip tight and painful. Lucas rushed to me but hesitated. He didn't know what to do any more than I did.

For a moment, he seemed to still be in the dream, then his eyes flashed with their vampiric icy-blue glow before settling into their natural color as he scanned the room, first landing on Lucas and then on me. His pallor was off, and based on his pained expression, whatever hell he'd been trapped in was still fresh. He ran his hands over my shoulders.

"Are you injured?"

What a strange question. He must be coming out of the dream having seen everything I had. Yet, he hadn't been with me when I'd been given a scenic tour through the shifter's house. At least, I hadn't felt his presence. Had he been living some other nightmare?

I shook my head, not sure how much to say with Lucas hovering over us.

Then Sergi was back. "Devon? Are you all right?"

He took a moment to answer, his gaze still a bit wild and focused solely on me. "Leave us."

Neither of his guards moved. I assumed they were doing that vamp stare contest between them because I didn't take my eyes off

Devon—questions, concern, and anguish still alive in his sapphire gaze.

He broke the hold he had on me and forced a smile as he turned to his cadre. "Give us ten minutes. I'll meet you in my office."

It was enough for the two vamps to step away, and Devon didn't say another word until the bedroom door closed.

"I'm sorry." I sucked in a ragged breath. "I don't know what happened. I'm sorry I have no control over these damn dreams."

He pulled me to him. His skin was sticky hot. I didn't care as I melted into his embrace, only now feeling the shakes overtake me.

"We were at the lake. You were comforting me."

I nodded against his chest. This would be easier if I didn't look at him. "Do you know why?"

He squeezed me tighter. "Not at first."

"Then you saw it. The shifter house."

His breath hitched, and I knew the answer. New tears traced a path down my face, and with his arms wrapped around me in a vice grip, all I could do was let them fall. "It's been some time since I've seen such carnage. Such waste. And Elijah..."

I hadn't remembered the name, but he could only be speaking of one person. "He was an alpha."

"Of the Humboldt pack. I met with him earlier this evening."

I pulled back as far as he would allow, at least far enough to see his face. If I'd expected any residue of his earlier shock, I should have known better. He'd pulled up a shield, his emotions safely tucked away, yet his arms wouldn't release me. "That seems more than a coincidence."

"I would agree."

I dropped my forehead to his chest. "I need to know more about these dreams."

"And I would agree again. I need to go to my office and calm Sergi and Lucas. Try to get some rest." He released me, and I stood, realizing we were alone in his bedroom, sitting in his bed. It had seemed so natural, I hadn't given it a second thought. But now, I needed to get out.

When I reached the door, something sprang to mind. "Did you see the blonde woman in white?"

His expression was blank, but his eyes narrowed in concentration. "No. I don't remember a woman."

I nodded, then left, forcing one step after another until I almost flew to my room. I slammed the door behind me, arms wrapped around my stomach, and collapsed on the window seat. My gaze brushed over the shadowy grave markers.

I didn't know why, but Devon had lied when he said he hadn't seen the woman.

Chapter Eighteen

DEVON WAITED for Cressa to leave and listened to her increased pace as she ran back to her room. She knew he'd lied, that sour scent he'd caught from her clung in the air. He'd deal with her anger later. He took five minutes to wash the drying sweat from his body and threw on his sweats before clomping down the stairs toward his office.

Sergi and Lucas waited for him, and the whiff of freshly made espressos filled the room, mingling with the wood scent from the fire glowing in the hearth, and gave him a second wind. A cup waited for him, and he picked it up after crashing onto the sofa.

The necklace lay on the table between them. It flickered with the reflection of the flames, almost alive with dark powers. He was projecting, but what else was he to believe considering the change in the direction of the dreams since it found its way to this house.

"Is Lyra all right?" Devon should have gone straight to her room to check on her, but Sergi would have handled everything. Though she responded well to everyone in his cadre, she had a special connection with Sergi. If only any of them could stop her sticky-finger habit. It was increasingly apparent he'd failed at the task.

"She was wearing it this time." Sergi's growl told him enough of his friend's thoughts on the necklace in general.

"Cressa said she was in her dream." Lucas's voice was soft, concerned for his new charge.

"I told her I didn't see the woman, but I did." His hand trembled as he sipped his espresso, and he set the cup down, running his hands through his hair in some vain attempt to settle his nerves.

"Can you tell us what you saw?" Sergi asked.

He blew out a deep sigh. At least this one wasn't erotic, though he was beginning to miss those. They didn't foretell of peril and devastation.

"We were at the lake, and I was wrecked. I didn't know why I'd felt so empty, so defeated. Something horrible had happened, but I had no reference as to what, just a deep sense of loss and failure." He released a shaky laugh that wasn't a laugh at all. "It's been centuries since I've had that feeling."

"The battle at Petumbra." Sergi would know; he'd been with him since the old days.

"That was a difficult period for vampires." Lucas was an expert in all vampire history. He would have been a better instructor than Anna, but his service as a guard was more crucial.

"And Cressa was at the lake with you?" Sergi kept to his questions, not allowing Lucas to sidetrack him.

It would be easier to share stories about the battles, not that Lucas hadn't heard them dozens of times as a child, then again during long evenings with his cadre reminiscing tall tales. Sergi was right to keep them focused, reviewing the details, no matter how much he didn't want to relive the dream. He could still feel the darkness—the evil—invading his soul.

"She was trying to comfort me. It wasn't working." He grunted. "Or maybe it was. I couldn't shake the bleakness, but when she laid her hand on my arm, it settled me. I can't explain it. She somehow balanced the raging emotions I couldn't control. I know it doesn't make any sense, it's just what I felt." The experience had been deeper than that, but they wouldn't understand. Perhaps Lucas would, but not Sergi, who relied on facts and what he could see. Yet, he couldn't forget her touch in that moment. It was like someone pouring a healing salve over a deep wound.

"She mentioned the dead. Was this from the House Wars?" Sergi always went straight to the heart of things. Nothing subtle about him.

He shook his head. "Could I get something stronger?"

Devon finished his espresso while Lucas fetched the scotch and three glasses. After the first biting sting ran down his throat and lit a fire in his belly, he relaxed into the sofa, leaning his head back to stare at the ceiling. And as much as it pained him, he let the dream return, flooding his senses with its dark despair.

"The only constant within the latest dreams is that it begins in one place, in this instance the lake, then it jumps to another. It was an abrupt shift. One moment, I was on the ground at Oasis, a piece of paper clenched in my hand, the next, I was in a house littered with the bodies of shifters. Blood everywhere. They went down fighting, and based by how much they'd been ripped apart, they must have been outnumbered."

He sucked in a breath, took another long sip of scotch, and shivered. "There were balloons and ribbons strung from the ceiling. It was someone's birthday. A woman laid on table, pieces of a smashed cake beneath her. She hadn't died quickly or easily. It was impossible to walk through the place without stepping in someone's blood or entrails. The kitchen was the worst." He wiped his face over and over before lifting his head to stare into Sergi's hard gaze. "Elijah had been nailed to the wall with crossbow bolts. The words 'had enough' carved on his chest."

Sergi paled. "You just met with him earlier tonight."

"Does Cressa know this shifter?" Lucas's porcelain skin tone which, on any other day, dramatically conflicted with his California beachboy appearance, had taken on a gray tone.

"No. I'd only met him once before, about a year ago."

They were quiet for several minutes before Sergi urged him on. "And Lyra?"

"She hadn't been in the room when I first walked through it. But after the kitchen..." Why couldn't he get that image out of his head? He'd seen worse, but that had been a century ago. Maybe it was the eyes. The eyes of the dead always condemned, always saw the truth. "She was standing by the windows of the great room, her hair rustling with coastal breezes, although I don't believe Elijah lives anywhere near the coast. Then she said this doesn't have to happen."

"This doesn't have to happen. Were those her exact words?" Sergi pressed.

He didn't hesitate in responding. "It's what I remember. Why?"

"Those were the exact words she said to me when she gave me the necklace."

A cold shiver stiffened his spine. "Was she in bed when you first got there?"

"No." Sergi refilled glasses, though he didn't drink. He held the glass in a tight grip, and for an instant, his cool facade slipped, and that unsettled Devon more than anything else from the evening. "She was sitting in her favorite chair, staring at the darkness beyond the windows. At first, she ignored me when I called her name and asked if she had the necklace. I thought she might still be in the dream with you. Something had to be holding you there. Then she removed the necklace and held it out in her palm as if it were some offering. When I took it from her, it was cold. She never looked at me. All she said was that you'd be okay now and that whatever you'd seen doesn't have to happen." He shook himself like a cat shaking off water. "I thought it was strange until you said the same words. I imagine Cressa must have heard them as well, though she didn't mention it."

"These dreams must be prescient. Some form of divination where the foretold future can be changed." Lucas had inched to the edge of his seat, his forehead wrinkled in thought, putting together a puzzle that still had far too many missing pieces.

"If so, they're not very helpful," Sergi growled.

"We need someone who knows how dreamwalking works. " Devon downed his second shot and waited for the pushback.

"Haven't you already tried that?" Sergi's tone matched his own frustration.

"We haven't used all our available resources. There's still one person who hasn't divulged all they know."

It didn't take long for Lucas to offer up a name. "Willa Underwood."

Devon hadn't expected him to be the one to mention her. He didn't believe his youngest guard would be willing to pressure Cressa's mother for answers. Sergi wouldn't hesitate. After Cressa's not-so-friendly meeting with her mother, perhaps her irritation would make her more understanding of what he had to do.

He laid out his idea. "I met with Decker this evening, and we've discovered Underwood has a weakness for beautiful young vampires."

"Did he know she was a vampire?" Lucas asked.

"He was at a fight club, drinking with a group of shifters and vampires while a particular lovely hung all over him."

Lucas whistled. "The question is whether Willa already knows about her husband's infidelities."

"There's only one way to find out." Sergi smiled, and Devon already pitied the position Willa would find herself in. "You mentioned Decker was following him?"

Devon nodded and slid his empty glass across the table. "He should have a few compromising photos by morning. Willa might have stonewalled Cressa for information, but if there's some part of her that wants to protect her daughter, we might be able to persuade her with the correctly applied pressure."

"And you think these pictures will be enough to sway her. That seems risky." Lucas frowned.

Devon could almost hear his friend's internal struggle. He would be weighing Willa's usefulness against Cressa's eventual outrage for using her mother. Yet, earlier this evening, she'd understood the necessity of controlling the dreams. Somehow the necklace was the answer, but it was too dangerous to use without more information. It unnerved him that Lyra had used it. Was it possible that she'd been the one who'd directed the dream?

"A meeting with Willa is a risk, and as you pointed out, she might already be aware of her husband's infidelities. I haven't decided how to use the photos, but it will be done one way or another. This entire issue has played out longer than it should have, and with the direction of the latest dreams, and Lyra's increasing participation, I no longer have a choice."

He didn't want to admit the situation had become more personal than just Lyra. His delay in discussing the dreams with Cressa hadn't protected her. At some point, she would have discovered her mother had lied to her about the date of her birth. What else was Willa Langtry Underwood hiding?

"We either need to find Rasmussen or someone that knows something about that damned necklace. And I've been more than patient on this. The Council, the dreams, Lyra, this business with Lorenzo searching for the necklace—it's a distraction to our goals. Yet, somehow, I can't shake the notion that something connects these events with our overall mission. I'll make my decision on this soon." Devon stood and glanced toward the window, the open blinds revealing the darkness. Several hours yet before sunrise. He strode to his desk. There wasn't any hope of returning to sleep, so he might as well work.

"Lucas, have you been keeping up with the Renaud libraries?"

"I visit them whenever I can."

"Sergi has the name of a book that had been in their main library eight centuries ago. We need to find it. I'd like you to lead that effort now that Ginger seems settled." When Lucas appeared torn between his passion for the libraries and those for his charge,

Devon chuckled. "Don't worry. You still have your duties guarding Ginger, but I think you can manage both."

Lucas blushed but retained his game face. "If the book is still in this world, I'll find it."

"Can you also check on Cressa before you leave?"

Lucas smiled. "Of course." He glanced at Sergi, who held up his tablet. The information on the book had already been sent.

Devon waited for Lucas to depart before he motioned Sergi to his desk. "I need to tell you about something Decker discovered."

"Does this have something to do with a message I received from Elijah?"

The alpha hadn't wasted any time contacting Sergi. It made sense, especially after the dream. Shifters, as well as unsuspecting humans, would be the first victims of a vampire's inability to control their beast.

"One of Decker's fighters was dosed with Magic Poppy."

Sergi's normally blank expression went rigid. His rugged face, clenched jaw, and steely gaze made men who faced him on the battlefield want to run home to their mommies. He had to admit, it scared him at times.

Devon filled him in on what Decker and Elijah had shared. "I want to keep this investigation close. No one else in the House is to be told. Work quietly with the shifters."

Sergi's brow raised. "Not even the inner circle?"

He sighed. He'd struggled with the decision on the drive home from the meeting. A major threat lurked among the vampires. A certain threat to his family, considering his past addiction. Yet, his decisions should be based on facts and not his own insecurities. After all this time, it was incredibly difficult. More than he'd ever imagined it would be. He'd been lucky to come back from that hell and still run a loyal House. Of course, it had been more than luck, and certainly more than just him that had built this House. In the end, his family would turn to him for their security and protection, and they would require more than just faith in his ability to provide it.

If he pushed aside his own apprehension over his earlier entanglement with the Poppy, what did that leave? One known case at a fight club and rumors from Los Angeles. He needed more before putting his family on alert.

"One week. I need facts not innuendo."

"You want me to go down there?"

"I don't see any other way. If these infected vampires belong to a House, they're keeping it quiet for obvious reasons. If there's something more going on in those Houses, they won't share it willingly. My gut says rogue vampires are being selected."

"It would be my first thought."

"If it is some type of experiment, the perpetrator would be foolish to involve more than one House. The last thing they'd want is a multi-House investigation, which the Council would get wind of. If it's some form of retribution against a particular House, then it should be easy enough to track down." He met Sergi's gaze with a harder one of this own. "You're not being sent to solve this. I don't want you taking any chances by getting in their way. Observation only."

When Sergi held his gaze and didn't respond, Devon leaned over the desk. "We have enough on our plate without this, but I need to know if this is widespread or contained. Perhaps Decker's vampire was a fluke, or he has some tie with the southern Houses. Once I know the level of threat, I can advise the family accordingly, then we can get on with our most pressing business."

Sergi relaxed his shoulders and nodded, but the grimace on his face said he was less than pleased. "Do you want pictures?"

He shook his head. "No. Your word is sufficient." He didn't think the trust he placed in Sergi was enough to assuage his displeasure, but this wasn't the first time he'd kept critical information from the rest of the cadre. The fact this information involved Magic Poppy might make his inner circle feel betrayed by his silence, but how could he expect others to let go of the past before he did?

When Sergi moved to the door with his usual stride, Devon stopped him. "Only stay as long as you need. Be careful."

His security specialist only nodded before closing the door behind him.

Devon turned his chair to face the window. The one question no one mentioned ate at him. Why reintroduce Magic Poppy into the vampire population now? He didn't believe in coincidences. Was someone luring him out? And if so, was it Lorenzo, or had someone else just entered the game?

Chapter Nineteen

STEAM FILLED the room and covered the mirror with tiny beads of moisture. The droplets bent beneath the force of the hot wind before finally breaking up to dissipate into the air.

I shut off the blow-dryer and blinked.

I was so frickin' bored, I was studying steam like a first-year science student.

Two days had passed since the dream incident. Devon hadn't mentioned it again, and I had no desire to relive that nightmare, but we'd have to talk about it eventually. I glanced up, still convinced someone lived in that room above me.

I'd spent the last two evenings staring out my bedroom window, searching for the dark-clad woman who visited the graves. I wouldn't be able to see her face, but it would be nice to confirm if it was the same woman who returned or whether various people stopped by in the middle of the night to pay their respects. While that might seem unusual, I was living among vamps. Regardless of their ability to walk about in the sun, night was kind of their thing.

Here I was, making up stories in my head to fill the gaps of who I was and what my dreams meant. But Devon's mission came first, as Lucas and Sergi continued to remind me. I stared at my reflection and ran my fingers through my dry-enough hair, but I was just stalling the inevitable.

When I'd finished my training with Sergi, he'd told me to clean up for a meeting with Devon, and as usual, gave no further explanation. That never failed to carry an ominous tone. I grabbed my jeans and sweater, rebellious enough to irritate him for no particular reason, before common sense took hold. Simone's words echoed like a harpy to play my role. So, I tossed the jeans and sweater onto the bed and selected black leggings, a long fleece shirt, and low-heeled shoes—all appropriate for a Blood Ward.

I was on my way to Devon's office when I heard laughter coming from the library. When I poked my head in, my suspicions —based on one particular squeal—were confirmed. Lucas and Ginger sat across from each other at a small game table, a map spread out between them.

"Hey, I didn't know you were here." I strode in, my curiosity on high alert to check out the map.

"I wanted to tell you I was here, but Lucas said you were freshening up from training, as if that's a valid excuse not to drop in. Like, how many times have we had discussions with one of us in the shower and the other on the toilet."

"Stop." Lucas appeared horrified, holding his hands against his ears as if that would stop him from hearing anything.

Ginger and I burst out laughing.

"Something tells me you don't have a sister." I meant it as a joke and not to pry, but Lucas's gaze became unfocused as he glanced off at nothing in particular.

"I have two, actually. But they were much younger than me when I left home. It's been some time since I've seen them."

"That explains the overprotectiveness." Ginger gave me a knowing look before her keen gaze flitted back to Lucas.

"All vampires are protective, some more so than others." He shrugged and stared down at the map.

One look at Ginger told me not to delve deeper. She'd eventually worm the story out of him.

"So, what are you looking at?" I asked instead.

"It's the map of the Renaud libraries."

The map was an internal view of a multi-story building. It had been hand-drawn on paper as ancient as the pages in Anna's history books. Symbols, painted in myriad of colors that appeared mixed with a metallic substance, dotted the sketch. A tingle ran over me. How did something this amazing not reside in the museum itself.

"For which library?" I didn't know what I wanted to do more —go over every nuance of information that had been packed into one map, or find the library and spend days, maybe weeks, exploring all its nooks and crannies.

"All of them." Lucas's eyes glowed a preternatural blue.

Ginger laid a hand on his arm. "He gets that way every time he looks at the map."

"You mean each of their libraries are built the same way?" I dragged over a monstrous chair, the legs leaving a sunken trail in the carpet, and took a closer look at the drawing.

He nodded. "They built their first one in the south of France, which is their home territory. This was centuries ago when the Council made House Renaud the Keepers of Knowledge."

"This was before the House Wars?"

"About a decade or two before. Their House was considered untouchable, even through the wars."

"Like Switzerland," Ginger offered.

He gave her a pleased smile. "Exactly. The Renaud family never took sides. They were chroniclers of everything vampire—the good, the bad, and the ugly as it were."

"I thought history was written by the conquerors." I ran a finger over the oddly-sketched stairwells, my gaze jumping back to the unknown symbols.

Lucas laughed. "That's true for the most part. But the Council, true to our nature as a long-lived species, understood that truth can't be hidden for long, so why bother." He gave us an evil grin and twirled an imaginary mustache. "But that doesn't mean the less-favored books couldn't be buried so deep it would be as if they hadn't been written at all."

A cold shiver went through me when I considered the illusive *De første dage*, still positive it was a book. My thief alarm blared that we were on to something as I stared at the drawing of a massive library that could hold thousands of artifacts, probably more. And this was just one of them.

I leaned over to re-examine the map, then pointed at what appeared to be the front door. "If this is the entrance, then only three levels are above ground."

He nodded. "And six below." That grin returned. "We are vampires, you know."

Vampires who preferred the dark. When I reviewed the upper floors, very few windows existed, and they probably all had blinds or heavy drapes.

"How do you know so much about this?" Ginger had stopped gazing at the map some time ago, her focus solely on Lucas.

He sat back and got that faraway look again. "My family are merchants, neither wealthy nor poor, though aligned with a powerful House. My father tried numerous times to teach me the business, doing everything he could to keep me out of our library in exchange for his office of inventories and financial records. Once I was old enough to travel on my own, I visited the Renaud Library in France and fell in love. I have visited them all, several many times over."

"A librarian turned warrior?" I teased.

He laughed and shook his head, but his fingers grazed the edges of the well-aged map. "It didn't take me long, having read hundreds of books by the time I was of age, to realize that our race survived on both good and evil. And with the rise of humans and shifters, it wasn't difficult to see that a horrible war was on the horizon. I was friends with several vampires from the Bertrand House and discovered that many Houses believed peace among the races was the only way to survive."

"As Devon believes," I said to no one in particular.

"But peace comes at a price," he continued.

"Whoever has the biggest guns," Ginger chimed in.

He shrugged. "For humans, yes. For shifters, they built packs and hierarchies. Vampires have their Houses and the Council. But it's all the same. Concerned for what might become another century of war, when I came of age to choose my own path, I wanted to be prepared to protect our knowledge and history. I begged my father to send me to a House where I could become a warrior."

"I bet he wasn't happy about that." Ginger had obviously spent enough time with Lucas to weasel out his story. We were way overdue for a drink night.

"No, but I think he knew he'd lost me years before that. And rather than face my mother, who protected her children, especially where their hearts led them, he sent me to House Lafitte."

"Not the House Trelane?" I had just assumed.

"That is a story for another time."

All eyes turned to where Devon leaned against the doorframe, impeccably dressed in a three-piece, chestnut-colored suit that emphasized the golden highlights in his hair. The light-blue shirt drew out the deeper shade of his sapphire gaze, and my insides melted to goo. I pushed down thoughts of the hard muscles beneath all that cloth and caught my tongue before I licked my lips. Good grief, where was a fan when I needed one.

"When no one came to my office, per my request, I decided to see where my errant family had strayed."

Lucas jumped up. "Sorry, Devon..."

He waved a hand and strode to where we sat. "Don't bother. I can see you were outnumbered." His lips twitched as he pulled a chair over that was a match to the one I sat in. While I had to drag mine, his movements made the heavy-wooded chair seem as light as a plastic patio chair. I wasn't sure I'd ever get used to that.

Lucas settled back in his chair. "I was showing them the map of the libraries, and we got sidetracked."

"It seems a fitting place to discuss a different library and our next mission." Devon glanced at the map as if to confirm which one it was before he sat back.

"This is where everyone went." Simone, dressed in an indigo caftan, her hair dyed to match, strolled in, and Lucas stood to offer his chair. She took the seat while Lucas brought over another one. "I confess I didn't search that far; you can hear the laughter all the way to the solarium."

Ginger stared at Simone, her mouth half opened. The only thing missing was the drool. It hadn't occurred to me she hadn't officially met Simone. The only time they'd been together was at the ambush at our old apartment, and Ginger hadn't been in the best shape to remember who'd been there.

If Simone was aware of Ginger's ogling, she didn't show it, but she had to be used to people staring. It was something vamps did frequently to my great annoyance having been on the receiving end more times than I could count.

"I asked Lucas to take over the hunt for the *De første dage*, which I should have done from the beginning. And now we know where it might be."

I leaned forward, taking a closer look at the different sections of the library, but if I'd been expecting to see labels like philosophy, science, fiction, or cooking like a human book store, I was out of luck. Those beautifully colored symbols appeared to reflect the contents of the various areas. If there was a legend to translate them, I didn't see it.

"I think you'll find it in the rare book collection." Lucas tapped his knuckle in an area on the third sublevel. The symbol looked like some ancient bird.

"Rare books? Aren't they all rare?" I surmised the vamps were still recording history, but considering how long they lived, I'd assumed the majority of the books were ancient.

"The levels are arranged in a couple different ways, but one is by the age of the books. Books written over seven hundred years ago that aren't still considered popular are housed in the rare book section. The third sublevel is the farthest the general members can browse. The lower floors include the massive inventory that are cycled through the main library displays, restoration areas, research labs, offices, and the like."

"And where is the one with the book we're looking for?" This sounded like my kind of job.

"Los Angeles." Devon had been watching me. I didn't know when I'd developed the ability to know when his eyes were one me, but I'd felt their weight since he'd entered the room. Not a heaviness, but a gentle presence that said he had my back. Maybe it had been the dreams, and considering the last one, I didn't realize how comforting his presence had become.

If he was waiting for my reaction to the location or the layout of the building, I wouldn't disappoint.

"When do we go?"

Chapter Twenty

I RELAXED against the headrest and stared at the palm trees superimposed against a hazy blue sky. The air was warm, and a breeze blowing through my hair would have been perfect except for the stop-and-go traffic that kept the convertible to a crawl.

Simone's fingernails tapped out an irritated staccato on the steering wheel. It was hard to believe anyone could be less patient than me in traffic, but considering how fast she preferred to drive, the crawl through Beverly Hills should be enough to flash fangs.

She'd insisted on renting the high-end sports car, even though we had a SUV with a three-vamp security detail at our service. We availed ourselves of the offered vehicle twice, but Simone preferred to be in control, so the SUV followed along at a not so discreet distance. The security team was provided by Carlos Ortega, the alpha vamp of the largest House in SoCal and a strong ally of Devon's.

Bella and Jacques were also out there somewhere, or so Simone said, although I hadn't seen them once since we'd arrived four days ago. But everything had been a flurry of activity during that time, and playing tourist, shopping, and clubbing had only been the beginning. Add on excursions to tea houses, one tea party, and a formal private dinner with fifty of one's closest vamps held in Simone's honor, and it had been a true whirlwind of activity.

Whenever I had an opportunity to stay in a hotel, I kept my room orderly. On this trip, the two of us shared a penthouse suite in an oceanside resort, and the place looked like it had been tossed by street thugs. Clothes, shopping bags, empty jewelry cases, and shoeboxes were everywhere. To my utter amazement, Simone did wear other things besides caftans, and her fashion maven was in full swing for rubbing elbows with the City of Angel's elite.

The first time I attempted to tidy up the place, her fangs dropped.

I got the hint and tossed a few of my own new purchases around, just to prove I could—although I picked most of them up before dropping into bed each night.

"Have I worn you out, human?"

I rolled my head toward her. "You'd think with all the daily training I'd have more stamina for shopping and museums."

She clucked her tongue. "This type of activity requires a different level of perseverance. A Blood Ward would usually spend all their spare time shopping and attending parties. The only reason Devon has restricted the activity is to prevent your face from showing up all over Santiga Bay."

"Thank heavens for small favors."

Simone laughed. "One does have to enjoy this type of activity. In the vampire world, shopping is second nature to us, or at least to those Houses that have money."

"Just one more similarity to humans I'm afraid."

She growled, but there was humor in it. With her disdain for humans, she allowed me a certain leniency when comparing our two species. At times, she appeared to soak the information in as if still trying to figure us out. I took it as a good sign and didn't look any deeper.

"I thought you'd be more excited about the library." She

checked the rearview and side mirrors. Something she'd been doing for the last ten minutes.

"I am. I think I'm in recovery mode from the tea house. Did you really know all those people? And why didn't that mob happen at the other three tea houses we visited?"

"I've been going to this one for years. It's almost a ritual. My friends don't go to tea parties, and most don't circulate in Carlos's circle of friends." She checked the rearview mirror again.

"Trouble?"

She gave me a side glance. "I'm not sure. Our escort flashed his headlights. I think they picked up on the same tail I did."

"Another vamp House?"

"Or rogue vamps checking us out."

"That's comforting."

A beep sounded, and Simone tapped her earbud. She didn't speak, her eyes focused on the road ahead of her, then a quick nod was followed by "got it" and another tap of her earbud.

At the next busy intersection, she took a last-minute right, and seconds later frantic honking soon faded behind us. I seized my first opportunity to turn around. Our escort was gone.

"Are they going to check the tail?" That seemed dangerous out in the open.

"Just slowing them down. Bella will be waiting at the library while our escort takes our mystery friends on a scenic tour of town until they realize they've lost us."

"Does this happen all the time?"

She shrugged. "It depends on the town and why we're there. Devon does the same thing when strange vampires arrive in town without known business."

I began to understand. "Is it always a requirement to notify the local Houses you're arriving?"

"If you're part of a House, then yes, usually. But it's not unusual for the courtesy to be ignored. In those cases, a vampire should expect to be followed, more as a warning than anything else."

I nodded. "You let them know you know they're out there so if anything goes down, they'll be first on the list."

She smiled with a bit of fang. "Then it's hunting time."

That didn't require any further explanation. Simone grabbed the wheel like an Indy racer and cruised the twists and turns of the back streets. I wasn't sure how much of it was a test for another tail, or her need to feel the wind stream through our hair after twenty minutes in traffic.

Ten minutes later, she turned into an open-gated drive. A small brass sign reflected the hours but gave no indication of the name of the institution. Fifty yards past the gate was a guard house, and several yards beyond that was a spot for cars to turn around. Something told me there were probably more cars turned away than allowed to proceed.

Simone stopped and stared at the guards. If she intimidated them, they didn't show it. They took note of her House bracelet, and she gave them her name. While one guard typed into a tablet, I scanned the building and camera locations, one of which was pointed at the car. No doubt taking a picture for facial recognition. This form of security was growing quickly in the corporate world as well as high-end residences and wasn't surprising for a library or museum, especially one owned by a vamp House.

Before another minute passed, Simone was following the long driveway that passed under large Sycamore trees and past lush vegetation before opening to a parking lot that could hold fifty cars. Emerald-green lawns and dozens of flower beds, sporting tropical and native varieties, surrounded the massive Greek Revival building. The floral scent was surprisingly heady, spicy, and sweet —intoxicating.

Five cars were parked in the row closest to the walkway leading to the library. It was midday during the work week, but I somehow expected more visitors. But then, how often would vamps visit a library? The turnaround at the guard stations would have deterred humans.

Simone led me up the low steps to a massive wooden door that she swung open as if it were made from balsa. "This particular library, like seven others of its kind around the world, is also a museum. The artifacts are displayed among the stacks on all six floors available for public viewing. The library opens in the afternoon and closes at dawn."

Strange hours until one considered the clientele. The cars out front were probably staff, unless there was a back parking lot I hadn't noticed. I didn't see any sensors, but cameras dotted the lobby.

"Hello, and welcome to the Renaud Museum of Vampirology and Knowledge." A wizened old woman, her hair as white and lofty as a cloud, peered up at us with bright green eyes the color of a meadow. Eyes that searched for any deception and made me want to squirm. She must be the head librarian.

"We're from out of town and couldn't pass the opportunity to roam the halls of this great building." Simone finished with a slight bow of her head. It was such a mirror image of what I'd expect Devon to do, I had to blink. Maybe Devon held a class on how to emulate him. Between his cadre moving in perfect sync with him and copying his deportment, it was downright eerie.

"There's a map in the basket. We only have a few guests today, but one can wander through the stacks for hours and never find another soul." The old woman pinned her gaze on me. "If you need help finding a particular reference, there is one custodian on each floor. Tables are located in the center of each floor for reading. The only items that require a custodian's assistance are the artifacts and any book in the rare book collection. Though with advanced notice, you can schedule a private viewing."

Then she smiled, and I wished she hadn't. Her yellow-stained teeth looked sharp, and the tips of her fangs hovered like they were stuck at that half-mast position.

"Thank you, custodian." Simone took one of the folded, brochure-style maps and walked off. I followed, but the itch to keep an eye on the old crone made me want to keep watching our backs.

"Are they all going to be that creepy?" It was meant as a joke, but it was all I had to fall back on since I hadn't thought to bring a flask of vodka.

"Yes."

Well, that was helpful. "Did we need the map?"

She handed it to me. "No."

I was going to ask her to elaborate until she added, "For appearances."

Of course. And when was I going to remember that? It was second nature for me to create a role when researching a job. Somehow, that natural instinct seemed to have vanished since working with vamps. I tucked the map away, deciding it couldn't hurt to keep it. With any luck, this map used words rather than obscure symbols to reflect the different sections of the library.

Our heeled boots on the marble floor announced our presence a good ten seconds before we appeared, and the sound echoed behind us. Otherwise, the place was quiet as a mausoleum. And based on the array of ancient weapons and paintings of bloody battlefields, it was close enough to one.

Simone stalked down the aisle to the central staircase and never slowed until we reached the third sublevel. She came to an abrupt stop at the base of the stairs, and I almost rammed into her. She lifted her head and made a complete circle—sniffing something out.

"What does that vampiric nose tell you?"

Her menacing glare came with a bit of fang, and I braced myself, amazed I didn't take a few steps back.

"Vampires have been here. Recently."

I sighed and rested a fist on a hip. "This is a vamp library. And based on the number of cars in the parking lot, it was probably a group of those custodians."

"The custodians all have the same smell. These are different."

They had the same smell? No doubt. They spent their lives buried in the book stacks and probably smelled of dust and mold.

"Four of them. Moving together." She lifted her head one more time and turned to her left. "I'm not saying they couldn't be here on legitimate business. Scholars or students. Maybe a family researching their history."

She moved into an aisle, and this time her boots were stealthy silent. I followed like a trained puppy, not nearly as quiet, but a vamp would have to be listening for me. After two turns to the left and three to the right down aisles of floor-to-ceiling bookcases, she stopped just short of another aisle. She gave me a sign to go around and flank whoever might be down here with us.

I didn't bother nodding, just turned and crept back to another main aisle. With no one in sight, I crossed the aisle and made a zigzag pattern until I was somewhere directly across from where Simone should be. I pulled my bone-handled dagger from an inner jacket and tiptoed to what appeared to be a small circular sitting area, wishing I had super scenting ability. Although, considering where I used to live, there were plenty of places where that gift wouldn't be a plus.

I kept my head low and crept to the right, using the gap in books on a lower shelf to provide a partial view of the reading area. No one was there.

Then a flash of forest green—Simone.

She moved so quickly, a glimpse of her flowing caftan was the only proof it was her. I turned to flank from another position, all the while, closing the net.

After another five minutes of quiet circulating, Simone called out, "Whoever it was is gone."

I straightened and stretched my back before sliding the dagger into my jacket. We met at the reading table, though we kept our eyes on the stacks. They ran in various directions, forming small circles in adjacent sections. I was curious how they would look from a bird's eye view. Lucas's map wasn't that detailed, but I couldn't help wondering if there was a pattern to it all and if it was the same on each level.

"Now what?" Simone stared at me, arms across her chest, and her caftan seemed to flutter with some mystical force.

"We look for the book."

"And how do we do that?"

Good question. There hadn't been any computer stations along the way. I made a slow circle and smiled when my gaze landed on a long cabinet with rows of small drawers next to one of the stacks. Old school it was.

It had been years since I'd been in a library where they still used card catalogs and didn't think any still existed. For the first time since we'd entered, I took the time to let the scent of books fill my senses, memories rushing past of days spent in libraries, anything to keep me from having to go home. Thinking of Christopher's house shook me out of the old days, and I pulled open one of the drawers.

The heavy wood drawer slid out easily, displaying dozens of index-sized cards. I flipped through several and wasn't surprised to discover they didn't use the Dewey decimal system. Vamps preferred their own way of doing things. The cards appeared to be filed in alphabetical order by title, although there was some type of alpha-numeric code assigned to each card.

I checked my pockets but no pen. Out of curiosity more than anything else, I scanned the top of the cabinet. Sure enough, on the far side there was a pad of paper and a short lead pencil. I was beginning to see why Lucas loved these libraries and would have to ask him if there was one closer to home.

When I stepped back, my heel clipped Simone's boot. "Good grief, Simone. Is this a date?"

Her expression revealed nothing as she continued to stare.

Personal space, or lack thereof, was another annoying habit with some vamps, especially the older ones.

"Why are you hovering?"

She blinked. "I wanted to see what you were doing."

"Could you do that from two feet over?"

When she continued her stare, I rolled my eyes and started opening drawers to find the ones starting with the letter D. This all seemed too easy. Devon never said where he got the information on the book's whereabout, and I hadn't thought to ask Lucas.

I found the right drawer on my eighth try. A tingle ran over me when I pulled the card with the book's name typed on it, and my hand trembled when I wrote down its location, which appeared surprisingly exact with stack and shelf number. The stacks were clearly tagged with labels, and it didn't take long to find what we were looking for on the third shelf, two-thirds of the way down the aisle.

I froze, checking the location on the slip of paper against the book label on the shelf. Then I read the name on the book's spine. This was it. I glanced at Simone, her eyes big as saucers, a smile on her lips. She nodded for me to do the honors.

I suspected right away that something was wrong. But sometimes, I think the brain pushes the thought aside to keep us in that state of heightened expectation for as long as possible before the inevitable crash. It wasn't a large book, but it should have weighed more than the light, airy object in my hand. Turned out, it was a box that had been painted to look like an ancient text, title and all.

My hands shook as I opened the box. It was lined with a soft, silk fabric and held a card the size of a wedding invitation. I choked out a laugh. Of all the frickin' luck. The note was short and sweet.

"De første dage is currently out for restoration services. Apologies for the inconvenience."

SIMONE TAPPED HER BOOTED TOE, the soft sound more like a drumbeat in the quiet room. Her other leg was crossed over her knee, her shoulders back in a regal posture. She would make an amazing House leader—or a queen if times had been different. Her brows knit over a faraway gaze, still stymied over the note and five minutes of what she referred to as a discussion, and I viewed more as a tirade of how the simplest of things could get so fucked up.

"We can't ask for a private viewing. That would leave a trail." This was the third time Simone had made the comment, as if all the earlier statements had melted the obvious problems away.

Simone's flaw, not that I would tell her, was that she'd never planned a job before. She'd been a member of many missions, and while she'd had to make last-minute decisions, it wasn't the same as planning a job from beginning to end. She was in a position to watch how Devon devised his missions, but the other players never saw how the pieces were brought together. From my experience in planning several heists, it's not the same until you're the one in charge—mistakes and all. To put it plainly, she couldn't see the trees for the forest, and the devil's in the details.

"It would have been helpful to put a date on the card." Her fingernails tapped a slow rhythm in time with her boot, her expression never changing as she continued to spit out her long mantra. "We have no idea if the book was removed yesterday or ten years ago. We need to get into the restoration room."

I'd sprawled in an overstuffed chair a few feet from her with one leg thrown over the arm while I perused two maps. One was a copy of Lucas's map, and the other was the one Simone had taken from the basket. A plan was forming, but I'd either need a crew or a diversion. I hadn't spoken to Harlow since the job where Sorrento had caged me, and though it was past time to discover who the snitch had been, his crew was currently a high risk.

Besides, after a glance at Simone and her wrinkled forehead, if there was a solution to this, it had to be soon. I turned my gaze to the room and considered our slim options—or lack thereof. For no other reason than sheer boredom after our anticlimactic moment and waiting for Simone to complete yet another review of our impossible task, I turned to the modern-day map of the library. I read through its brief history and a list of coming events when I turned the page to find a list of weekly happenings. The library was busier than I thought, and whether it was the alignment of stars or fate resting her hand on our shoulder, luck was on our side today.

I popped up, grinning like an alley cat with an opened can of tuna.

"We have a way in."

Simone's gaze snapped to me, and her fang-tipped smile matched my own. "It took you long enough."

Chapter Twenty-One

SERGI AND LUCAS were quiet in the front seat of the sedan. That wasn't anything new for Sergi, especially since his unsuccessful return from SoCal that morning, but Lucas was usually chattier, even when on a mission. He'd been unhappy when Devon had first laid out the plan for Willa Underwood. More so when he'd selected a meeting for when Cressa was conveniently in Los Angeles.

Lucas had become personally involved in Cressa and Ginger's life—the lives of humans. If he ran his House like many in the aristocracy, Lucas would be moved to another assignment, or possibly traded to another House. It was a harsh reality and cruel. When a vampire was traded like that, some retained their rank, but some lost all they'd risen to and were forced to start over, almost as if they were freshly made. The practice disgusted him.

He stared out the window. And worse, it would make him the largest hypocrite of them all. He kept Cressa at arm's length—until he couldn't. Then he would build back his defenses and remember what was at stake. The actions he'd taken regarding the dreams and the necklace had been for Lyra's sake, but that wouldn't be the complete truth. So, he couldn't punish Lucas for feelings of protectiveness for the humans in their midst when he couldn't control his own.

The meeting today, however, had to happen, and he didn't have the time or energy to fight with Cressa about it. Not when it interfered with his business, his livelihood, and the safety of his family. He didn't want to think about dealing with Cressa after the fact, but perhaps that would maintain their personal distance, because there wasn't any doubt she would be spitting mad about this meeting.

When Sergi pulled in front of the posh restaurant in the Castle Street district, Lucas made a call.

"She's waiting at the table with a glass of wine." Lucas's tone was warm, and when he opened the back door, he gave Devon a wicked smile. "The hostess mentioned your guest was a bit irritable."

Devon squeezed Lucas's shoulder. "Thank you."

He strolled past the front entrance with Lucas trailing behind him. They followed a path that wove around the building to a side entrance leading up to a private section of the rooftop patio. This exclusive dining area was reserved for privileged clientele.

Lucas left Devon when they reached the roof to wait at the bar with other drivers and bodyguards.

The host, a young man with olive-toned skin and dancing amber eyes, bowed his head before greeting him. "Mr. Trelane, it's an honor to serve."

Devon grinned at him. "Hello, Thomas. Are you still enjoying Santiga Bay?" Thomas was a rogue vampire, and the only one working at this restaurant as far as he knew. He'd moved from Egypt a couple of years earlier and had found it difficult to find acceptance. Another vampire societal issue. If he wanted to live in the Hollows, no one would question him. But he wanted to live in a better neighborhood, specifically one close to the galleries. He had skill with a paintbrush, and when Devon had heard of the young man's plight, Devon found a job for him and granted him permission to live anywhere in the city.

Devon didn't have an issue with rogue vampires. It was a fallout from current Council policy. He didn't see a reason not to use someone to their full potential, and what a waste for the world if this young man's talents weren't shared, assuming the vampire kept to the rules. If he stepped out of line—well, that was different story.

So, whenever he saw Thomas, he asked the same question. If Thomas was being persecuted or hunted in any way, this was one way to inform him.

"It reminds me of springtime in Cairo. Your guest is reviewing the menu with an exquisite merlot." He strode toward a table that faced west, an umbrella tilted to block the sun.

The woman watched the horizon with a hand resting on the wine stem. He couldn't see the other side of her body but thought she might be twirling a lock of chestnut-colored hair that hung to her shoulders. Though he and Thomas barely made a sound, he detected the slight bend of her head as she sensed their approach. She took a long sip before Devon reached the table, and he nodded at Thomas that they'd be fine.

Each of the five tables on this side of the rooftop were separated by twelve feet and a glass partition. With the sound of the city streets just one story down and the soft coastal breeze, even elder vampires would have difficulty picking up full conversations —nothing but bits and pieces floating in the wind.

Devon sat without preamble, preferring to keep her rattled, if she wasn't already.

"Thank you for meeting with me, Mrs. Underwood."

She stared at him, and though she had a lighter coloring than her daughter, it was easy to see signs of Cressa hidden behind the heavy makeup, and based on her smell, Valium. Was that simply to calm her nerves or more of a habit? Based on her eyes, complexion, and mild scent, she didn't appear to be a regular user.

"Somehow, it didn't seem you'd take no for an answer."

"Or maybe you were curious?"

She fidgeted with her napkin and glanced around the patio. "I've been up here once before. A couple of years ago, I had lunch in one of these private cubes with Christopher and some man from eastern Europe, who'd brought his mistress. The men huddled together, whispering amongst themselves, all smiles and chuckles. The man's mistress didn't speak English, so we sat here and gazed toward the ocean as if we could see the waves and hear the gulls."

He wasn't sure how to respond to that. "How's the wine?"

She blinked before staring down at the table. "It's really rather good." She took a sip as if to prove it.

He drank to calm a nerve or two of his own and agreed with her assessment of the wine. "I have a feeling you know why I'm here."

"If you're going to tell me my husband is cheating on me, I already know." Her eyes remained clear, but they were shadowed, and fine lines formed around her mouth as she pursed her lips. Something she must do frequently.

Devon removed the envelope from his inside pocket and laid it on the table between them. Her hands were steady as she opened it and dropped a handful of photos on the glass tabletop. She spun them around with a perfectly manicured sunset-colored nail.

She bent over to get a better look, then clucked her tongue. "Well, this is a new one."

He grimaced. "I'm sorry."

She appeared shocked by his response, then she snorted, sounding so much like Cressa. "They say we make our own beds. Or perhaps it's the sins of the mother coming to collect their fee."

"Which brings me to why I asked you to meet me." He studied

her, and to her credit, she didn't flinch. He imagined that came from years of practice, living in a house that had turned Cressa into a thief.

"Why do I have a feeling this has to do with my daughter?"

"If you mean Cressa, you'd be correct."

She sighed. "It's that damn necklace, isn't it?"

"Several nights ago, she wore it to bed."

She'd been staring at the napkin that was crumbling under her tight grip, but now her gaze flashed to him. The mixture of fear and concern confirming all he needed to know.

"Why didn't you tell her the danger it posed?"

She pushed a lock of hair behind her ear, and for a moment, he saw the woman she'd been when Cressa was only a child. "Ras said she should wear it all the time. He'd been adamant about it. But three days after he left us, she had her first nightmare." She lifted her chin and didn't waver, though her hand trembled as she lifted the glass and gulped a couple swallows. "There's nothing you can say that would make me believe Ras knew that would happen."

"I agree."

Her lips twisted, and her eyes narrowed. "Then why are we playing this game?"

"I need to know where I can find Ras."

Her laugh was harsh. "That would be like chasing the wind."

"I don't understand."

"No. You wouldn't. Ras was a unicorn. A leprechaun. A man as mysterious as the lost city of Atlantis." She glanced away, and when she turned back, her eyes glistened with shattered memories. "He was the love of my life, who gave me a beautiful daughter, then disappeared into the night."

"Is he still alive?" His heart hammered against his chest.

She gave him a half shrug and leaned back. "I don't know. Does Cressa know you're here?"

He didn't answer.

She tapped a nail against the stem of the wineglass and met his stare. "What is it you want?"

"Is there anything you can tell me about the necklace? Or maybe someone that can explain the dreams."

"And why should I tell you? Who are you to my daughter?"

"Her protection." His tone hardened as did his gaze, and though her gaze flickered, she held her ground.

Her laugh was broken. "That's good. It's more than I can do." She reached into a pocket and pulled out a business card. She rubbed her thumb across the face of it, and he sensed she might put it back, but then she handed it to him. "Something told me when Christopher asked where the necklace was that old debts were about to come due. I told him I hadn't seen it in years. That it probably got lost somewhere along the way, but he instantly blamed Cressa for stealing it." She laid her palms open. "There wasn't anything I could say that wouldn't confirm she had it. So, I played dumb, hoping he'd never find her." She sniffled, but it was so low, it might have been his imagination.

"Then Cressa came looking for you."

Her smile was filled with pride. "It had been so long since I'd seen her. I'd forgotten how much she looked like him."

"Thank you for what you've been able to do." He collected the pictures and shoved them back in the envelope, sorry he'd had to play that hand. Once the envelope was back in his inner pocket and the unread business card tucked away in his outer pocket, he gave her his most sincere look.

"Underwood has partnered with very dangerous people. If there's any way possible, I would suggest planning a way out."

Her chuckle was dark, the sound throaty. "I've been planning it since that lunch on this very patio."

He nodded. "Thomas will see you back out through the main entrance so no one will be suspicious about who you might have been meeting. He'll also give you a number. It's a burner, so it can't be traced, but someone will always be monitoring it. In case you need help."

She finished her wine and stood, her back straight and her head held high as she turned toward Thomas, who waited a short distance away. After a couple of steps, she glanced back to him. "You never gave me your name."

"It will be safer for you if you don't know."

Chapter Twenty-Two

FOUR SETS of eyes stared at the vehicles that filled the parking lot and those still waiting in line to reach the front of the Renaud Library. Strategically placed lights reflected the architectural nuances of the aged building that would have been built sometime during the early nineteen hundreds, most likely considered new in the world of vamps.

Jacques was our chauffeur for the evening, driving the sedan we'd driven down from Santiga Bay, and the vehicle he and Bella used for their surveillance. Bella would be our bodyguard and would assist with any help we might need on exiting the building.

"This seems like a lot of vamps for a weekly event. I'd expected maybe a couple dozen faithful members. There must be over a hundred of them in there." This was more than I could have hoped for a diversion, but I'd be lying if I said images from my fall through the window weren't bouncing around in my head.

"Vampires bore easily, yet we find comfort in the rituals." I'd never heard Bella speak before, let alone in a response to one of my comments. Though her voice was low, it came across strong and husky. With her dark-as-night eyes, thick black hair tied back in a braid, and bronze skin that almost glowed, it probably didn't take her long to mesmerize someone.

I considered her words and found them similar to what Devon had once told me. "So, every Thursday, they gather among their closest hundred friends surrounded by their own history."

"Poetic, isn't it." Simone's dry statement sent a shiver down my spine.

I was so overdue for a quiet movie night.

Our car inched forward. For fast-as-lightening vamps, it took them forever to get out of their vehicles. "There are three doors that lead to the lowest levels, each requiring a passkey." I'd been repeating the plan since we left the hotel. We had extra time while we waited for our turn to unload, and one last review couldn't hurt.

"I'll get the passkey." Simone flicked a nail as she stared out toward the parking lot.

"We won't know if there's a different key required for the restoration room until we get there. So, this might be a quick evening." This was the risk I'd explained to Devon when I called him to discuss the plan, fulfilling my promise to get his approval before I did anything that could jeopardize the larger mission. He'd listened to my entire proposal before asking Simone's opinion. I would have preferred if he'd agreed on my word alone, but Simone was in charge of our trip, was part of his cadre, and would eventually earn her own house name. Of course, he'd ask for her opinion.

"If we get in, we grab the book and get out." This was one of the simplest plans I'd come up with, though it was similar to Gruber's tea party when I'd gone rogue and stolen the handwritten letter. We had to be discreet, preferably not leaving any sign the book was taken. With any luck it would be weeks, maybe months, before the loss was detected. This restriction meant if I couldn't unlock the door to the restoration room, I couldn't make this a smash-and-grab.

"Once I see either of you head toward the exit, I call for

Jacques." Bella purred his name. "If I see any trouble start, I call for Jacques."

Jacques nodded, a wicked smile on his lips that suggested he'd be ready with the car but would be equally fine if we brought a fight to his door.

Bella and Jacques had been instrumental in creating a believable diversion when I'd met with my mother. With any luck, they'd come up with something just as splendid if we had problems extricating ourselves.

"Simple, Cressa." Simone turned her dark gaze to me. "Just like I said." She radiated confidence in her sleek tawny-colored bodysuit. Her caftan was various shades of forest green and deeper browns, providing a stunning camouflage to move in and out of shadows.

I gave her a nod. I'd seen more simple jobs go awry than complex ones. People got lazy and didn't stay sharp. If these weren't vamps I was working with, I'd be more concerned by their blasé attitudes.

When our limo made it to the red carpet, I had to roll my eyes. I mean, really, this vamp aristocracy crap was getting old. Would they even notice if one evening the carpet was blue? I snorted, attracting two couples who'd gathered to talk before moving into the building. I gave them my dazzling smile before joining Simone.

We walked in side-by-side with Bella behind us. When we'd passed into the foyer, Bella positioned herself twenty feet from the door where she blended in with the other vamps conversing, snacking, and drinking. Simone didn't break stride as she strode to the central staircase, and I breathed a sigh of relief to find them open for the patrons to tour the museum.

So far, so good.

"I'll get the passkey." Simone bowed her head and, after greeting several of the guests, wandered toward the banquet table where most of the human servers would gather.

I strolled in the opposite direction, perusing the art while occasionally stopping to pull out a book, glance through the pages, and then return it. I stopped when I came face to face with an immense portrait of a flower.

At first, I thought it was a rose. No. Similar to a rose but not quite the same. The petals were a snowy white and appeared to be tipped in crimson. I reached out to caress the life-like image but stopped myself, unsure what made me do that. I knew better than to touch artifacts in a museum whether there were alarms or not.

"A flower as beautiful as the woman that beholds it."

The accent and voice were familiar. I turned, and though I'm sure my eyes widened in surprise, it was difficult to hold back a grin. His ruggedly handsome face hadn't changed in the last few weeks, emphasized by his close-cropped hair that was the same color as the flower I'd been admiring.

"Is it a rose? It seems out of place here."

He gave me an odd glance before shaking his head. When his focus turned to the painting, he had a faraway look. "It's the Blood Poppy."

Blood Poppy. That sounded—creepy, yet eerily familiar. He seemed as drawn to it as I was. I changed the subject.

"I remember you. So, who won the billiards game?"

"My brother and I owe you a drink. The woman, as you predicted."

I glanced over his shoulder to find his twin, or close enough to it, sitting at a table with, yep, a bottle of vodka and a stack of glasses. Their traveling bar, just like at Gruber's tea party. I laughed. "What are you betting on now?"

His smile widened. "Various things. But our largest bet is whether someone will start a fight."

My brows rose. "In a library?"

He shrugged. "It's happened before. I admit that was back in Norway. That raging Viking blood and all." His fangs slipped a bit when he smiled again.

I was probably naïve, but he didn't scare me. Devon and Sergi hadn't mentioned they were dangerous, nor had they said they weren't. They were vamps after all.

"I'm told you're the Oslo twins."

"You've heard of us?" He seemed rather pleased by that.

"Not enough, I'm sure."

"Come, have a drink with us."

I tagged along. My original direction had been to the bar where I could listen to conversations and get a feel for the crowd. But this would do.

"This is my brother, Ulrik. And my name is Erik." He turned to his brother. "You remember this lovely."

"From the tea party! Yes. Did your Father spank you when you got home?" His brows wiggled, and his eyes twinkled.

"That's getting rather personal." When Ulrik's smile faded, I leaned toward him and added, "How do you know I wasn't the one doing the spanking?"

He roared a laugh and poured me a shot. "We knew you were our kind of woman. And a Blood Ward, no?"

"And one who hadn't heard of the Blood Poppy." Erik chimed in.

"No? How long have you been a Blood Ward?"

"Slow down, boys." I grinned and downed the first shot handed to me. "My name is Cressa, and I've been a Blood Ward for less than a month."

"Ah, that explains it." Erik shook his head. "There's too much to learn, it's a wonder anyone bothers anymore. So what are you doing so far away from home..." He glanced behind me and then around the room. "I don't see your Father among us."

"I'm here with one of his bodyguards. He had to travel for some business, and he's allowed me a few days to vacation in the City of Angels. Funny that we should both meet here."

"We haven't been to the United Sates for several decades. We are getting reacquainted with your country."

"They do say it's a small world." I finished off the second shot and held it out for another pour which Ulrik was happy to do.

I'd downed that one when I noticed Simone make her way toward us. She was halfway across the room when someone bumped into her. My blood ran cold. Simone's cool gaze never missed a beat when she sneered at Lorenzo Venizi. What the hell were the odds of that?

I lowered my head and placed the glass on the table. "It's been great to see you again, but I must be on my way."

I didn't dare turn around, not wanting to give Lorenzo the chance of glimpsing my face. Thank heavens I'd gone for the casual look with black wide-legged pants and a matching puffy-sleeved shirt belted at the waist. A somber vest completed the blend-into-the-background ensemble that wasn't worth a second glance.

The twins glanced toward Simone, and by the time they turned back, I was scurrying behind groups of vamps, steering for the crowded bar. When I was in the thick of them, I took the chance to glance back. Lorenzo had moved past the twins, who ignored him as they huddled in deep conversation, glasses of vodka gripped in their hands. This was the second time I'd met them and made a rude exit. Someday I'd have to make it up to them.

Simone was nowhere to be seen and was probably on her way downstairs. Once my heart stopped pounding, which was bringing more attention than I wanted from the vamps that surrounded me, I continued to weave around the crowd as I made my way to the stairs on the east side the building.

Simone waited for me in the reading circle on the third sublevel. She prowled from one end of the dimly lit area to the other.

"What did Lorenzo say to you?" I scanned the area, focusing on the dark aisles.

"Get out of my way."

"Excuse me?" I was ten feet away from her.

"You asked what Lorenzo said."

I stared, finally understanding. "He didn't recognize you?"

"It might come to him later. His mind seemed elsewhere, and it was only a brief glance."

"That's good, right?"

She shook her head. "You do have a knack for the obvious."

"And you're a laugh a minute. Did you see anyone on your way down?"

"There are several people on the first sublevel, one or two on the second, but I sense no one on this level."

"Let's not take a chance of someone coming down. We should try one of the doors close to the stairs we used."

"Agreed. Let's try the east side." She led the way, stopping short at the secure door that should lead to the lower levels, assuming the library maps were correct. She pulled out a plastic passkey from a small pocket at her waist. Without waiting for a prayer or words of encouragement, she ran the key over the door pad.

A green light flashed, followed by the sound of the lock disengaging. She pulled open the door, took one step onto the landing, then stopped.

She lifted her head as she'd done the day before, and I swore under my breath. She caught a scent.

Would I ever get lucky with one of these jobs going easy? "The same vamps from yesterday?"

She nodded, and I pulled out my bone-handled dagger, quietly thanking Devon and Sergi for forcing me to learn how to use it. We crept down the stairs, and while I didn't have the ability to sense anyone or have near as good hearing as Simone, I strained to pick up the slightest sound. Quiet as a tomb they say, and as we reached the first landing, we were now four levels below the surface. This floor was different. No wide-open areas, just hallways honed out of rock—and no light.

I retrieved a penlight, keeping the narrow beam focused on the floor as I followed Simone. She paused at each intersection before quickly moving on. At the third intersection, she turned left then right before stopping two doors down.

I moved the beam of light to the door and then around the doorframe. The sign confirmed we'd reached the restoration area, and the only thing preventing us from entering, assuming the door was locked, was a traditional door that needed a good old-fashioned key. Thank heavens for small favors. Simone tried the door to confirm it was locked.

I held the light in my mouth as I pulled out my lockpicks. In less than thirty seconds, the door opened. I moved back to let Simone enter first. Once I'd closed the door behind us, the room blossomed in light, blinding me after the darkness of the halls.

These vamps never failed to surprise. The halls were taken straight from one of Sergi's favorite Bela Lugosi flicks, minus the cobwebs, but in here, state-of-the-art technology dripped from every corner. Stainless steel cabinets and counters lined two of the walls, and the floor was spotless concrete. Ten long rows of tables occupied the center of the room and seemed to stretch forever. Each table housed clear storage boxes which held various items— ancient manuscripts, scrolls, paintings, books, and other miscellaneous artifacts. I stopped in front of the first box. Seals and locks kept the items safe and snug in what appeared to be automatically regulated environments. Displays showed temperatures, humidity levels, and other measurements that meant nothing to me.

"You start here and move right; I'll take the left side." Simone prowled the aisles, only stopping at the displays with books and only long enough to check titles.

I followed her pattern, moving down each aisle before moving to the next. There were thirty tables per row, and though most of the artifacts were books, it didn't take long to reach our conclusion.

The book we sought wasn't here.

Chapter Twenty-Three

WHEN THE TWO of us met back at the main door, the tip of Simone's fangs showed. "Tell me again why we couldn't have done this yesterday while we were alone in the library, rather than creating an elaborate ruse for no reason." Simone had been chafing to go home after the second day in L.A. She had become accustomed to living at Oasis, and more than a day or two away always made her testy.

"It was exactly because we were alone that we couldn't. Without spending a couple of weeks here, we have no idea how often they have staff in this room, and we'd prefer no one noticing the book missing after we've taken it. That means, no one can know we were looking for it."

Her response was a fang-filled scowl. "The note clearly stated the book would be here."

"Do you detect our vamp friends being in here?"

She shook her head. "Could there be another room?"

"Maybe. The map only showed one, but maybe it was more representative of the area and not that it was all in one room."

"I need to check the rest of this floor and the ones below."

I didn't like it, but she was right. Something was off about the whole thing. We couldn't leave until we checked everything. "All right. Let's go."

"I can move faster without you. If I find anything that might be another restoration room, I'll come back for you." She nodded to the far side of the room. "That looks like it might be an office. Maybe you can find something there."

I nodded and glanced the direction she pointed, grateful I wouldn't have to sneak around if the other vamps were still here. When I turned back, she was gone. "And good luck to you too." My grumbling wouldn't do any good, so I strode to the office, glancing around a second time for cameras or any other security but didn't spot anything. The office door wasn't locked.

This was a room I could handle. It was an office like any other. A desk brimming with stacks of papers, files, and books. Bookcases and file cabinets lined each wall, and two simple, wooden chairs faced the desk. I took the time to review the labels on the file cabinets and the titles of books on my way to the desk. Nothing popped out at me. The desk drawers were my first priority, but the six of them held nothing more than standard office supplies. I ran my hands over the walls of the drawers and the frame of the desk, searching for secret compartments.

Nothing.

I stared at the mess on top of the desk and went with the easiest approach, starting on my left and working my way right. Under the second stack of files, I found a name plate laying on its side. It was one of those old styles that sat at the edge of a desk with a black background and white lettering. Philipe Renaud. That made sense. But that didn't help with where the book might be.

I sat back and scanned the office. At my first glance at the desk, it appeared Philipe was one of those messy intellectuals, perhaps an old professor who didn't notice the chaos around him. Yet, the bookcases were neatly arranged and the top of the cabinets bare. The only clutter was the desk.

I flipped through some of the files. Most held a single form with a request to either move an artifact from one library to another, loan it to an outside museum, or request restoration. The rest appeared to be induction forms for new inventory. Reference books filled the remaining space.

If I'd bothered to look at this with a more open mind, I might have noticed right away that this was an office that hadn't been used in a while. Requests were simply added to the pile as if Philipe would return one day and restore everything to order.

The question I couldn't answer was how long Philipe had been gone. Without knowing how often these requests came in, he could have been gone a couple days or several months. And that gave me a new perspective.

I stopped looking through the top portion of the stack and focused on the bottom, searching for anything that might have made Philipe not want to return. It seemed a sinister thought, but it was interesting how many roadblocks we'd faced looking for the book. There was no reason the state of the office had anything to do with the missing book. Was it nothing more than a coincidence? Possibly.

I returned to the file cabinets. The folders were arranged alphabetically, and I searched under every name I thought might provide insight on where the book might be—*De første dage*, House Trelane and Venizi. Again, nothing. Disappointed but feeling I'd covered all the bases, I went back to the desk.

The note was buried under two inches of papers that had been scattered across the desk. The name on the empty folder was Aramburu, the fourth House created at the same time as Trelane, Venizi, and Renaud.

An itch crawled up the back of my neck, and I was still scratching it as I tried to read the pages that had fallen out of the file, but they were written in French. Great. Other than pulling the pages together, I had no idea if they were related, so I shoved them back in the file anyway. And that was when a portion of the desk was clear enough to see the note partially hidden beneath a stapler.

It was a thin slip of paper, no larger than a sticky note, and although the note had been ripped from something larger, the remaining words were clear enough.

"a *threat to all magical creatures and humanity itself.*"

That earlier itch spread to race down my spine. I took a deep breath. The scrap of paper could have been ripped from anything. Maybe vamps had a secret passion for creepy suspense thrillers, or it could have been written centuries ago. On the off chance it was part of the Aramburu file, Devon would have to decide. I shoved it in the folder as Simone appeared in the doorway.

"We have to go. Now."

I stuffed the folder in one of the deep pants pockets, and though bulky, it didn't seem to hamper my movements. Before stepping away, I scattered another file to replace the one I'd taken so at first glance everything looked as I'd found it. With one more quick glance around the office, I raced for the outer door to the hallway where Simone waited.

"Keep your flashlight off and stick close."

I slipped my dagger out, and tracking the soft sound of her boots, managed to keep up without falling on my face. It was a quick race up the stairs, and we sprinted across the third sublevel until I ran into Simone, who'd stopped and spread out her arms to keep me from passing her.

Two vamps, arms crossed over their chests, leaned against a bookcase, blocking access to the stairs that lead to the main floor.

"Edgar said to be patient and wait for the mice to come to the cats." The vamp on the left glanced at his buddy.

"Edgar is always right." The second one smiled. His fangs gleamed in the low light, and his eyes glowed an eerie electric green. That was disturbing.

"I hope he wasn't the smartest of your group, assuming that was him and his partner I left on the west staircase." Simone didn't move, her feet already planted for an attack.

The two glanced at each other, and the first vamp's eyes flickered with a soft amber gleam.

Good grief. While I was messing around with office supplies, she was out killing vamps. I had to admit, two were better than four.

The two didn't bother with any further discussion and launched themselves at us. The one with the neon-green peepers came at me with amazing speed and agility. If he thought I'd run like a frightened human, he was only half-right. I waited for him to get within striking distance, raising my dagger as if ready to swipe down, and he watched my dagger rather than which foot I'd placed my weight.

With his next step, I swung a roundhouse kick with my right leg, planting it squarely in his solar plexus. While the kick wouldn't have done much damage, I couldn't help grin at his shocked expression as he flew back and hit one of the stacks, knocking several books off the shelf.

I cringed, hoping I hadn't damaged any of the rare books, but before I could take a step, he was up and charging again.

I managed to duck the expected blow and twisted, sweeping a leg out from under him. On his way down, I kicked out, landing a solid hit to his head, and the sound of his jaw colliding with the cement floor was gratifying.

Devon's training slammed into me. Don't be a hero. Attack and run. The vamp will ultimately win. It was a bitter pill, but I swallowed it, noted that Simone was doing just fine on her own, and ran for the stairs.

"What's going on here?" The voice was muffled, still several stacks away, probably hearing the fighting but not close enough to see us.

I flew up the stairs and was approaching the main level when Simone caught up to me and touched my elbow, but I'd already slowed.

"Are they dead?" They'd seen us—our faces.

"Quite. Just stroll. It will take a minute or two before they sound an alarm."

We were on our way to the exit, the lobby in sight, when a man raised an alarmed voice.

"There are murderers among us."

Well, that was a bit melodramatic. And while some turned their heads, many either hadn't heard, or for some unexplainable reason, didn't seem to care. That might change before we reached the exit.

I grabbed Simone's arm and pushed her toward the bar, stopping next to two men who appeared to be in a disagreement. Vile words were being thrown while arms swung widely to emphasize whatever point they were making, but their eyes weren't glowing. I needed someone to help turn that tinder into a blaze. A few feet beyond them, a threesome, two men with a young woman, conversed as if they couldn't hear the argument behind them.

I pulled Simone with me until we stood between the two groups, then glanced around, looking for inspiration. I found it in a six-foot floor vase. I leaned against it, but it was sturdier than it looked.

"Come here and push this over." My whisper met shocked eyes.

"I will not damage priceless artifacts." Simone planted her fists on her hips and gave me that look that said I was painting outside the lines again. I scanned the room. A group was starting to form around the area where the man had screamed. We couldn't afford to get caught. There hadn't been time to tell her about the file I'd taken.

"There are dozens that look just like it on this floor alone. And god knows how many they've collected around the world. I think one can be sacrificed for Devon's mission."

She hesitated, then glanced over her shoulder. Her eyes widened a split second, and I turned in time to spot Lorenzo storming over to the yelling man. Any moment, and he'd have the place locked down.

I sighed. "And Devon had such high hopes for his new House leader."

Her eyes glowed a bright yellow, and I stepped back, pointing to the vase, beads of sweat sticking to my shirt. "Push it toward the guy behind the one waving his hands."

"He hasn't done anything."

"Exactly."

When she smiled, her fangs had dropped. "We'll have words later."

"Yeah, yeah, let's just get out of here, then you can bitch at me the entire drive home."

Simone barely nudged the vase and it teetered, the timing perfect with the vamps flailing arms as it smacked the man behind him, knocking him and the woman to the floor. His partner glanced at the trio and started to apologize, but in the next second, he was flying across the room, knocking over a table and several chairs when he landed.

That was the match that lit the tinder under a bored aristocracy.

I turned when Simone grabbed my arm, and I locked eyes with Erik, who stood on the table where their minibar had been. He grinned and waved cash at me—he'd obviously won the bet as to whether there'd be a fight. He nodded his gratitude before he stuffed the bills into a pocket then dove into the fighting. I saw a flash of Ulrik's white hair before he slammed into two other vamps.

I was still smiling while we skirted the fray. If they had any intention of locking the doors before, it now appeared they just wanted everyone to leave before more priceless artifacts were damaged. I kept an eye out for Lorenzo, but he wasn't anywhere to be seen. When we reached the foyer, Bella threw a cape over each of us and rushed us outside.

The sedan waited for us, and Bella opened the back door. I dove in first, Simone behind me, and I sucked in a large gulp of air, releasing it slowly, trying to slow the exhilaration of the getaway. Bella jumped in the front and barely closed her door before Jacques hit the gas, dodging around the other cars and keeping to a respectful speed until we exited the gate.

Turned out, our theft was a smash-and-grab after all, if you could call the four dead vamps and a fight the smash part of the plan. I hoped no one noticed the missing file for some time. And while we didn't find the book, we didn't leave any evidence that we'd been searching for it.

Jacques made several turns down backstreets until he hit the 405 north. With it being somewhere around two a.m., the freeway wasn't void of vehicles, but there was plenty of room for Jacques to put the car in cruise for our race home.

Simone poured a scotch, then held the bottle up to me.

"Vodka."

She complied without question, but before she handed me the glass, she said, "Tell me that wasn't a waste of a priceless artifact."

"If there's a price Devon won't pay to find a way to defeat Lorenzo, someone should fill me in." I ignored the sharp glances the vamps in front gave me as I lifted my ass to tug the folder from my pants pocket. "I can't read French, but something tells me Devon might be interested in this."

She handed me the glass of chilled vodka, but her eyes had narrowed. When she didn't take the folder, I had no doubt I'd gone too far. But honestly, what was the price of a stable vampire council compared to an old vase?

When she took the folder, I released an imperceptible breath that the danger had passed. Without looking at it, she stuck the folder in a leather satchel by her feet, sipped her scotch, then leaned back and closed her eyes. She could have been a stone statue of a regal heiress in repose. The only sign she was pleased was in the slight twitch of her lips.

Chapter Twenty-Four

THE FINE-LINEN BUSINESS card Willa had given Devon the day before laid on his desk. The cream-colored card was a blank piece of canvas. He found it odd, as if the bearer had no identity and created one depending on the situation. Was this how she ended up marrying Underwood after Rasmussen left? Rather than take another chance at love, she simply remade herself into what was required in the best interest of her daughter. Who could blame her for not anticipating where it led? Or perhaps she had loved him at one time and, instead of leaving him, she'd honed various personas after years of living with the man.

It was easy to blame Rasmussen for everything—what the humans called a deadbeat dad. But there were two sides to each coin, and it was difficult to judge without seeing both. The more important mystery was why Willa hadn't protected Cressa from Underwood's indifference.

Perhaps something changed after April was born. Maybe it was the dreams, or that Cressa simply reminded her too much of Rasmussen. He would never know, and the relationship between mother and daughter was Cressa's to own.

The bottom line was that the past didn't matter. Not now.

Willa's story, whatever the truth was, belonged to her and Cressa. He understood enough. His focus moved past what the blank card represented and to the neatly printed name—Colantha Dupré. Written below it was the name of a city. New Orleans. It twisted his gut, yet it made sense. A piece of the puzzle locked into place.

If he only understood why the piece fit, he'd have a sunnier disposition. New Orleans. A city filled with voodoo, mysticism, and the undead. A city strife with rich and terrifying history. Interestingly enough, the American home to the House Renaud. Their true ancestral home was in the heart of Southern France, but a segment had moved to the Big Easy and entwined their House with the city. The question wasn't only about what answers Colantha Dupré could provide about dreamwalking. The strings, as thin as they were, seemed to tie the necklace with the book in Renaud's Library.

He never believed in coincidences, and too much was at stake to think any differently now.

The knock at the door pulled him out of his musings. "Come."

Lucas strolled in, his eyes dancing with amusement, a smile on his lips. "Good morning. We missed you at breakfast. Can I make you an espresso?" He moved to the machine after catching Devon's slight nod.

"How's Ginger?" Devon had to ask, if only to tease his friend, and he smiled at the light blush that tinged Lucas's cheeks.

"She's comfortable but restless."

He rubbed his forehead then accepted the espresso. "I forgot she had to quit her job when we moved her. Was that a hardship for her?"

"She seemed genuinely relieved to give her notice at her last job, but I've seen help wanted ads hidden under magazines."

"What sort of jobs was she looking for?"

Lucas lifted a shoulder and moved back to the espresso machine to make himself one. "I didn't want to pry."

When Devon let the silence build, Lucas returned with his cup but still seemed to squirm in his seat. He couldn't ever remember speaking to Lucas about a woman, and he shifted in his own seat. It wasn't something vampires typically discussed. It was more of a shifter and human thing for men to share intimacies.

"We go for walks around the neighborhood. Usually while we're out for lunch or a late breakfast. She has an eye for fashion and once mentioned working at a diner. But..." He paused and stared past Devon's shoulder to the window beyond. At first his expression was pensive, but then he smiled. "She loves flowers. I buy her fresh ones every day, and she makes the most beautiful arrangements." He brought his focus back to Devon, his shoulders giving a slight shudder as if shaking off the images. After sipping his espresso, he finished with, "She knows it's too soon to return to a normal life."

Devon had watched Cressa chafe over the last week. Her weapons and martial arts training combined with Anna's history lessons kept her busy, but even with her limited free time, the walls of the mansion were confining. What would it be like for someone with limited boundaries and nothing to occupy her time?

"I've been neglectful." There wasn't any other way to say it. He'd been a poor protector. "While Ginger might not be involved with our mission, she has been put in harm's way on more than one occasion. Starting tomorrow, I want her training for self-defense." When Lucas's brow lifted, he added, "Escape methods only, including options for hiding until help can arrive if it's impossible to run."

"I've gone over a few methods with her after the incident at her old apartment."

Devon picked up his crystal, though he didn't roll it around like normal, it was enough to just hold it. "That's good. Have Bella participate in the training as well. I assume you're already sharing information about the vampire world. Its rules and such."

Lucas nodded.

"Then offer her the opportunity to take a class."

"A class?"

"Like the ones they offer at the community center or college. Anything she wants. Let's see where her talents and desires lay." He gave the crystal a toss. "I'd like to prevent Cressa from storming in here demanding I do something about making Ginger happy."

Lucas snickered as he placed his empty cup on the desk. He sat back and swung a leg over one knee, his hands clasping behind his head. "I almost hate to deprive you of the moment."

"Trust me. She'll find another reason."

They were both smiling when a pounding sounded on the door. Sergi strode in, his face expressionless except for the tightening around his eyes.

"What happened?" Devon asked, and Lucas straightened.

Sergi had always maintained a stoic persona, but there were slight tells when he was angry, frustrated, or scared, which was, thankfully, a rare phenomenon. If Sergi was scared, it was time to call a full level-three alert. So, unless Lucas was watching for it as Devon was, he would have missed it. But Sergi's shift in expression didn't slip by Devon, and his heart pounded with concern for Cressa.

"A small pack of shifters outside of Los Angeles were slaughtered last night."

Devon's stomach dropped, and the pounding in his chest turned into a tight band that constricted his breathing. "Slaughtered how?"

"From what Elijah was able to share, it sounded eerily like your dream minus the crossbow bolt. This was a group of rogue shifters, committed to no one, but they got along and had banded together for protection."

"For as little good it did them." Lucas kicked the desk, his face mottled with color.

Devon pushed up from his chair and ran his hands through his hair as he paced in front of the fireplace. If his friends were saying anything, he couldn't hear over the roaring in his head. Unsolicited visions from the dream filled his head with blood, destruction, and unnecessary brutality. Was it a message or the start of something viler?

It wasn't a stretch to connect the dots between the rumors of Magic Poppy, the wolves asking questions, and a massacre at a shifter house. And as obvious as it might seem, seen from that perspective, the answer could be as simple as one of the wolf packs cleaning house. If the local alpha thought the rogues were causing trouble, it was the best way to take care of them before something unfortunate happened. Another group of rogues would also be suspect.

These possibilities alone made this the perfect crime—the perfect kill.

He paced until his blind rage settled, and though the beast inside roared for vengeance—for answers—he couldn't do anything until his more rational side returned. So, he continued to wear a path on the Persian rug until his sight returned to normal and the glow in his eyes receded.

He wasn't sure how much time had passed, but Sergi and Lucas sat in front of his desk, quiet and expectant.

"Do they have any clues? Anything left behind like a message?" He was grabbing at the proverbial straw, but any little detail might spell the difference between shifter-on-shifter attack or, heaven help them, a vampire attack. If vampires had done this, it wouldn't be enough to start a war, not with it being a pack of rogues. But it would send the wrong type of message, stressing a fragile peace between the two species. It wasn't a far-fetched idea to believe that outcome might have been the ulterior motive.

"It wasn't mentioned. The local alpha was at the scene, but I'm not sure how much he'll be willing to share." Sergi shrugged. "The only thing Elijah could confirm was that these weren't the shifters he'd asked to help with." He glanced at Lucas, and Devon understood his reticence at not mentioning the Magic Poppy with Lucas in the room.

"What if these wolves were minding their own business, staying off the grid," Lucas said. "Even so, someone in the vampire community would be aware of them. They have no protection from an alpha or The Wolf. Maybe one of the shifters got wind of something they shouldn't. Or it might be as simple as someone testing how far they can push a vampire."

That brought an eerie silence of something larger and uglier if Magic Poppy was involved. He glanced at Sergi, whose hand trembled as he focused on his tablet. It was the first time in a long time that Devon sensed his friend's beast rising to the surface.

"Did you check in with Decker?" he asked.

Sergi nodded, and his gaze had turned to a soft red glow, confirming Devon's suspicions that they all needed some space.

"I'll ask Remus for a meeting." He might not be able to help his friends through the emotional hit, but he could remove some of the burden. "Decker will go with me."

Sergi raised a brow, then simply nodded, releasing an almost imperceptible sigh.

Devon understood. No one wanted to relive old memories, and if anyone was going to face this new threat that appeared to bridge his sordid past with his shared dreams, it had to be him.

"You should have someone else with you." Lucas edged to his seat, and his tone hardened, ignoring Devon's slow shake of his head. "I don't have to go in, but you'll need a driver. And Bella should be back soon. We can both wait outside. It would be expected."

Devon trudged back to his desk. The weight of everything—his censure, Lyra, the dreams, Decker—it seemed insurmountable. And while Sergi struggled with his beast, Lucas remained focused, ready to help. He sat and turned to stare out the window. It would be another warmer-than-usual day, though clouds currently dimmed the sun. He needed a trip to Oasis, if nothing more than to ground him. If he only had the time.

Images from his dream continued to bombard him, and as horrific as the actual massacre was, the unnecessary waste of life, it might have provided an opening. A tragedy that might help set everything right. But it had to be quiet with no one the wiser.

Devon spun around to find his guards staring out the windows themselves. "I'll contact Remus and Decker. The women should be home in the next hour or two. I doubt Remus will be able to meet any sooner than tomorrow, assuming he's in town. That should give Bella time to rest and join Lucas as my guards for the meeting." When Sergi began to protest, he held up his hand. "I'll need you to retrieve Ginger this afternoon. Ask Greta to make up the room across from Cressa. I want everyone close until we know more."

Sergi, satisfied for now, moved to another topic. "How did the job go?"

He frowned. One more problem to deal with. "Not as expected and a continuing mystery. I'm calling a meeting for this evening. Simone will want to check in at Oasis, and Cressa will need rest. Then we'll have the women debrief us."

He'd been disappointed to hear the book wasn't where it should be. But if Cressa had lifted a file she considered worth taking, even on a hunch, the book might not be completely out of reach.

"That's all for now."

After the men left, he glanced down at the linen business card with the delicate and precise handwriting. What to do about this and Cressa's rage when she learned how he got the information? For a brief moment, the issue with the shifters and the Magic Poppy seemed the lesser of his troubles.

Chapter Twenty-Five

THE GENTLE CARESS of the warm water left my body lazy and boneless. The tension from the last few days seeped away, dripping off me and melting into the beads of water tickling my skin. The muffled chiming of a clock the only sound to interrupt my daydreaming.

This was something I should do more often.

"Cressa."

His voice sent shivers over my bare skin, and the touch of the water brought back memories of his hands roaming my body, stirring my blood. I stretched my arms wider and arched my back on the chance he'd touch me again.

"Are you going to float there all afternoon?"

I floundered. My arms and legs flapped in the water as I choked out a gulp of chlorinated water. It wasn't the beginning of a dream; Devon stood at the edge of the pool with a wide smile greeting me.

He chuckled. "I didn't mean to startle you."

I dunked myself then pushed my hair back before turning to swim back to the stairs. After quickly drying off, I slipped on a terry robe and wrapped my hair with the towel. By then, the heat in my cheeks had cooled.

"I thought I'd see you as soon as you returned, but I understand you must have been exhausted."

He was sitting on a bench near the windows, the sun illuminating him in a shiny glow. There wasn't another chair close, and rather than dragging one across the floor, I dropped onto the opposite side of the bench, grateful for the warmth of the seat.

"I slept the entire drive home and could barely stay awake to find my room." I stared at my toes and cringed at the chipped polish. "You'd think all Simone and I did was run from party to party." It was pretty clear I should have taken the time to find a salon.

"From what I hear, you managed to see quite a bit of L.A."

There was tension running through him, regardless of his smiles and light banter. All the telltale signs were there—the pinching at the corners of his eyes, the tapping of his fingers on the arm of the bench, and the stiffness of his posture. Something was bothering him, but I didn't think it was from anything I'd done.

"I'm sorry we didn't find the book."

He studied me, and I pulled my robe tighter, ignoring the butterflies that erupted in my belly and swarmed through me, igniting every nerve in my body. Devon was dressed casual with his shirt unbuttoned enough for me to see the silver chain around his neck, but not far enough to see what I was positive had to be a medallion dangling from the end.

He played with the cuff of his sleeve. "But now we have confirmation that it does exist and that others are searching for it."

I scratched my head, forgetting the towel was there. "Because of the other vamps that were prowling around? Maybe. But it is a museum. They could have been looking for something else."

"Tell me. Did you believe the vampires to be a coincidence? Or did you think it odd they were there at the same time and place where you were searching for something? And then they show up the very next evening in a restricted area where none of you should have been."

I shifted on the bench, now scratching at my knee. It was a decent question, and one I'd been asking myself. Simone and I had assumed the same thing at the time. But five hundred miles and a different setting, it all seemed a bit surreal. "You're right. It was too much of a coincidence."

"And then add the fact that Lorenzo was attending an event so far from home."

"The same could be said of Simone and me."

"True. But your goal was to actually steal the book."

"Borrow." I had every intention of ensuring the book was returned once Devon was finished with it. I'd never stolen a library book in my life. Pilfered with the intent to return—yes. Stole—no. Odd, but that's how I looked at it. When I glanced at Devon, my cheeks flushed at his slow cat-gobbled-the-meek-mouse smile.

"I get your point," I continued. "Simone and I thought it odd as well. I'm not sure he recognized Simone, but I'm sure he'll piece things together once he discovers his missing vamps, assuming they were his. I made sure he didn't see me."

"If they weren't Lorenzo's, we might have a third player in the game."

"Who else could it be?"

He shook his head. After a silent moment, he turned in his seat, the movement bringing him closer. "I've spoken with Lucas about the condition of Philipe's office and the folder you brought back. That was very smart thinking."

And there I went, preening at the simple praise. Good grief. What a good puppy. Would I be acting the same way if he were a dull and ordinary man? Not answering that one. "I wasn't sure I should bother. It just seemed to be out of place, and the name on the file. It was one of the names of the Houses created at the same time as yours. So, what was in the folder?"

"Several things, but the interesting piece was the itinerary with copies of tickets, local maps, events, and other information that a person either going on vacation or on the run would put together."

"On the run?" I hadn't even considered it, but the more I thought about his office, it made sense. The place was orderly with no dust or clutter, except for his desk. And I recalled my original thought that people were piling projects or reports on the desk for his eventual return. "I have to admit, that does make sense with what I saw in his office, even though I don't know the man. Everything else was so spotless."

Then my head shot up, momentarily frozen by how close he seemed now. I had to back pedal to remember what I was going to say. "So, if we have his itinerary, we know where he went, right?"

"Doubtful. From what Lucas tells me, Philipe is too wise to leave evidence behind. Our best guess is that the folder was left behind to leave a false trail."

I could feel the blood drain from my face, my voice barely a whisper. "And I took it."

He hooked a finger under my chin and lifted my face. "If the other vampires had gotten there first, they would have taken it. Then we'd have nothing but a mystery. I have no doubt he'd given advanced notice of his absence and was most likely vague on how long he'd be gone. He might have mentioned where he was off to, but it wouldn't have been the truth."

His thumb rubbed a trail along my jaw, and a sizzle ran through me. I inched closer. His lips were so close. His breaths came in shorter rasps.

"You were gone a long time." His words brushed the air.

I smirked. "Four days."

"It seemed longer." His eyes simmered with that glow I'd seen so many times in our dreams and so rarely in reality.

I touched the hand that was now caressing my face. One of us leaned in. I thought it was him, but it could have been me.

His lips were soft, eager, gentle.

Mine were anything but.

I pushed against him with a hunger that had been building for days. There'd been no safe dreams, no closeness since the dreams before the ball.

He hesitated. I should have pulled back, but I ran a hand along his thigh, and any second thoughts vanished as his arm came around me. He tugged me close until I was almost in his lap. All thoughts disappeared, and I gave in to the sensations that burst through me when his hand slipped past the robe. He pulled down a strap of my swimsuit, trapping an arm as he uncovered a breast.

He traced a finger across my nipple as his tongue explored my mouth. I might have whimpered. With one arm locked in my suit, I could only hold on with the other as his mouth left mine and trailed a path along my jaw and down my neck, pausing at the vein that had to be calling to him.

For an instant, all I could think about was how it would feel, the pierce of his fangs, the touch of his tongue as he drank from me. Would my blood taste as sweet to him as his had to me?

His palm covered my breast, a gentle squeeze, and I waited for his mouth to move lower. But the strap was pulled back up, and though his mouth moved back to mine, he pulled the robe closed. The kiss turned from heated passion to a gentle touch on my lips before he sat back.

My head dropped against his chest. The pent-up frustration burned deep, and I wanted to beat my fists against him. His willpower was greater than mine. We'd gone so much further in the dreams. Why was reality so different?

I pushed away, needing the space. What I wanted was an explanation.

He moved back to his side of the bench, desire still smoldering in his gaze that forced me to look away.

"I don't understand you." I barely spit the words out and had to clear my throat. "I didn't realize vamps ran so hot and cold."

If my words stung, he didn't show it. Instead, his gaze turned neutral, the way he and the other vamps got when they did their stare thing. Then I understood. There was something else he hadn't told me.

"Is Ginger all right?"

"She's fine. In fact, she'll be arriving soon and will be staying here for a few days."

At first, I was thrilled. Someone to fill my lonely hours, but that didn't answer the real question. "What happened?"

"A shifter pack outside of Los Angeles was slaughtered."

Bells rang, and the stab of a piercing headache shook me. He didn't pull any punches when he shared news. And it didn't stop there.

"From the way it was described, it mirrored our dream of the northern pack."

If there was any blood left in my upper region, it was enough to keep my heart beating but did nothing to supply much-needed air. I ran a hand over my chest. Could I beat on it to get the air circulating? I closed my eyes and focused on Devon. Not from that dream, but an earlier one. The burn of his lips on mine and the excitement of his fangs trailing a course down my neck. Just keep the nightmare away.

"I have a meeting with The Wolf tomorrow evening to discuss the problem."

I couldn't seem to get my brain to think. The heat I'd built with memories of Devon's lips had dulled the images of that grotesque scene. I blew out a breath and opened my eyes to the bright sunshine streaming through the window. His words finally sank in, and I caught up.

"The problem?"

"Whether this was shifter on shifter or..."

"Vamps." My gaze shot to his, and though it was only there for an instant, his fear shook me. Not fear for himself, but what it could mean to the fragile balance if vamps had done this. "Why would vamps attack a shifter pack?"

"It wasn't a true pack. It was a group of rogue wolves who'd gathered for protection. From what Sergi was told, they had the approval of the local pack alpha. But that doesn't mean they didn't have issues with other rogues." He stood and moved toward the windows. His expression was unreadable as he stared at the view. He could have been staring at the manicured lawn that stretched to the cliff, the ocean beyond, or nothing at all. "There are other things at play that might have spurred the killings, we just don't have enough information."

"What other things?"

He turned toward me, and I no longer saw Devon. It was the alpha vamp, the leader of a great House who stared back at me. "We're still pulling the pieces together." He hesitated for a moment and seemed to gather himself. "There's something else you need to know."

I tugged my robe closer, wishing he would have waited until I had something more decent on. It didn't feel right getting bad news in a swimsuit, and I was pretty sure I wasn't going to like what was coming next.

"Underwood was spotted in the Hollows with a young woman. A vampire."

I snorted, and my earlier worry evaporated. "That doesn't surprise me. I guess that confirms whether he knows Lorenzo is a vamp."

His nod was quick. "And I used that information to gain other, more critical information."

My stomach clenched. Here it came.

"I used the photos of him with his girlfriend to learn more of the necklace."

"My necklace? How would photos..." The world tilted. He wouldn't have. Couldn't have. A coldness swept through me. "You took them to my mother?"

He didn't respond.

"Without asking me first?"

"It wasn't your call."

"Wasn't my call? It's my mother." I was off the bench, pacing alongside the pool. The earlier chill turned to a burning anger. "Is that why you sent me to L.A.? To get me out of the way? You had no right."

"First, I'll remind you of something I've told you before. My business and the protection of my family comes first. The continuation of our race, and the safety of your own, which I shouldn't have to remind you, comes second."

His words penetrated, but I shoved them away.

"We're not talking about that. We're talking about my mother."

He moved closer with a predatory grace I'd come to recognize as a danger sign. His gaze took on that silvery glow.

"Your mother. The one you barely speak to. The one you said all but abandoned you once she married Underwood. That mother? I just want to be sure we're talking about the same woman."

"That's not fair." The hot burning tears rose, and I spun away from him. So stupid to put my back to a raging vamp.

"She had more knowledge about the necklace, and your attempts were proving too slow. We have to know more, and we've lost the time to be subtle."

I whirled back around. Something must have snapped in me because he took a step back. "She didn't need to be dragged into your world. And whatever that necklace represents, that's my business. Not yours. It's between her and me." I was so angry, I could have spit blood.

"Let me break it down further for you. Because this is more than just you and your mother. There's a reason Lorenzo is looking for that necklace. I don't know why, but if he's looking for it, it poses a grave danger. And here's another startling truth. I wasn't meeting with your mother. I was meeting with Under-

230

wood's wife. One, I might mention, who was quite aware of her husband's infidelities. A woman, whose proximity to a man who's dealing with vampires, has found herself in a very dangerous predicament. By no fault of hers, her husband has put her in harm's way. Lorenzo plays for keeps, and if he has Underwood under his control, your mother's life as she knows it no longer exists. She needs to pick a side. And quite frankly, she's too immersed in guilt over you and worry for April to make a sound, logical decision."

He strode toward me. "I knew you'd be angry. And I didn't wait for you to leave to do this. I would have met with her without your knowledge or approval whether you were in town or not. Too many things are happening. Events that not only impact our greater mission but lives. I don't know if my move to repeal the censure has unwittingly cracked other secrets, or it's all bad timing. But I'm not going to sit around to find out."

His gaze softened, almost remorseful. "I need to get a handle on what happened with the shifters. In order to accomplish that, I had to give my guards assignments, which removes them from Ginger's security. I have others that can guard her, but for your benefit and hers, it's easier and safer to guard one position."

He heaved a sigh, and I thought he might reach for me. How silly was that?

"Take time to recover from your trip. Then get your head settled on our mission."

He strode toward the door, leaving me to stare at the sun blazing through the windows. The earlier anger had burned out, and not even the warmth of the room could dispel the chill from all he divulged.

He stopped at the doorway. "Willa is full of guilt over your separation. Everything she's done was to protect you. And while it wasn't the best way, that it hurt you, she never stopped loving you. Rasmussen was the love of her life."

Then he was gone. I had no idea how much time slipped by as I continued to stare out the window into sunshine that still couldn't warm me. Then the anger rekindled. He never mentioned what my mother had shared with him.

Asshole.

Chapter Twenty-Six

DEVON GLANCED at the tall stone columns and massive oak doors. Large windows displayed a busy bar, most likely a high-end pickup bar for shifters. The restaurant was near The Wolf's compound, though it catered to humans and shifters alike, or the occasional vampire with no hard feelings toward shifters. It was a safe location, and he'd been here a handful of times before.

He'd been surprised when Decker declined the invitation to join them. Based on current events, the shifter felt it sent a better message for the two alphas to meet on their own. No matter how much Remus trusted Decker, more could be shared if he wasn't in attendance. Devon couldn't argue his friend's reasoning.

He knocked on the glass that separated him from Bella and Lucas. They decided the limo made more of an impression than the sedan. When the window lowered, he said, "I expect this to take an hour, two at the most depending on how much Remus wants to rage."

They both smiled. Everyone in his family had met The Wolf at some point, especially when the two of them had become friends and not just partners. He credited Decker for his ability to make friends among the shifters. Over the decades, he'd taught Devon how tough, loyal, and trustworthy shifters were—unless you double-crossed them. He grinned. No different than how vampires took care of business.

He left the limo with Lucas two steps behind him. Once inside, Lucas went to the bar while he continued on to the maître d', who was prepared for him, and with nothing more than a nod, handed him over to a hostess who led him to a private balcony that looked out over the city.

Remus was already seated. A glass of single-malt—the bottle of Glenfiddich opened nearby—gripped in one hand as he scrolled through his tablet with the other. A bucket of ice sat at the edge of the table so it could be replenished throughout their meal.

He'd dressed in a sports jacket, shirt sans tie, and tailored pants from what Devon could see. And he breathed easier. Remus always dressed for the particular occasion, and if this was going to be a beat down about the rogue shifters and the delay of the mission, he would have worn an expensively tailored suit.

Remus closed the tablet and moved it to the side as the hostess pulled back the chair for Devon. The woman disappeared after pouring a glass of scotch for him. He never took his gaze from Remus, and when he lifted his glass, Remus tipped his toward Devon. They both drank.

"I think this has always been my favorite." Devon wasn't lying to impress. "I'm not sure why I don't stock more of it."

"That security man of yours doesn't know good scotch from rye. He's a vodka man, and you should never let a vodka man buy your scotch." Remus took a long sip, and when he smiled, his fangs reflected the bite of the slow burn.

"You'll be glad to know I've given that role to Cook. He's really the only one in residence who has the appropriate taste for the good stuff."

"Ah, wise decision." Remus glanced out the window and then to the glass wall that separated them from the other diners. "I appreciate you taking the time to come out this way. This place is famous for their steaks, but they also have a fine selection of organic meals."

Devon lifted a brow and after taking a quick glance at the menu tossed it back on the table. "Are we going to sing sweet adulations to each other while we wait for a slow song?"

Remus threw back his head with a hearty laugh. "That's why I trust you. No subterfuge. Straight to the matter at hand."

When he smiled, he let a bit of his own fangs show. "Who has the time these days?"

Remus frowned. "More truth than I care to admit." He was going to say more but paused when the server stopped by to take their order. Once he was gone, The Wolf gave Devon a hard look. "I've been patient, and now a new threat is upon us."

"Possibly." He felt the urgency as well, but their opponent seemed to be directing the play. "What have you heard about the rogues?"

Remus lowered his gaze, his lips thinning. "They'd been promised safe haven. The alpha of the local pack is very angry. It was difficult to rein him in."

"He believes vampires did this?"

"There were bite marks, though the bodies were so mangled it was impossible to discern anything other than fangs being involved. Several of the bodies had been ripped apart."

"Still not conclusive."

"True. Shifters that haven't gone through their first change can be equally violent in human form. Saliva and blood samples were taken to our labs."

Devon paled. "If it was vampires..."

Remus waved him off. "This is for my eyes only. I agree a war now would be poor timing with our own goals so close at hand. But I won't be able to hide whatever answers we discover for long."

They paused in their conversation as dinner was served. Remus rubbed his hands together when the thirty-ounce prime rib was placed in front of him, complete with garlic mashed potatoes, and a vegetable medley. Devon's halibut was succulent and accompanied by the same mix of organic vegetables. And as delectable as it was, he picked at his meal.

"I know I've been distracted, but the last artifact is proving illusive. To add to that, another issue has taken more time than I anticipated."

Remus buttered a roll and sucked a spot of butter from his thumb. "And this is something you can't share with me?"

"I'm afraid the pieces are currently too scattered to provide a coherent picture."

The Wolf wiped the breadcrumbs away and sat back, sipping his scotch, the roll forgotten. "How long have we been planning our mission?"

Devon refused to drop his gaze, but a flash of caution forced him to change direction. This wasn't the time to test The Wolf or hold secrets. "We've recently discovered the existence of a book that might provide the truth behind the House Wars."

The Wolf's gaze widened at that, and he leaned into the table, pushing his bread plate aside. "Go on."

"It's not easy to explain." He pushed a hand through his hair then refilled their glasses. He stared down at the city, and, for a moment, thought about Cressa and what she might be doing. Probably watching old movies with Ginger and eating Cook's specialty popcorn. For an even crazier moment, he wished he could be there to share it. He gulped two swallows and savored the tang of the amber liquid, giving him the courage to lay it all out for The Wolf.

"We discovered the name of a book that, up until now, seemed to be hiding in plain sight. It's almost imperceptible as anything more than the chronicler's random musing. But after further investigation, we traced it to the Renaud Library in Los Angeles."

Remus grunted, and Devon wasn't sure if The Wolf found the story interesting or noticed the coincidence that the City of Angels had become the center of perplexing activity. Perhaps it was both.

"But it's no longer at the library, and though we haven't had time to confirm this, it's possible the curator, Philipe Renaud, might have made a hasty departure."

"Meaning you have no idea if he had anything to do with this missing book, and you have no idea if his absence was planned or unexpected."

When he nodded, Remus shook his head. "So you have nothing."

"Except for the four vampires who were sneaking around the restricted areas of the library at the same time as my team was attempting to extract the book."

Remus fell back in his chair, a low whistle escaping. "Now we have something."

"My team coordinated the break-in to occur during the weekly vampire gathering at the library. An event that Lorenzo was attending at the time."

Remus's earlier whistle was replaced by a low growl. "What are your plans?"

"I'm sending one of my guards to track down Renaud and see if he can tell us something about the book. It's a stretch, but too many questions are without answers." And now came the tricky part. "He could use an experienced tracker."

The Wolf barked out a laugh. "And now you finally admit that shifters make better trackers." He winked. "When you need one."

He smiled in return. "Is there a better time?"

Remus shook his head, and he suddenly looked his couple hundred years. "No. I don't suppose there is."

They stopped their conversation again as plates were removed and espressos were served. "Will you keep Sergi involved in the investigation of the shifter deaths in addition to the rumor of Magic Poppy?"

"We believe there's a connection between the incidents, so yes, Sergi is at your disposal. We need answers before we can proceed with the larger plan."

"This should be our last communication for a while. Will you continue to use Decker?"

"Yes. For all things that need to pass between you and me."

"You still trust that old wolf?"

"Aren't you some years older than him?"

Remus's sharp white teeth appeared in a mischievous smile. "You must admit I look years younger." Then his smile faded. "I hope he finds the solace he seeks when this is all done."

But when their gazes met, it didn't seem either of them held out much hope of that happening.

Chapter Twenty-Seven

THE FIVE-STORY APARTMENT building was in a decent neighborhood. No bars on the windows, and a flashy awning covered the front door. No doorman, but that would be out of character for this part of the city where young Millennials made their homes. There was even a quaint park across the street with a playground for the local kids, which was currently occupied by two moms and three kids.

I'd watched the building for the last two days. Training and classroom sessions had been postponed in favor of special meetings. Devon and most of his inner circle had moved to Oasis for three days of meetings, including an afternoon with shifters. At least, that was as much as I was able to drag out of Cook. Even Anna had gone with them, leaving Ginger and me behind in the mansion.

I couldn't complain about spending quality time with Ginger, we'd had so little time to spend together that it was like a mini vacation. After the first evening, our days of doing nothing seemed to be quickly filled with sleeping in, movie nights, and lounging by the pool. Ginger spilled the beans that Lucas has been giving her defense lessons, and to keep up with my own training, we spent an hour every morning going over simpler yet highly effective martial art moves.

I borrowed a six-inch dagger from Sergi's supply for Ginger to use, but after the first thirty minutes, it was pretty obvious it wouldn't be her weapon of choice. Besides, if she got that close to a vamp to use it, she'd end up dead. So, we sneaked down to the armory, and I punched in Sergi's security code I'd figured out weeks ago. That was before he'd understood my skills as a thief.

Devon kept a well-stocked supply of swords, daggers, rifles, handguns, throwing stars, and other weapons of death. Ginger's eyes danced when I pulled open a drawer and found a collection of derringer pistols. It didn't take her long to select one with a rosewood grip that fit her grasp perfectly. After a couple practice sessions, I discovered my bestie had wickedly good aim.

Needless to say, no perfectly good armory existed without a fair amount of ammo. In the Trelane House, that included a walk-in closet the size of a master bath with wall-to-wall shelves that ran from floor to ceiling. There was a wide array to choose from, but I grabbed a box of 9mm silver bullets. Sergi would eventually notice a missing box. I had no doubt he kept a tight inventory, but I'd worry about it later.

Between my dagger and martial art skills, and Ginger with her defensive training and silver bullets, we knew better than to think we could take on vamps, but we felt empowered enough to survive until the calvary arrived.

Security had been tight after the incident with the shifters, but Bella and Jacques, who'd been assigned as our bodyguards, took us shopping each day. Ginger requested they take us to the same eastside mall. The vamps never asked why, and after a couple hours, we always returned with bags from various stores. They parked outside and let us go in alone as long as we promised to keep our phones attached to our hips. The general consensus was that no vamp in their right mind would launch an attack at a mall.

What was really happening when we went to the mall was that

Ginger spent the time doing what she did best—wandering the stores, trying on anything and everything, and purchasing a little bit of this and a lot of that. I'd leave her immediately, giving her a small fist bump before walking out the back door of the mall that bordered the local metro stop.

Within thirty minutes, I stepped off the bus to this lovely, tree-lined neighborhood. And on this third day of our own little world, it was time to rattle some cages. The fire escape was in good condition and faced the alley between buildings. It was the middle of the day when most of the neighborhood was at work, and though it was a bit risky, I guessed that even in this neighborhood, no one would be surprised by someone on the outer stairs.

After standing in a doorway, scoping out the windows of the next-door building and not seeing anyone, I pulled on a knitted hat and tucked my hair inside. I wore my jeans and sneakers with an oversized T-shirt and a loose windbreaker. With any luck, no one could discern if I was male or female, and most would assume male.

I caught the bottom rung of the ladder on my first try, which was easy after all the wall training Simone had put me through. Once I reached the third-floor window, it took less than a minute to shake my head at the sloppy security and bypass it. Some things never changed.

I didn't need to take the extra time but decided to play it safe and waited for something loud to pass by. It didn't take long for a delivery truck to cruise by the main street, and I used the sound to mask sliding open the window, just in case it stuck.

I checked my watch. If he was on time, I had five minutes to spare. I grabbed a hard cider out of the fridge and made myself comfortable on the leather couch, flipping through one of several magazines sprawled across the coffee table.

When voices filled the hall outside the apartment, I smiled at the familiar argument. Keys rattled at the door—first the dead bolt, then a second one, and finally the doorknob. The door burst open and two people stumbled in, both still grumbling until the man and woman came to an abrupt halt when they spotted me.

I flipped another page and smiled up at them. "Hello, Harlow. Trudy." When the two people from my old crew stared open mouthed like bass after a worm, I grinned wider. "Shut the door, Lucy. You have some 'splaining to do."

Trudy slammed the door, took the bag Harlow was carrying and walked to the kitchen which was separated from the living area by a long counter. She smiled at me, pulled a beer out of the fridge, and held up a hard cider. "Need a fresh one?"

I nodded. "You might need to get something a bit stronger for Harlow."

He was still at the door. He'd shut his mouth, but I could see the wheels turning, deciding the best approach.

"Cressa, luv." He sauntered in, going for the casual approach, and I almost smiled. He dropped his keys in a crystal bowl on the coffee table, then sprawled in the plush leather chair, his grin in place as his gaze rolled over me, making the usual stops at my breasts and crotch.

Trudy smirked when she joined us, handing me a new bottle and Harlow a beer. "How did you know we'd be here or that you'd catch us coming home?"

I chortled. "Late breakfast at the diner, a stroll to the local bars to check in with the crews, a little shopping, then back home." I gave Harlow a pointed look. "You know better than sticking with a routine."

He grumbled when Trudy snickered. "Told you."

"Hasn't been a problem until now." His cocky expression disappeared, and his shoulders slumped. His hand was shaky as he ran it over his head, moving it back and forth, making his mess of locks more of a rat's nest.

I waited to see if he'd say more, but he wouldn't. Not because he didn't care. The guilt had been eating at him. He was a specialist at covering his emotions from most people. A quick glance at Trudy, who was frowning at him, only confirmed it.

"Sorrento refused to tell me where he took you." He broke sooner than I'd expected, and he laid it out in a simple matter-of-fact approach. "I heard him and his bodyguards rubbed someone the wrong way."

I didn't have time for chatting over Sorrento's disappearance and what I knew to be a grisly death. "I'm only here for one reason." I didn't have to ask it. He knew.

"It was Stan."

I shot another glance at Trudy, and she grimaced. But Stan? "Then he must be one helluva an actor. He looked ready to piss himself every time Sorrento stalked by him."

Harlow cackled, short and dry. "Oh, yeah, he was. That was no act. Sorrento had his hooks in a few of crew members. Mine, Jaconi's, and Webster's."

The big three of the north. Made sense. All it took was Pandora joining any of them for a job, and Sorrento could spring his trap. And to rat out a crew? If they were caught, they'd never work in the region again. In California, that meant they wouldn't find a crew anywhere up and down the West Coast.

I considered Sorrento's choice of crew member to target. It had been perfect. There was no doubt Stan was the weakest link. And when Sorrento made an offer, he might as well be the godfather. Still, he had to have had something on Stan to get him to turn on them.

"What happened to him?" I had to know.

"All three of the snitches were rounded up and driven out to the state line and dumped. They can find work in Reno or grab a bus for Vegas. Either way, they won't be back."

Word of their betrayal and punishment would have spread faster than a grass fire. No. They wouldn't be back. They'd been in a tough spot, but in the end, they'd made a bad decision and would have to live with it. They'd find other crews, and hopefully they'd be more loyal. But some never learned.

When the silence became deafening, Harlow tapped his empty beer bottle on the arm of the chair. The soft thuds shouldn't have bothered me, but for some reason, I wasn't sure how to take the next step any more than he did. After hearing the snitch was really one of our own, it kind of took the wind out of a person.

Trudy seemed to be the only one not stressed, but she'd scrunched up her brows as if finally remembering something. "So, what happened to you?"

"Ah, man." Harlow stood and picked up his empty bottle before striding into the kitchen.

"It's a fair question." Trudy raised her voice as if the kitchen was down the hall rather than fifteen feet away.

When Harlow was seated again with another beer, he picked at the label. "Was it bad?"

I nestled back in the sofa, pleased that the worst was over. "I woke up in a catch cage after he kept me drugged for a couple of days. Then he traded me off to clear his own debt." When they both looked sick, I eased their worry. "I can't complain about where I ended up." As angry as I'd been with Devon the last time I'd seen him, our separation made a perfect salve for wounded pride. It grated that I actually missed him. "I'm working off my debt in a decent place, and I'm protected."

"And how exactly are you working off that debt?" Trudy's smile was all evil and mischievous.

I reached over and slapped her knee but couldn't hold back the grin. "I had the same conversation with Ginger."

Harlow burst out laughing. "How is my girl?"

I laughed. "She's living uptown now. At least temporarily. The boss wanted her someplace safe."

Trudy whistled. "It sounds like you bounced to a better place."

I shrugged. "The work is dangerous. I'm basically the house thief, but I have to admit, I don't miss the old apartment."

When silence descended a second time, I got to the heart of why I was there. Ginger would be expecting me soon. "Who's your new hacker?"

Trudy stretched back in her seat and placed her boots on the table, her hands behind her head. "Go ahead, you tell her."

"A lovely lass by the name of Roxie."

"Who's all of twelve." Trudy was holding something back, but all she did was smile at him, her eyes brimming with humor.

"She's twenty-three, or something like that." He glanced at me but pointed his beer at Trudy. "She's just jealous Roxie is smarter than her. A real sweetheart."

Trudy shook her head and leaned toward me. "The first job, Harlow tripped over his big feet, or so he says, and ends up staying upright by grabbing Roxie's boobs."

I laughed. He'd done the same thing with me. It was comforting to see he never changed. "How did that go over?"

"She punched him in the face."

This time I barked out the laugh. "Oh my, I think I'm going to like her."

"It's a good thing she's fucking good at what she does." Harlow's mutter was said with a scowl, but there was amusement behind his hawk-eyed gaze.

God, I missed this motley group. "How's Jamal?" He was our driver and backup muscle.

"He's good. Seeing that waitress from Donna's."

I finished my drink and set the bottle on the table. "He always had dreamy eyes for her."

"Who would have thought it would take so long for him to ask her out?" Trudy gave me that look that said it was time for me to get to the point of my visit.

"I might be in need of a crew over the next few weeks. Maybe more than one job. I can't give you any specifics at this point, mainly wanted to see where we left things. The only downside is the short notice on the jobs." When the two eyed each other, I figured they wouldn't just jump in. "I'm not looking for a commitment, just a show of interest."

Harlow studied me. No joking, no easy smiles. All business. "Is it dangerous?"

I shrugged. "Depends on the job. But the pay is top notch, and like always, you can say no."

"Who's running it?"

"Ultimately, my boss. But he'll listen to me when it comes to a job. And while I have the final word on what I propose to him, I'm here because you know how to put a job together. And that's what I need."

He glanced to Trudy, who got up and grabbed the empty bottles without saying a word. It was a sign that it was up to him. "Same rules as before. If we're not already committed to something else, we'll give what you bring us full consideration. But I'll expect extra for the risk of someone else running the job."

I stood and stuck out my hand.

He stood and faced me, his expression still stern, but he grasped my hand and shook it. Then he pulled me in for a hug. "I'm glad you're okay. That was a tight spot." Then he squeezed my ass, both buns, and I pushed back, grinning.

"You just can't leave well enough alone."

He laughed, and Trudy joined him at the door, her arm around his waist.

"Don't be a stranger, sugar," she said.

I trotted down the inner staircase, not worried about anyone seeing me. Those two were a strange couple, but I felt lighter than I thought possible having the crew back.

Now, I just had to talk Devon into my mad plans.

Chapter Twenty-Eight

DEVON FELL INTO BED, exhaustion ripping at him. He needed blood, but had turned away donors, too busy with meetings that went nowhere. He'd been pushing hard, working with the shifters to track where the Magic Poppy might be coming from and who had murdered the rogues. The Wolf was still incensed by their tragic loss, and he couldn't blame Remus one bit. Yet, the results from the lab work Remus ordered had come back inconclusive. That had stunned them all. Further tests were being done, but without more to go on, the final resolution had been to send out more field teams to quietly pursue more leads.

He'd been so obsessed with the pending threat, he hadn't been available to Cressa, and though Bella had assured him the women were fine, he wasn't convinced. They'd parted in anger, and even with Ginger around, he found it difficult to believe that three days of shopping and leisure activity had been enough to keep her out of trouble. He thought the mission to locate the book would have been enough to reduce the binds of her confinement, but she needed a purpose beyond the training and classroom sessions. She was like a dog after a bone. Once her mind had pinned on that damn book, she'd lost interest in the rest of the story.

If she'd been able to find a single item, or a series of events, that explained the House Wars all those centuries ago, she would have been satisfied. He'd been buried under the same frustrations the first time he'd delved into those books and found no real reason for the shattered loyalties.

Now, they had a missing Renaud and a missing Rasmussen, who both could shed light on the mysteries surrounding them. Cressa needed a project of her own. He'd take her to New Orleans and find the link Willa had given him. Soon. He'd take care of all of it soon.

He tossed for another hour before sleep enveloped him, and his troubles fell away like leaves in the fall.

A light fog rolled in, and Cressa was in his arms on the widow's walk as they watched it blanket the yard in shadows and dew. The mist left minuscule beads of moisture on her skin, and he kissed her neck, tasting the sweet sheen mixed with her desire.

She stepped away but took his hand and led him down the stairs and through the halls until they reached the library where a roaring fire had been started. A blanket had been placed in front of the hearth, and she pulled him down to it.

"Let's dry off. The fire feels good." She removed his jacket, her fingers caressing his neck as she tugged it off him. She left a kiss on his ear, her breath warm against his skin.

He grew hard when she returned to remove his shirt, and he grabbed her wrist before running his hand up her arm. "You need to warm up. You're chilled."

She pushed his hand away. "There will be plenty of time for that." She took her time as she unbuttoned his shirt, her knuckles scraping along his skin, sending short bursts of lightning with her every movement. Once the buttons were free, she moved behind him to slowly draw the shirt off his shoulders, featherlight kisses trailed behind, and he struggled to free the shirt. But when the shirt tangled around his wrists, she left it to trail her fingertips up his back and over his shoulders, her nails gripping hard as she traced her tongue up the same path, light and teasing.

A growl slipped from him as he tried to untangle his hands, but she leaned her body into him, her breasts against his back. And though he couldn't feel her skin under the soft silk of her dressing gown, he felt her warmth.

"Stop struggling. This is my dream."

He stopped, but not because she'd asked. Memories from an earlier dream—an aggressive Cressa. Before he could wrap his head around what was happening or what he should do, she was back, once again pressed against him, but this time the dressing gown was gone.

Her skin was on fire, her nipples hard, and the kisses resumed along the side of his neck, her tongue sliding along his artery as if testing for the best place to bite.

"Cressa." The word struggled out as soft as the cry of a baby bird.

"Shh. All is well. It's only me, and it's been too long."

Whatever tension had been building inside him released with those words, and he gave in to the sensations she aroused in him. She laid sweet kisses across his back as her hands slid to his chest and rubbed his nipples until they were nothing but hard buds. When her hands slid lower, his mind broke, and he struggled again for the release of his arms.

Her laughter was erotic and devilish. "Let me." Her hands worked at the sleeves that bound him. "You need to learn patience, my sweet."

"Set me free, and I'll show you patience."

She only laughed again, this time it was huskier, more sensual. "We'll see."

When an arm came free, she moved it above his head. "Don't move. Just let me get this other one." She pushed him to the floor as she moved over him to reach the errant sleeve. Her bared breasts hovered over his face, and he did the only thing that made sense with the offering she placed in front of him.

He lifted his head and took one of her nipples into this mouth, his tongue circling until it was as hard as she'd made his. A soft moan escaped, and she stretched with feline grace. Her spicy scent invaded his thoughts, and nothing existed but this moment—this woman. He moved to the other breast, her skin taut as she continued to stretch, and the tips of his fangs scraped along the underside of her soft flesh creating goosebumps that he kissed and teased until they disappeared and her skin warmed with an internal flame.

Then there was nothing but air as she slid down the length of him. When he tried to reach for her, he found his wrists still bound, this time to the leg of the coffee table.

She'd kept her gaze on him, her light brown eyes aglow with passion. "As I said. My dream, my rules." Her smile was loving and wicked. Then all he saw was the top of her sable-colored waves as she kissed her way down his chest, slowing as she reached the light hairs just below his waist. She moved to his left thigh as his manhood pulsed with need, becoming unbearably hard as she teased her way around it.

When her fingers wrapped around him, he thought he'd blast to the moon, but somehow, he retained control, tugging at the table that drew closer.

Then her mouth was over him and sweet delight flowed through him. Her lips were soft yet firm, her tongue busy as heat roiled, his nerves bursting with need, the table drawing ever closer as he struggled against her constraints. She never slowed, never stopped as she took him over the edge, his toes curling, his hands tightening into fists as he arched into her and could no longer stop the release that gave way. It was nothing short of a dam bursting as his body melted into the blanket beneath them.

She dropped across his chest and untied his wrists, rubbing along the muscles that had strained. When his arms wrapped around her, she rested her head on him and ran a soft circle around a nipple.

There were no words. None needed. He didn't think anything like this was possible in a dream. They'd touched before in the earlier dreams, but nothing in those erotic moments could have prepared him for this.

Once their combined heartbeats slowed to a normal rhythm, she rose and once again took his hand.

"Come."

He didn't question her but simply rose, leaving his clothes behind as he trailed after her. She led them up the stairs and down the hall to his bedroom. Once inside, she shut the door, the soft moonlight revealing her naked beauty.

Her eyes glimmered with unsatisfied lust. "Let's stop playing games."

Then she was gone.

His eyes popped open. He blinked and glanced down. His cock lay spent along his leg. That had never happened in one of their dreams.

When he turned his head, she was still there, lying next to him.

He was in his bed with a naked Cressa beside him. She was on her side, leaning on her elbow, and she smiled.

"Your turn."

I HELD MY BREATH. I'd never done anything quite so daring, but after all our erotic dreams, dreams we'd both shared, it wasn't like we didn't already know each other intimately. And as real as those dreams felt, lying here next to him, bared body and soul, I second-guessed my rash decision.

I'd been in his home a month, and while so much had happened between us, there was a distance between us that didn't feel right. We'd come so close to this moment, his attraction to me so obvious, the heat so consuming, that if he turned me away this time, the man had more control than I thought possible. Although, I'd already witnessed how much control he had when his beast had raged, and he'd held it in check.

Time crawled, and my breath caught as I took in his mussed hair, his droopy, sleep-filled eyes, and his bare chest shimmering with a light sheen. Had that sweat been caused by our dream? Something to file away for later. This whole evening had been somewhat of a test. More than that, but a test all the same.

He stared at me for ages, his expression never changing. His eyes were the key, and they glowed with that dusky iridescent blue, darker than his normal eye color but not the pure silver of his beast. They were filled with heat and a deeper passion than I'd seen before.

I didn't move. I wasn't lying—this was his turn. To reach out or to leave.

He reached out a hand, first to my arm and then my face, as if testing to confirm I was real. That this wasn't a dream. I turned my face into his palm and closed my eyes, savoring the feel of his strong fingers, the warmth of his touch.

When I opened my eyes, I knew I wouldn't be leaving anytime soon. I smiled.

He was on me in a flash, his lips devouring mine, his hands sliding down the curves of my body as he pulled me close. Then his kiss gentled as his tongue caressed my lips before it slipped inside, then his urgent need wasted no time—as if he'd been starved for days. Hot and hungry, I could no longer tell the difference between dream and reality. I never could. His taste was the same, his tangy scent of cinnamon and cloves wrapped around me until I was encased in everything Devon.

When he moved his mouth to my throat, I arched into him. His tongue flirted along my neck, while his fangs tested and teased. How would my blood taste to him? Would it be as sweet and addicting as his had been to me?

He moved over my body, using the same triad of pleasure—kisses, tongue, and fangs. The farther down he moved, the more my nerve endings came to life, almost raw as heat built in me. He never rushed, once again proving his control, even though I felt his body shudder when he hit a sensitive spot and my body leaned into him.

He wasn't the first man I'd been with. There had been a few, but none came close to evoking the feelings, the passion, the torturous heat this man coaxed from me. Whether it was mere lust, proximity, or the pull of the dreams, I didn't know. And I convinced myself it didn't matter. He was a vamp. I was human. Nothing more than a thief. And if this was all that could ever exist between us, it was good enough for me.

Ginger taught me that. Take pleasure where you could find it. Don't waste a minute of it.

So, when Devon spread my legs to continue his exploration, I stretched like an alley cat and gave into the heat. The pulsing need threatened to split me open, and when his tongue touched that sensitive bud of my core, neon lights flashed, and the sound coming out of me was somewhere between a moan and a cry of sheer bliss. My body trembled with a fierce need for more, for him to never stop, until the dam was breached, and wave after wave of pleasure swept through me. I almost wept from the intense release.

He didn't give me a break as he slid back up, his lips reclaiming mine. The taste of me on his tongue drove me wild as he ravaged my mouth. I barely noticed him centering himself between my legs, and while he sucked my tongue, he pushed inside. I welcomed him with a wild abandon I'd never felt before. My legs wrapped around him, pulling him deeper until I heard his own satisfied moan as he drove harder.

I lost track of time, of the world, while he continued to take and give. Whether on my back, my side, on top, or on hands and knees, there was only Devon long into the night. And I reveled in every second of it.

When I opened an eye and noted the light seeping in from under the blinds, the only question was whether I was still in one piece. Not that it mattered. After the long evening, if I died right now, I'd die a happy woman.

I couldn't move my body. Every muscle was limp with nothing more to give. I couldn't even muster enough energy to move my head.

I was laying on something hard, yet it moved. Devon. My head was on his chest, which would explain the light dusting of hair that tickled my nose and the soft thumping I heard. His heart beat. Huh. Vamps had heartbeats. I guess something had to push that vampiric blood through their veins.

Then he was caressing my hair. "Good morning."

I blinked. The awkward part. The morning after.

I stretched, determining which muscles would obey, and found enough energy to inch my way from his chest to rest my head against the crook of his arm. He wrapped one around me like a band of steel holding me against him. I guess he wasn't reconsidering our actions. My brazen seduction.

I ran a tongue over my teeth. "Morning."

"Should I ask about last night?" His tone was light. No judgment.

I released a sigh. "You mean the dream?"

"That's as good a place as any."

"It's the first time I've been able to control the dream without the necklace."

"At what point did you know you had control?"

I bit my lip, forcing myself to wrinkle my brow as if in some deep concentration as I relived the dream. But I knew exactly when I'd become aware. It was right from the beginning when I laid my head near his and ached for him. His touch. I'd missed the dreams where it had just been the two of us and some inexplicable, lustful attraction. Those dreams felt safe. They seemed like the most real part of my whole disastrous life. And how much of that truth did I share with him?

"Be honest with me. It's the only way I can help you." He gave me a squeeze.

I should have been ashamed that he expected me to lie. Instead, I ran an arm across his chest, circled his nipple, then glided south.

He grabbed my wrist. "As much as I would prefer that distraction to talking, we have to know how your dreams are manifesting." When a minute passed, and I remained silent, he sighed. "I'll share a tidbit with you if you promise to do the same. Agreed?"

I nodded against his chest.

"Have you ever heard of someone named Colantha Dupré?"

"No." It came out rather fast, but it was more from a desire to hear more than any memory it dredged up. "Did my mother give you that name?" If this was about the dreams, then it must be the lead she'd given him.

"Yes. That and a location. New Orleans."

I shook my head this time. "None of it's familiar. Not even a spark."

"Until we can locate this person, it's critical to understand everything we can about these dreams. Especially your part in them—whether you're being pulled along for the ride of if you're directing them."

I sighed and pushed away from him, pulling myself up to lean against the headboard. I pulled my knees up so I could circle my arms around them. Devon sat up to lean next to me, his shoulder touching mine.

"From the minute my head hit the pillow, I'd been thinking about the widow's walk and the day you first took me up there." I turned my head toward him and found him watching me—waiting. "We'd gotten pretty passionate until something called you away."

"I remember."

My deep breath was shaky. "I just thought about what I

wanted to do, where I wanted to go, and the dream made it happen. One minute we were here in your room, the next everything else. I almost forgot it was a dream." And my cheeks burned remembering how assertive I'd been, especially sneaking into this room and crawling into his bed while he slept.

"Did you influence my reactions?"

I flinched. Some part of me understood why he'd asked. Another part was hurt by it.

"Don't answer. I'm sorry I asked."

I shook it off. "No problem. I get it." I forced a smile. "Your reactions were your own."

I was not going to talk about this and was halfway across the monstrous-sized bed when he caught me and rolled me over. He stared down at me, and I squeezed my eyes shut. He shook me until I opened them and got caught in his gaze.

"Don't do this. Don't overreact."

When I stared daggers, he released me and laughed. "If the tables were turned, you would have asked the same question."

I opened my mouth, but after an absurdly long moment, I shut it.

"Just one more question. Do you know how you did it?"

The words wouldn't come out. I wanted to say hell no. That I needed his help to figure this out, but it was too soon. I wanted time to think about what had happened. It was just as new to me. I hadn't any time to consider it, roll it around, see how it tasted, and figure out if I could do it again. I would tell him, after I had time to reflect on this new magical part of me. Until then, I did the only thing I could think of to stop him from asking more questions.

I flung myself into his arms, planting a fierce kiss on his lips. And he must have decided the discussion could wait for another time, because neither of us came up for air for the next two hours.

Chapter Twenty-Nine

I HAD to get out of the house. Good grief. Last night kept replaying in my head all day, and I'd barely heard what anyone said. That might have explained a couple blank stares I'd received. But my evening with Devon—turning the tables on him—I hadn't expected the evening to be so passionate, so carnal, so frickin' amazing.

I was itching to talk to Ginger, but there wasn't an inch of this place safe enough to talk without a vamp being within earshot. It wasn't that I was embarrassed, but Devon hadn't mentioned if the evening should be kept a secret. The best recourse would be to stay silent until he said something.

The clock chimed four and knocked me out of my musing. I dropped the book I'd been not reading on the side table and jogged up the stairs, stopping at Ginger's door, which was partially open. I knocked before peeking around the door.

"Hey, is it safe?"

A short laugh. "Is it ever?"

I had to agree after pushing my way past a pile of clothes dumped on the floor and glanced around. It just got deeper every day. Other pieces of clothes were strewn around the room—a few

257

shirts here, a couple of sweaters there, and a skirt over a lamp of all places. Jewelry was scattered across the dresser and a tray of sweets laid on the bed, where Ginger had sprawled to paint her toenails.

"I do admire your ability to make anyplace immediately feel like home." I shoved shoes off a chair before dropping into it and heaving a leg over a stuffed arm.

Ginger grinned like a cat. She had no shame. "I'm too bored to clean. This place isn't exactly walking distance to anything. Not like our new apartment. If I spend any more time in the pool, I'll permanently prune. Soon I'm going to be forced to watch one of those shop from home channels."

"Heaven forbid." I feigned outrage, and we both giggled. "Hey, seriously, want to go out tonight?"

"Lucas is on assignment."

"I mean without a bodyguard."

Ginger closed the bottle of polish and frowned. "I doubt Devon will allow that."

I gave her a wink. "Leave that to me."

Four hours later, after pampering in front of a mirror and a long dinner at a posh downtown restaurant, the two of us sat with our back to the bar as we watched the dance floor.

"What exactly did you promise Devon to get him to let us go out on our own? I thought there was a reason I was staying at the mansion." Ginger sipped her mojito, her gaze moving across the dancers but not doing her normal ogling in a search for some hunk to dance with. That spoke volumes for whatever was going on between her and Lucas.

Now I paused in how to answer her. This whole evening had been to get her advice on what to do about Devon and our incredible night together. And as silly as it was, I had no idea how to bring it up. I didn't want to take the shine from her own relationship with Lucas, which she hadn't shared with me. Whatever it was, it was enough to cool her jets while men watched her every move.

I grabbed my drink from the bar and used the spear of olives to stir the dry vodka martini. "We have an arrangement. I'm a thief and can take care of myself. I've proved it enough times. We have a nondescript car with no route or plan in mind. And no one has been trailing us." I shrugged my shoulders as if it were no biggie.

He and I had made a deal that came with promises of more classroom training mixed with options that were too intimate to share, considering I hadn't told her about the previous evening. But I couldn't stop grinning thinking about the suggestions he offered for the optional tasks I would owe him.

"Should I ask or ignore that canary grin of yours?"

I finished my drink and stood. "Drink up. Let's check out that bar on the corner."

We were on our way to a third bar when someone yelled my name.

"Yo, Cressa."

I didn't have to turn around to know who it was, but Ginger stopped, her arms waving in excitement.

"Harlow!" She tripped over a piece of broken concrete, and Harlow caught her. His hands, as usual, roaming more than they needed to. "Hey, Trudy. What are you guys doing in this part of town?"

My thoughts exactly since Harlow lived closer to the Hollows.

"One could ask the same of you." He was all smiles, and when he turned to me, he winked. "Twice in one week, luv. How could we be so lucky?"

Ginger gave me a slide glance. "We were just club hopping." She pointed to the bar across the street. "We were headed to that one next." The line was half a block long, and Harlow shook his head.

"There's a nice lounge just a block over. It has some local talent, not as busy as these other cheap places. Why don't you have a drink with us, then you can come back here?"

Trudy smiled, but she scanned the area. A look I knew well.

They were on a job. And what were the odds we'd meet them here? Yet, I didn't sense any deception from Harlow, and that was something I could usually pick up after years of working with him. It's why I knew he hadn't been the one to call Sorrento when he'd surprised us on that job.

"Ooh. Let's do it." Ginger grabbed my hand, and we followed the couple as Harlow launched into sordid tales about jobs they'd worked since the last time we'd all gone out together.

The lounge was quieter than the other clubs. After ten minutes and a martini, I couldn't argue the talent was better, but the place was a dive in every other aspect.

"So, what's the job?" I asked it right after Trudy shared the antics of their new neighbors, who apparently had more frequent and louder sex than they did. That was saying something, which I'd unfortunately discovered on an out-of-town job with the crew.

Harlow flashed me a look before hunching over and scanning the room. "Why do you think there's a job?"

I rolled my eyes, and Trudy just grinned into her beer. I pointed at her mug. "Trudy's drinking beer, scanning the street, and keeping an eye on all the exits. You've hardly touched your drink, and the only time I see you this sober is when there's a job."

Ginger giggled. "Even I know you have a job."

Harlow scowled, then his brows rose, and I sighed. He always got that look whenever an idea popped. I didn't like it. "It's an in and out. Snatch and run. Some jilted lover wants an expensive piece of jewelry back."

"I guess they'd been dating for six months, and he gave his lover some diamond earrings." Trudy tapped her right ear. Her hair had been shaved to a buzz cut with just a touch of curls left on top. She reminded me of Pink. "Then he caught her cheating on him, yet she was the one to kick him to the curb. Now he wants the earrings back. Says they cost him a cool hundred grand, and he's willing to pay half that to get them back."

Ginger whistled. "Wow. Will the jewelry store even take them back?"

Trudy shrugged and tugged at her bra strap. "The guy's not hurting for money. It's the principle."

The women grinned then looked at Harlow.

"What?" Then the lightbulb went off. "Oh, yeah. We men have such low self-esteem that we get all in a twitter when rejected. Now, don't tell me if the tables were reversed, you wouldn't sneak back and grab those earrings."

"We'd take the earrings and probably cut up a couple of his favorite suits." I grinned at him.

"Exactly."

We listened to the music for a bit before Harlow tapped the table. "You know. It's a simple hit, but the woman has a safe."

I snorted. "I suggest you keep with your original plan. Nothing good comes from changing the job in the middle of it."

"Technically, we haven't started the job yet." Trudy was usually the one who cautioned against straying from the plan.

"Look at it this way," Harlow said. "Roxie, our new hacker, will be working on the security. This would be an opportunity to meet her. See how she works."

Ginger fidgeted beside me. "I didn't think you were looking for work."

"I'm not."

"Then why did you stop by yesterday?" Harlow's grin made me want to kick him.

"It wasn't to look for a job, and you know it." I looked to Ginger. "I just wanted to see if they could be trusted after Sorrento. In case I need backup for my current employer."

Ginger nodded, but I saw the caution in her eyes, and I squeezed her leg under the table. She shrugged. "I get it."

"I'm not interested."

Harlow pulled his chair closer and leaned his elbows on the table. "The job is a couple of blocks over. Roxie will be waiting for us. You can meet her. Get a sense if you think you can work with her. Then, if you want to go along, we'll give you a cut of whatever's in the safe. Or you can walk away."

A new song started up, and Trudy stood and tugged on his shirt. "Let's dance and give her a second to think it over."

When they were gone, Ginger wasted no time. "What were you thinking going to see Harlow?"

I pushed the martini away and drank half the glass of water Harlow had asked the server to bring. "The last few jobs I worked for Devon have been where he and I have both been seen. The only exception was the L.A. job, but the place was crawling with vamps, including Lorenzo."

Her eyes went wide.

"Sooner or later, someone's going to put it all together. I wanted to see if Harlow could be trusted as a possible backup. Someone different to send in where I won't be hanging off Devon's arm."

She nodded then picked at the paper napkin that doubled as a coaster. "Change up the scenario so the robberies appear to be different perpetrators."

"I don't know if they're needed, and I haven't discussed it with Devon yet." I rubbed my hands along my black leggings, then pulled at my neckline, needing to get out of the warm club and let the cool night air clear my head. "I needed to know who gave me up."

"Oh, honey. I know. It's just..."

"You don't have to tell me I'm walking a line. But Harlow's right about one thing."

"You need to checkout this new hacker."

"At least meet her. Get a sense of what she's like."

After a minute ticked away, Ginger nodded. "I'll wait here."

I snorted. "That's crazy and not likely."

She ignored me. "I have my phone, the band's not half bad, and there are more than enough people for me to blend in." She winked at me. "Besides, how long does it take you to lift something, assuming you decide to. What, like an hour, two tops?"

"Exactly. Even sooner if she doesn't take to Roxie." Harlow winked at me, too.

I growled at Trudy. "You better not wink at me."

She laughed and punched my arm. "Not in a million years." Then she slammed her fist on the table, making the glasses shake. "Let's go, Harlow. We're on the clock."

"Yes, princess." He gave Ginger a hug. "It was good seeing you, little one. Let's not be strangers, especially now that you're living in plush comfort."

She pushed him away, laughing as she stuck her nose in the air and struck an aristocratic pose. "That'll be the day I'll let riffraff into my home."

"That's what I used to say." Trudy shook her head in mock despair, and they all laughed, except Harlow.

He wrapped an arm around her waist and kissed her on the neck. "You always say the sweetest things."

Once they'd headed for the door, Ginger pulled me close. "You know I trust you, right?"

I nodded.

She glanced toward the door where the two waited. "Just promise me you'll remember the deal you made with Devon."

"And which one was that?"

Her expression hardened into something I rarely saw—Ginger laying down the law. "You know exactly what I'm talking about. Don't do anything that could impact your mission without his approval." Then she moved closer and whispered the rest in the same no-bullshit tone. "I don't know all the little details about your mission, but I can pretty well guess he wouldn't take kindly to finding you in jail for burglary."

I winced. "Jinx me already."

Her face fell. "You know that's not what I meant."

I gave her a quick hug. "Eyes wide open on this one. You have my word."

Her grip on me was fierce, then she pushed me away. "Order me another drink on your way out." Then she winked and turned to the band.

The girl had spunk.

Harlow led us down back alleys until we'd gone a block past the mark. Then he walked us past a short strip of retail shops including one Italian restaurant, a bookstore, and a combination coffeehouse and bakery. I'd have to remember this area; Lucas and Ginger would love it.

We circled the block then returned to the strip of shops, except we were on the opposite side of the street. Harlow stopped next to a cream-colored panel van. It might have been a lighter shade of some other color, but it was difficult to tell with the glare of the streetlights and reflections from the storefront signs.

He tapped the van once and, after a couple seconds, the side door popped open. Harlow nodded at me and slid the door open. I jumped in and stopped. Trudy pushed me forward so Harlow could get in. The inside looked like something you'd expect in any cop surveillance van. We'd never had anything like this before.

I whistled. "An upgrade?"

"That would be me." A small voice floated out from around a high-backed leather chair.

"Pardon me?"

The chair swiveled around, and a young Asian woman stared at me with hard, squinting eyes that peered at me through brilliant pink bangs. "You asked if this van was an upgrade. From what Harlow tells me, you've never worked with a mobile hacker. So, yes, that would make me an upgrade. I'm the van, and the van is me. We're a single unit. You can't have one without the other."

"A real hacker?" The excitement bubbled over, and I felt like doing a little jig. "Hell's bells, tell me I'm not drooling."

Her lips quirked, and I'm pretty sure I was definitely drooling. "You must be Pandora."

Chapter Thirty

I MIGHT HAVE BEEN LATE to the party, but the job was the slickest I'd ever been on. I don't know where Harlow found her, but Roxie was the bomb. Each security sensor popped off before we got there, then turned back on once we were on our way out. I had to admit, I was a bit disappointed I didn't have to climb the outside of the building. From what Roxie said, it was doubtful the security company would even know someone had messed with the sensors. How sweet was that?

I also couldn't deny that over-the-top nipple-tingling excitement of going in stone cold with no idea what to expect. It reminded me of stealing that note under Gruber's nose at the tea party. And for a quick minute, I wondered what happened to that note and whether it helped Devon. Something to store away for later.

The earrings Harlow was looking for were exactly where his contact said they would be. The safe, also high-tech, would have been more of a challenge if the mark had bothered to use something other than the default combination. A tinge of guilt had swept over me stealing from someone I didn't know anything about. Was this just a hard-working woman we were stealing from?

But then Trudy started bitching about her being the spoiled daughter of a multi-millionaire slumlord, who hung out with drug dealers. The kind of slumlord who owned buildings in my old neighborhood with broken heaters, bad plumbing, and leaky roofs. All I had to do was glance around at her ill-gotten wealth, and I grinned in delight when I lifted out three hundred grand in cash and a handful of gold coins. The woman would have the money back in the safe with one call to Daddy. I'd give my share of the take to Bulldog. He'd know the best way to help the neighborhood. It was the best I could do.

We parted company outside the woman's apartment. Roxie shut down the cameras as we each made our way to different exits, me out the back, Harlow and Trudy out the front. Jamal was stationed with a car to pick them up a block down the street. Roxie would stay where she was until the team was across town.

The walk back to the lounge where Ginger waited was exhilarating. In and out in less than an hour. I was buzzed with excitement—the thrill of the job, the score, and a bit of nostalgia. Harlow had definitely upped his game with Roxie. And the best news, with Roxie on board, Harlow had a crew that could be of benefit to Devon's plan. I just had to find a way to broach the subject and convince him without giving away this little escapade.

I hummed to myself as I strode down the alley that led to the lounge when hairs on the back of my neck tickled and brought me to an abrupt stop. For a reason I didn't understand, I slipped into the shadows, vamp quiet, and spent five long minutes scanning the darkness. I almost shook the whole thing off when the slightest movement from the left froze me. Then I noticed movement a few yards on the right. Both figures were positioned at the entrance to the alley, and it didn't take a genius to know they were watching the front door of the lounge.

I don't know how I recognized them as vamps, other than the way they moved, or more accurately—barely moved. But it was more than that. It was the way they lifted their noses to the sky, just like Simone did when she scented something.

A slight breeze rolled in from the coast, and I smiled knowing I was downwind from them. That's why they didn't smell me. I'd stormed down the alley like I owned the world, but with the number of training sessions under my belt, my footsteps had been light. They hadn't heard me.

They were probably from Devon's House, trailing me as a precaution. Yet, my senses stayed on high alert. I backed my way out of the alley and jogged a block over, coming in from behind the lounge and hiding behind a dumpster. This time it took five minutes to spot another vamp. There might have been another one, but if they were out there, they were staying well hidden.

With the front and back doors being watched, would they let me enter?

I should check in with Devon, but he was in another meeting at Oasis, along with Sergi and Simone. Lucas was on assignment. There was only one vamp, and I knew I was being insanely stupid, but what good was my training if I couldn't handle one vamp.

I reached into my jacket and felt the cool touch of my dagger. It was most likely the high I was still on from the job, but I was ready and more than willing. I texted Ginger.

You there?

A long pause before her response. *Just got another drink.*

I'm in the back alley.

Already?

All went well but vamps watch the lounge.

A full thirty seconds rolled by. *Closing out tab. What's the plan?*

Text me at back door. But don't come out.

I split my time between watching the vamp and checking for a new text. It was another five minutes before the vibration signaling an incoming text made me jump.

At the door.

Cross alley to right blue dumpster. Run like there's a Prada sale. Past dumpster to last club. Stay and call help.

What about you?

I'll keep them away.

Cressa?

I'm trained. You're not. Don't argue.

FINE.

I grinned. I needed her to be feisty.

Count three. Run like hell.

I stuffed the phone away, pulled my dagger, and bounced on my toes as I waited. An image of Simone circling me with her fangs bared came to mind, and I couldn't stop the wicked smile. Even miles away, the fierce vamp was my inspiration tonight.

The back door flung open so hard it slammed against the brick wall. A flash of hot pink and curly hair raced across the alley. Ginger made a beeline for the dumpster, then past it.

The vamp hadn't expected it, but it didn't take him long to catch up. He would have caught her before she made it to the end of the alley, except he didn't notice me until he grew even with the dumpster. He wasn't expecting a well-placed kick to the side of his knee as he ran past.

He went down, and I didn't hesitate. I stabbed him in the chest with the dagger and almost stumbled when he released a bloodcurdling scream. I hadn't expected that. Guess that silver really hurt. But he was already rolling to his hands and knees, so I kicked him in the head. When he reached for me, I kicked him in the groin, then again in the ribs.

I glanced back to make sure Ginger had run, but she'd stopped at the alley entrance. I think I'd made a mistake. It appeared I wanted her scared, not feisty. I checked our surroundings as the vamp rolled around, but if there had been another one out there, they'd run. I stabbed again, this time in his side, the blade just missing a rib. I'd been aiming for his chest, but he'd rolled away from me.

This better not be one Devon's vamps, but if he had been, they should have called out. It wasn't like I was doing anything that would kill them, so I stabbed a third time, and closed with one more kick to the head, hoping to disorient him for a while.

Then I ran for Ginger. When I closed in on her, she turned and ran. But she didn't make a right that would take us to the last club. She made a left. How did she run so fast in those damn shoes? I caught up with her two blocks away and pulled her to a stop. We were in a quiet neighborhood, but we needed to be where there were people. Lots and lots of people.

"Where the hell are you going?" I heaved a breath, turning to see if the vamp was behind us. I pulled Ginger into the shadows when someone stumbled out of the alley. Before the first vamp turned our way, the other two vamps stalked down the street toward their buddy.

Shit. Shit. Shit.

Ginger pulled on my arm. "We just need to get to the next block."

I had no idea what she was talking about, but she continued to tug on my arm while I watched all three vamps turn our way and start jogging.

Then I was dragging her with me as I took the lead. I didn't know what was at the next block that would deter three angry vamps. I wasn't familiar with this neighborhood, and the streets seemed too damn quiet.

I didn't bother glancing behind; it would only slow us down. We were breathing hard, air rushing out with heavy pants. The vamps had to be close.

Ginger tugged hard, yanking me to a stop when we reached the magical get-out-of-jail-free block. I was ready to scream at her to fill me in on the secret when a car screeched toward us from the left. It slammed to a stop in front of us. The front passenger-side window was down.

"Get in." Bella made a motion with her hand to speed it up.

I didn't ask. I flung open the door and turned toward the approaching vamps as Ginger dove into the back. They were close enough to see the glow of their eyes and, without a second thought, I jumped in behind her. The car took off before the door slammed shut. I turned around to look out the back. The vamps stared at us speeding away.

"Why didn't you run?" My ragged voice competed with the air I was sucking in.

"I wasn't going to leave you. I called for backup while I was waiting to clear my tab." She was breathing hard, too, but her eyes shined with satisfaction that she'd outsmarted my false bravado.

I glanced to the rearview mirror where Bella's gaze met mine. "Why didn't you show up in the alley?"

I caught the lift of her shoulder and the crinkle of a smile at the corner of her eyes. "It sounded like a solid plan. Hiding in the club would have probably worked, but I was close enough."

"What if something had gone wrong?"

That shrug again. "Then Sergi and Simone would have been disappointed that your training hadn't been good enough."

I stared at her. So did Ginger. And though I still sucked in air like a three-pack-a-day smoker—I laughed.

Then Ginger laughed. Then Bella.

The laughter filled the car, and I rested my head against the soft leather of the sedan.

Ginger grabbed my hand. "God, I feel alive."

I could only shake my head.

When Bella pulled to a stop in front of the mansion, I waited until Ginger got out and reached the steps before asking, "I suppose you have to tell Devon?"

"I have to tell him you had a tail. You were leaving but spotted two vampires crossing the street. I'll also have to tell them you and Ginger sneaked out the back and that you defended an attack by a third vampire before I arrived. He ran off before I could detain him."

She held my stare. Had she been fabricating an alternate story on the drive home? She knew I hadn't come out the back. Had known that I'd originally come from the front before circling around. Bella had been our tail all evening, and I'd never been the wiser. So, why hadn't she called me on it? Of all of Devon's inner circle, Bella was the rebel of the group, almost an outsider. And here she was, giving me the benefit of the doubt for a reason I couldn't explain, and she obviously wasn't going to share. I gave her a slight nod before I opened the car door.

Ginger waited for me on the top step. I raced up and grabbed her arm to pull her inside, and we stormed up the stairs to our rooms.

Ginger hugged me in the hall in front of her door. "That was the most fun I've had for some time."

I stepped back and gave her a stern look that I couldn't hold and just smiled. "Is it us, or is it the company we're keeping that makes us live on the edge?"

"I can't even believe you're asking that."

Her smile was mischievous as she entered her room and waved goodnight.

I stripped off clothes as I made my way across my room to the bathroom. After I peed and brushed my teeth, I crawled into bed and pulled my knees to my chest. The rush of the evening faded as I relived the highlights of the evening.

I'd get a lecture in the morning as soon as Devon heard about it, but that wasn't what bothered me. Who were the vamps, and how had they found us?

Chapter Thirty-One

EARLY THE FOLLOWING MORNING, Devon glared at his tablet after reading Bella's report from the previous evening. He wasn't sure whether to put her on probation for the obvious gaps in the report or race upstairs and pin Cressa against the wall for her foolishness.

He couldn't stop the heat that rose in him when he considered the two times he'd actually done just that. When his beast had risen to the surface. He'd smelled her fear, her anger, and something more delicious—her attraction to him. Even with his burning fear for her, and the force required to keep the beast at bay, he knew exactly where a third encounter would likely end. The both of them tangled in the sheets of her bed.

He blew out a frustrated sigh, keeping his expression bored, knowing Lucas watched him. He could put Bella on probation for letting the evening get away from her, but it would be a knee-jerk reaction the rest of his guards would know was more personal than professional. Besides, Bella wasn't the only one of his guards that had grown protective of Cressa. Holy hell, they all had. Even Simone. The one who was the least to cave to any human, to show any amount of concern or, god forbid, friendship. Yet, there it was. The more Simone denied it, the more he knew it was true.

He tossed the tablet on the desk. Cressa had gotten home just a few short hours ago. He didn't have the energy to deal with facing a badly woken Cressa. Not when she wouldn't back down from what she'd done. Christ. Fended off a vampire by herself. He just couldn't understand why the two of them felt the need to run. Maybe Ginger had been too frightened, considering her last run-in with vampires.

"Is everything all right?" Lucas asked.

He rubbed his face. "We had a difficult enough mission ahead of us. Everything intricately planned over the last two years. In my need to help Lyra, I hadn't given any consideration to the chaos a dreamwalker might bring. Let alone its impact on her."

"I'm not sure anyone could have predicted that, let alone believe a dreamwalker actually existed." Lucas scratched his chin and rose to make espressos. Devon sometimes thought he received visits from his guards for the coffee more than a need to check-in with him. "But you didn't bring Cressa onboard because you thought she was a dreamwalker."

He grimaced. "You're right. I brought a thief into the house. I'm not sure that was any better."

"Yet, she's retrieved two critical items necessary to appeal the censure on your Council seat. And now she's given us a new lead with Philipe Renaud."

He took the cup from Lucas and immediately drank half. He wasn't sure he needed anymore caffeine, but he had a long day ahead of him. "There seems to be more mysteries and not near enough answers. We need to pursue the lead Willa gave us. If nothing more than to understand why Lorenzo is so interested in the necklace. It might have nothing to do with our mission, but if it's important to him, I can't help but think it's important to us."

"The possible source is in New Orleans, right?"

He picked up the crystal and rubbed its rough edges. "I know the timing is bad, but I'll need to go down there myself, assuming I can get Renaud's permission to enter."

"Is it worth spending the time tracking down Philipe and the book with everything else going on?" Lucas's tone came across as disinterest, just a good guard considering the best path forward, but Devon saw past that. Lucas wanted to track down the book. The minute the Renaud Libraries were mentioned, Lucas had jumped at building a file on it. He believed in the Keepers of Knowledge as Devon did, and the importance of keeping their origins, their history, and culture alive.

He gave Lucas a tired smile. "In the scope of our mission and all this business with dreamwalkers, Magic Poppy, and a shifter massacre, taking time to find some ancient text seems like lunacy." He turned to gaze out at the soft morning light, only an hour since sunrise. One of the most beautiful times of day.

When he turned back to Lucas, his resolve had never been more certain. "I can't explain it. Call it a hunch or some voice in my head, perhaps some long ago dream, but that book could hold the key that unlocks everything."

Lucas never dropped his gaze from his, the only hint of emotion set in the deep lines marring his forehead. "Or it could hold nothing at all." His voice was filled with the haunting promise of loss and disappointment.

"Or nothing at all." He set the crystal on his desk, and his fangs inched down. "But if that turns out to be the end result, we won't be the only ones disappointed."

Lucas nodded. "The other vampires who appear to be searching for the book. Which reminds me, where's Sergi? Wasn't he trying to determine who the vampires were from last night?"

"He messaged that something had come up, and he'd be late." Devon checked his watch. "But he should have returned by now." He checked his tablet but no new messages. "I need to see the guard schedule for the next two weeks and which family members are being assigned to the cases we have going. You're the lead for finding that book. Sergi and Decker will continue their investigation into the dead shifters and the Magic Poppy outbreak. I still believe those two incidents are related."

He'd finally updated his cadre about the Magic Poppy during their three-day meeting at Oasis. They'd been unhappy but understood his reluctance to bring them in too soon. And he'd decided then and there—no more secrets.

He continued with his agenda, "Simone has her hands full with Oasis. Bella will be responsible for guarding Cressa and Ginger until your mission is complete."

Lucas took notes in his own tablet. He didn't need to. Vampires remembered everything, but mistakes happened, and Devon preferred a trail, so his entire guard was up to speed on all active assignments.

"And you?" Lucas glanced up from his notes.

"I'll be tracking down the dreamwalker connection until something else requires my attention. We also have one last missing artifact to complete our plans for Lorenzo. Something tells me, any one of these other issues could alter our course, or with any luck, maybe do part of our work for us..." Before he could continue his thought, the emergency ring from his phone caught them both by surprise.

Devon grabbed his phone, noted Sergi's handle, and answered with the speakerphone. "What?"

"Underwood's been murdered."

THE SEDAN RACED through the streets in the early morning hours of a sleepy Santiga Bay, but I imagine any town would be quite this early on a Sunday, except for early church risers. I sipped the coffee Cook had been kind enough to hand me on my race out the door.

Christopher dead. Murdered.

What had the fool expected working with a vamp? I gave Devon a side glance, feeling somewhat silly since I also worked for one. But Christopher had been working with Lorenzo, who wasn't nearly the vamp Devon was.

Although, I had to admit I didn't know much about Lorenzo other than what Devon or his cadre shared. I'd only met the vamp on a few short occasions, but those encounters had told me all I needed to know. And knowing Christopher as I did, with his shady dealings and even shadier friends, the man's eventual link to Lorenzo hadn't been that surprising once I had time to think it through.

What would my mother and April think? What would they do? In the end, they'd be wealthy and relieved to not have to deal with the asshole. When Devon had barged into my room, tossing me from bed with the news, I'd wanted to call my mother until he rightly pointed out she probably hadn't been told yet.

The police had discovered his body less than two hours earlier and were still working the crime scene. Sergi had heard the call over a police scanner and arrived before forensics. Either through some arrangement with the local cops or with mesmerizing, Sergi got the okay for Devon and me to enter the crime scene.

I glanced out the window. A jolt hit me, and I almost dropped my mug. The neighborhood Bella drove us through was where Ginger and I had been clubbing. Where I'd worked the job with Harlow. Where we'd run from the unknown vamps.

My gaze shifted to Bella, but she kept her focus on the road, only occasionally checking the rearview mirror. I sucked down the coffee, still hot in its insulated cup, but I barely registered the heat as she slowed, turning into a back alley no more than a block from the main strip of clubs.

My blood turned to ice as I peered through the front window to see the line of squad cars, unmarked vehicles, and the crime scene van. I couldn't look at Devon, though I felt his warm gaze on me.

"Maybe I shouldn't have brought you." He slid closer and touched my shoulder. "Are you all right?"

I leaned against his shoulder, and he wrapped an arm around me. "I'm in shock, I guess. But I don't think I'm surprised."

The passenger door opened, but it wasn't Bella who'd opened it. Sergi stuck his head in.

"We don't have much time. They want to move the body. The detective is an old friend, and he's aware of who we are. I told him we were working a case that might have crossed with this. He's given us ten minutes to review the scene."

He held out a hand for me. I set the coffee cup in a holder and got out. Devon scooted across the seat and exited behind me, and though he didn't touch me, he stuck close. Close enough I could feel little flickers of his breath against my temple when he turned his head toward me.

I took in the scene, forcing myself to look at it with dispassionate interest, forgetting for a moment that I knew the victim.

Sergi walked on our right. "How are you holding up?"

Everyone so concerned about the delicate little human. "I'm fine. Just wondering what took so long."

When he gave me a questioning look, I shrugged. "Even if Christopher hadn't been involved with Lorenzo, this ending was only a matter of time. He's worked with questionable business partners for a long time. It wouldn't surprise me if this had nothing to do with magical creatures."

I didn't have to watch the two vamps to know they were making eye contact, wondering how dark Christopher's past might be. The things they didn't know or hadn't yet uncovered. All part of the brutal truth as to why I'd run after graduation, knowing I was leaving April behind. But April was his daughter. I wasn't. It didn't get any more complex than that.

Sergi stopped us when we were six feet from the limo. "They don't have a lot at the moment. The limo was rented from a private party. No one knows where the driver is. There's no evidence that he was harmed or had anything to do with this, but they're looking for him. There's no murder weapon and no sign of robbery."

"Do they know if anyone else was with him?" Devon had gone still, his nose slightly lifted. He was assessing the scene with all of his senses. Then his gaze pinned on me. "This might not be anything you want to see."

"She needs to see it." Sergi didn't look at either of us. "You'll see why. And they're not sure if there was anyone else with him. They'll need to wait for the crime scene report to determine that. Unless they find the driver alive."

A chill blew down my spine, but I squared my shoulders. "Let's just get this over with."

My first step was faulty, but it could have been from not enough caffeine after a late night. But an early morning with little coffee and even less sleep didn't explain the raging tremors as I took one step after another. The drips of blood were apparent as I grew closer, and with each step even more of it appeared.

That wasn't the horrible part. The smell was. The thick coppery scent of blood mixed with the smell of decay already working through the body. When I stepped next to the door, mindful of where I stepped, my hand flew to my mouth.

Blood. So much blood.

It was everywhere—on the cream-colored upholstery, the carpet, the windows, the doors. A deeper smear formed a wide arc as the blood had spurted from his body. It was probably from the killing blow. The rest appeared to be done after, as if in a rage. But what did I know? I wasn't big on the forensic TV shows.

Christopher was dressed in a somber charcoal suit, the coat unbuttoned, and no tie that I could see. His shirt had also been unbuttoned or ripped apart. A wide gash at his throat was plainly visible even through the splatter of blood that now clotted over his throat, chest, and suit. Other slashes had been carved across his chest and stomach. The seat looked like someone had dumped a bucket of red paint. It was a pool of crimson gore, congealing as if it were blood pudding.

I took a step back, but Devon was there. His hard body pressed to mine, his arm around my middle, holding me up as he provided comfort. Or maybe he needed someone to hold onto as he reviewed the carnage.

"Come around to this other side. You need to see what was left on the seat." Sergi took my arm and led me around the vehicle, taking a wide berth to keep me away from any possible evidence that might be outside the vehicle.

Devon put an arm around my shoulder as we both stepped close enough to see the piece of paper, no larger than a greeting card. It had been wrinkled as if it had been folded and unfolded dozens of times. Droplets of blood were sprinkled across the page as if someone had used a spray bottle. Splotches of red on a snow-white page.

Any doubt whether this involved vamps evaporated like ash. Which is what I tasted in my mouth, along with the bile that crept up my throat.

The image had been hand drawn, but there was no doubt what it was.

It was the perfect image of my necklace. The one my father had left for me. The one my mother had given back. The one thing that could connect me to this brutality.

I felt nothing as Devon led me away. Not the warmth of his touch, the blowing heat he asked Bella to turn on, nor the rays of sunlight glaring through the window. The tremors only got worse.

Devon positioned me in the middle of the back seat so the heat would blast on me, which put me in direct line of sight with Bella whenever she looked in the rearview mirror.

I only had to glance at her once to see the question in her eyes. Where had I gone last night?

Chapter Thirty-Two

LUCAS WAITED NEXT to the massive oak door as Bella pulled to a stop in front of the steps. Devon got out first and raced around the sedan to open the door, holding a hand out to Cressa. When she didn't appear, he stuck his head in.

"Cressa?"

She startled and turned to him, her expression sheepish. "Sorry. I was miles away."

"Understandable. Come. Let's get inside and warm up. Brandy or hot chocolate? Your choice."

She scooted to the edge and grabbed his hand. Hers were ice cold. "They both sound good."

"Together?" He gave an exaggerated shiver and scrunched his face in distaste. "That would be horrible."

She laughed. A good sign. "You'd be surprised."

He put an arm around her as they walked up the steps even though she was steady on her feet. It felt good to hold her, but she was still pale.

When they reached the door, Lucas took her hand. "Ginger has a hot bath ready for you."

"I'm not an invalid, you know." She still held a smile, but he could hear the annoyance.

By Lucas's expression, he could also. "Maybe not. But you're shivering and ice cold. You must know you're in shock."

She didn't argue and let him lead her up the stairs. Lucas gave him a nod before they turned down the hall.

Devon strode to his office, his thoughts moving away from Cressa and to more pressing matters. Like who the hell had killed Underwood.

Sergi and Bella waited in his office.

"How did you get back before us?" Devon picked up the glass of scotch that one of them had waiting for him.

"Bella drives like an old woman." Sergi had his tablet out, scrolling through pages of what were most likely his notes from the scene.

"Shut it, old man." Bella stood next to the espresso counter.

"Bella, take a seat," Devon said. When she hesitated, he added, "You have a habit of hovering, and it can be annoying."

She did as he asked, though her scowl told him she only did it because it had been a command.

"With that drawing of the necklace, that puts Cressa on the suspect list." Sergi continued to scroll. "It will take the police a day or two before they discover the connection. They'll notify the wife and daughter. The detective said they'd wait a day before questioning them, depending on their reaction to the news. He'd like to have a preliminary report before moving forward with the formal interviews."

"That seems rather cordial." He searched his desk before pulling out pen and paper.

"The Underwoods, whether we like it or not, are upstanding citizens and philanthropists. The police will need to act accordingly or hear from the mayor."

"God forbid the wealthy are disturbed for something as messy as the murder of one of their own." He jotted down a few notes from what he'd observed at the scene. "Bella, did you see the women meet up with anyone while clubbing last night. Or see anything strange?"

She leaned against the counter and stared up at the ceiling, a normal pose when she thought. After a few moments, she lowered her head. "I didn't have eyes on them all the time. The couple times I saw them on the street, it was just the two of them." She paused. "There was a couple that followed them into the last club they were in. They all seemed friendly, but they'd been moving from club to club. You know how chatty Ginger gets after a few drinks."

Sergi, in his normal deadpan expression, said, "She's chatty without drinks."

Bella remained detached, but Devon had to grin. Sergi wasn't wrong. Regardless of what friends they might have picked up along the way, they couldn't prove without a doubt where the women had been all evening. Sergi would speak with them, but if they had a story to cook up, they were probably running through it while Cressa bathed.

He shook his head and reviewed the notes he'd scratched down. The words were a jumble of first impressions—the condition of Underwood's body, the possible methods of killing from the perspective of human, shifter, and vampire, and lastly, everything about the necklace including the paper it had been written on and how well it had been rendered. As if someone had a recent firsthand look at it or had seen it in another drawing or book.

He'd kept his eyes on Cressa from the moment they drove into the alley until Lucas took her down the hall to Ginger. She'd already been a bit shaky on the drive over, but when she looked into the limo, the horror on her face wasn't an act. Her face had drained of all color, and her hands were ice. When he'd caught a whiff of her, his senses confirmed both anger, fear, and most importantly, shock. Unfortunately, his reading of her emotions wouldn't confirm her innocence with the police.

"Your thoughts?" He turned to Sergi.

"I'd like to see the coroner's report. I need a better look at the cut radius. My initial assessment ruled out shifters. The slices appeared to have smooth edges, so I assume the coroner will suggest some form of sharp instrument as the murder weapon. I suppose that doesn't completely rule out a shifter, but it would be a rare occurrence."

"Not if someone is trying to pin this on Cressa." Bella was hovering again, but he let her be.

"Maybe." Sergi responded when it seemed Devon wasn't going to. "But that assumes the police are being led to believe whoever has the necklace was the killer. If Cressa was the killer, why would she leave such damning evidence behind?"

"The police might think she was rattled afterward. People who commit rage killings aren't usually thinking straight," Bella countered.

"Agreed." Sergi placed his tablet on the desk and turned toward her. "But what if the killing was an execution due to an unsatisfactory performance? The drawing the reason for the hit, or more accurately, his failure to obtain it was his undoing. This would make the drawing a message to others of what happens when you don't perform."

"Or a way to draw out the one who has the necklace." Devon's blood chilled at his own enlightenment.

Sergi and Bella both nodded as they each mentally raced through the implications.

Bella was the first to respond. "If anyone discovers Cressa has the necklace, it could lead Lorenzo straight to your doorstep."

Sergi gave Devon his first concerned look of the morning. "Perhaps this would be a good time for that visit to New Orleans."

～

THE BREEZE off the ocean was cooler than yesterday, and I wrapped the blanket tighter. High-peaked clouds were nothing more than a haze far off on the horizon. Perhaps a spring storm was on its way. Or maybe it was the gods sending me a rare gift in an attempt to wash away the earlier images of a horrific death.

After Lucas had delivered me to my room where Ginger waited with a hot bath, I made Ginger leave. She'd wanted to talk but had guessed correctly that I needed time to process the last few hours.

When she'd gone, I drained the tub, preferring the stinging beads of a hot shower. I blow-dried my hair until every drop of moisture had been whipped from it, dressed in my sweats and sweater, then sat in front of the cold hearth. Too tired to start a fire, I found an extra blanket and wrapped myself in it. I was still chilled to the bone with dozens of thoughts bouncing around in my head, yet I couldn't sit still.

I found my way to the kitchen and mumbled something about hot chocolate and brandy. Devon's last words to me were the only thing I seemed capable of holding onto. I must have said something else because Cook pushed me out the door, and next thing I knew I was on the widow's walk. Maybe not the best place to be, but the wind on my face worked as well as rain.

I don't know how long I stared out to sea before I heard the barest sound of footsteps. Maybe it wasn't their sound but the connection between us that told me Devon had found me. I closed my eyes, not wanting to see his condemnation, his questions, or anything to do with reality.

"I intercepted Cook on his way here. It's not often he leaves the kitchen for any place other than the dining room."

His words wrapped around me like a warm blanket. Not enough to stop the soft tremble in my hands or legs, but enough for me to turn to him. I couldn't help but smile at the insulated mug one would expect to find coffee. Somehow, I'd expected a big cup that could have been used for soup, but the one he held would keep the hot chocolate hot.

He handed it to me, his hand brushing mine. "How are you?"

I took the mug, and when I opened it, the combined scents of chocolate and brandy rushed over me. For an instant, I remembered the sweet taste of his blood. The spicy drink warmed me even though I hadn't taken a sip. Then I did, and I closed my eyes as the ice fell away like glaciers calving into the sea.

"Better now." I turned toward the ocean and waited for Devon to step close, our arms touching.

"I asked Sergi to stay involved with the investigation."

"Doesn't he have enough to do?"

He laughed. "He's good at multitasking."

"You know this is going to blow back on me. This will impact your mission."

He turned me to face him and lifted my chin. I closed my eyes. "Look at me. Look at me and tell me you didn't do this."

It took me a moment, and when I opened them, I could tell by his raised brow he'd seen the anger burning in them. "You think I could have done this?"

"No." Not a second of hesitation. "I wanted to hear you say it. I can see the frustration in your eyes, hear it in your voice. But I also see doubt and fear. That with your history with Underwood, no one will believe you didn't do it."

There wasn't much I could add. He'd wrapped it up rather succinctly. And when it appeared he wasn't going to let go of my chin until I said what he wanted to hear, I caved.

"I didn't do it." Each word whispered in short gasps.

His sapphire-blue gaze held mine. "I believe you."

When he finally released my chin, he steered me to a chair like I was some feeble old woman who couldn't think straight or put one foot in front of the other. Though he might have been right on the latter. He took the seat next to me, holding my hand while I sipped brandy-laced cocoa with the other. He rubbed his thumb over the soft web of flesh between my thumb and forefinger, and a low hum ran through me, soothing my nerves. My shoulders dropped, and I snuggled into the blanket. Content.

Until Devon went where I didn't want him to go. He'd been prepping me like some smooth-talking trial lawyer.

"Was it just seeing him dead or the manner of his death that bothered you most? You seemed more shook-up than I expected."

I took a longer swig of the cocoa, giving me time to sort thoughts I'd already tucked away. "I'm not sure how I feel about it. It's been something I've been wishing for years. But now..." All I saw were Christopher's expensive oxfords in a thick puddle of blood. A slow stream drained from his wounds. There had been so much blood pooled on the seat that a thin trail flowed to the edge. Every few seconds a drop would fall and thud into the puddle below. Bile rose, and I used the cocoa to wash away the foul taste. "This has to be a vamp kill. Lorenzo no longer having use for him. Right?"

"It's one of our suspicions, but until we see the lab results, we won't have the information we need to determine if it was a knife, vampire, or shifter that killed him. From there we can determine possible motives. But with the sketch of the necklace, it's a reasonable assumption to suspect Lorenzo."

He never let go of my hand as time passed, and we stared out to sea. The sun had risen high enough to warm this side of the house, and I let the blanket drop to my waist.

"What else aren't you telling me?" I glanced at him, and his jaw tightened. "Just get it out."

"Our leading scenario is that Lorenzo killed Underwood, or more likely had him killed, then left the drawing of the necklace on purpose."

"As a sign of what happens when you don't complete a mission." If I heard the doubt in my voice, I'm sure he had, too. When he didn't respond, I reconsidered his words. A dawning realization squeezed with an icy grip, and I pulled the blanket back up. "Not a sign of failure but a lure."

I turned to Devon, and he nodded.

"It was a smart move. Get rid of a risky, too-flashy partner who's probably overstayed his value, and let the police dig up possible candidates. Then Lorenzo can sweep in and pick them off until he finds the necklace."

"So now what?"

"Now we go on a trip."

I snorted. "I'm pretty sure a murder case stays open until someone is caught."

"We just need to be gone long enough for Sergi to confirm our suspicions. Then we'll know how to move forward discreetly. Until then..." He fished into his pocket for something, then handed me a small business card.

"Colantha Dupré, New Orleans." I rubbed the card. Fine linen. Expensive. "My mother gave you this."

"Yes."

"Do you think my father is alive?"

He released a long sigh that gave me my answer, but he put it into words anyway. "I don't know. But I don't think Willa would have given me this much if it wasn't going to lead somewhere." He pushed a lock of hair behind my ear. "She really does want what's best for you."

My laugh was bitter with all she'd hidden from me. "That doesn't mean finding my father."

"Perhaps. But I do believe she wants you to learn how to control your dreams."

"This could be a dead end. Then what?"

He took the mug from my hand, then knelt in front of me. Like that wouldn't terrify a person. He wasn't going to ask me to marry him, so this had to be really bad news.

"Before we leave for New Orleans in the morning, I need to tell you about the woman on the third floor."

Chapter Thirty-Three

WE'D MOVED to my room, and now I sat in front of the fireplace, my chair turned toward the door, Devon in a chair next to me. He ran a hand through his hair and sat back. If I'd expected him to launch into his story, I should have known better.

After he dropped his bombshell on the widow's walk, neither of us spoke as he led me downstairs. He'd stopped at my door long enough to send a text, then pointed toward the fireplace that still hadn't been lit. That was okay. I wasn't cold anymore. I was simmering on a slow boil and was tired of waiting for him to get his thoughts in order.

"Does this have anything to do with the woman who visits the gravesites? Is she one in the same?"

"Her name is Lyra."

I blinked. "I knew it."

"You were a stranger in the house, and I couldn't put her at risk. When the shared dreams began, I could only hope the miracle I'd been searching decades for had simply walked into my life."

Okay. That was a lot to unload.

"Lyra is my sister. Though many years separate our ages, she's quite dear to me. She's my one remaining true blood family."

Sister. I breathed a sigh of relief as thoughts of *Jane Eyre* and a crazy wife in the attic flitted through my head.

"She's suffered from nightmares for decades. But not ordinary dreams. She claims they're other people's dreams that she's pulled into. Realistic dreams, as if she's really in another place."

I fell back. Was she like me? "A dreamwalker?"

He shook his head. "She's vampire. From what I've discerned —and you have to understand that I've dug through hundreds of books searching for any mythical legends about dreamwalkers— one can be one or the other but not both. Anything written on the topic is extremely rare, but it appears that dreamwalkers are a different species in the way vampires, shifters, and humans are all different."

"And these dreams she's pulled into, does she recognize anyone?" I wasn't sure that was the best question, considering everything he just dumped on me, but there was someone else experiencing what I was. It was hard to track what that meant.

"I believe another dreamwalker is trying to communicate with her. Or perhaps they have, and she simply refuses to share the details." His laugh was short and possibly half-mad. "For all that she's suffered these years, she has a strong personality, and while she has her—I suppose episodes is the best word for it—she does what she wants and when she wants, though she's learned to live within certain boundaries."

I leapt up and began pacing. Devon stopped talking and simply watched me as I blazed a trail over the carpet. The woman I'd seen at the grave markers was thin and on the smaller side. I'd only seen drapes shift in the third-floor window. Was it a trick of the light or had I spotted a flash of blonde hair?

"She was the woman in the shifter house. The one with my necklace." I had turned to face him, and his expression confirmed it.

Before my legs gave out, I made it back to my chair, and he took my hands again. His were so warm, mine must be freezing.

"I don't know how it happened. The two of us never shared a dream. It's only happened with you. Maybe if she'd been able to share with me, I would have been able to help her sooner."

"It was the necklace." Nothing else made sense. And I croaked out a laugh. Did any of this?

"That's my belief as well."

"Did she fall into a coma afterwards?"

He shook his head. "I want you to meet her."

I nodded. "Yes." Maybe he was right, and she wasn't a dreamwalker, but it appeared she could control the necklace. Maybe control was too strong a word, but she could wear the necklace without repercussions.

There was a brief knock at the door before it opened. I hadn't expected the meeting to be right now.

Sergi walked in holding the hands of a pixie. There wasn't any other word for it. She was tiny, yet it was easy to see she wasn't a child. Though slight of build, she filled out her diaphanous gown with all the right curves.

She gripped Sergi's hand, but there wasn't any fear in her shocking blue eyes, so similar to Devon's. And though her hair was a light golden blonde to his darker ash color, the resemblance was obvious from the eyes to the nose. But her lips were different.

She never took her eyes from me as the two walked hesitantly toward me.

"Hello, Cressa." Her voice was like lyrics on the wind. Her eyes smiled at me, though her lips barely twitched. So like Devon.

"Hello, Lyra."

She seemed to like that. We stared at each other for what seemed like forever until Devon cleared his throat.

"Do you have something to say to Cressa?"

Her gaze dropped, and while her expression came across as sheepish, I caught the rebellious glance she gave him. Good grief, I knew that look. She could have been my twin.

"I'm sorry for taking your necklace without permission."

I laughed. I couldn't help it. The little imp was an exact duplicate of me. A quiet soul as she hid in her room, her fake ladylike responses, the rebel she tried to hide—had I been that transparent growing up? She was me right down to her sticky fingers.

"Should we sit?" Sergi asked.

Lyra tugged on his hand as she backed up. "Not now. This isn't the right time." Then she pulled away from his hand and ran for Devon. She jumped into his lap, surprising him as much as Sergi.

She hugged him before kissing his forehead then placing her palm on his cheek. "It will all work out. She'll save you. You'll see."

Then she jumped off and almost skipped back to Sergi to clasp his hand. She stared up at him. "I want to go back to my room now."

They were almost out the door when she tugged Sergi to a stop and turned to me. "It was nice meeting you, Cressa. We'll see each other soon."

Then they were gone.

I stared at the door for several minutes before turning to Devon. "What the hell?"

He shrugged. "Her words rarely make sense. But I think she's prescient. Just like you."

"Like I said, what the hell?"

He reached over and stroked my cheek, and I covered his hand with my own. "I know this is a lot to take in. I've not been able to put much together, but that's why we need to either find your father or someone who can tell us about the necklace and the dreams."

I had dozens of questions but no idea where to begin. I needed time to soak it in and put some type of order to it. So, I asked the one thing foremost on my list. "What time do we leave?"

❧

Thank You For Reading!
But don't go! Keep reading for more Cressa and Devon.

AN ENEMY STRIKES WITHOUT WARNING. A cunning attempt to take down the House Trelane.

They say cut off the head and the snake will perish. But when it's Devon Trelane they want to take down, they might discover the snake has many heads.

Cressa must admit to her growing attachment to Devon and hope it will enough to save him from his old demons. And to succeed, she'll need to learn everything she can, as quickly as she can, about controlling her dreams and how to use them to her advantage.

And now... (with a placeholder cover)

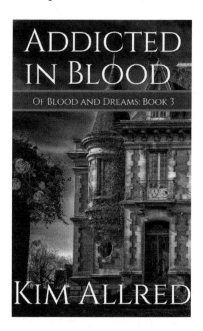

Addicted in Blood

~

Prologue

The beast lumbers through the dark, empty streets. He stops and lifts his nose to the air. His blood stirs at the scent. He doesn't run, but his pace quickens as he moves toward his prey.

They're close.

More than one, and his hunger calls to him. Ravenous. Burning. Unquenchable. And the beast rages from within, demanding to be fully released to hunt and eat.

He turns down an ally. His prey stands in the shadows. Two of them. They hold long sticks in their hands, but he is not afraid.

He slows, slipping through the shadows like his prey; his movements silent in the night. Yet, they turn toward him. Somehow, they know where he is.

He stops and lifts his nose in the air one last time. The scent is sweet. The meal worthy.

He springs, and is if perfectly choreographed, a blinding white light fills the sky. The shadows are gone and so is his prey. He falls back and snarls, raising an arm across his face, shielding his sensitive eyes from the light as fierce as the noonday sun.

Someone calls a name. A distant memory flickers. The voice— at first familiar and then not.

He turns and runs. The voices trail behind—urgent and incessant.

The corner. He must get to the corner. Safety. Without warning, a net falls from the sky, but it misses him. He runs and runs until his legs are leaden and the streets are far behind him. There is nothing but forest and the cool ocean air. When he reaches the familiar den in the base of a large cedar, he crawls in and pulls his knees to his chest and fights against the pain that fills his joints.

He howls at his hunger.

$$\sim$$

Chapter 1

I ZIPPED up my duffel bag then dropped my overnight bag on top of it. Devon didn't mention how long we'd be in New Orleans, but knowing him, if I didn't pack the right clothes, he'd simply buy me new ones. It was annoying but saved on shopping and worrying about what to bring.

Last night, after my introduction to Lyra, Devon's sister, who'd been living in secret on the third floor like a bad family secret, Devon and I had discussed our next plans. Number one on his list was finding the person who might be able to tell me about my dreams. My mother had given him a name and a city, now we just had to find them.

He'd wanted to get an early start, so I was surprised when I woke to find the sun already up. He must have decided to let me sleep in, and while I didn't want to look a gift horse in the mouth, I could have slept on the plane.

I moved the two bags to outside my bedroom door, knowing Sergi or Lucas would have them put in the car. There wasn't anyone in the dining room, so I backtracked to Devon's office. The door was closed, but I knocked and waited a full minute, surprised when he didn't respond.

I knocked again, then turned the handle and peered in. If he was in conference with his personal guards, I wanted to give him enough time to shout an order to close the door. When that didn't come, but a cacophony of voices immediately ceased, I threw the door wide.

His entire cadre of personal guards—Simone, Sergi, Lucas, and Bella—stood around Devon's desk. Jacques, who always seemed to tag along with Bella, his usual partner, was also present.

Devon's chair was empty.

"Where's Devon?" A pit opened in my stomach when they all stared at me, leaving me shaky with a rapidly growing anxiety. They didn't have to say it. They were hoping I knew.

"That answers that question." Sergi rifled through a folder on Devon's desk.

"Come in, Cressa." Simone's face revealed nothing.

I walked in and leaned against the sofa that faced the cold fire-place, telling myself it was to keep distance between me and the vamps and nothing to do with my unsteady legs.

"He was supposed to have someone wake me for an early flight." The words trickled out of my mouth as if his cadre didn't know his schedule to the minute. Based on him not being here, I guessed not every minute.

"Someone must have seen him leave." Simone sat in his chair and rifled through his top drawer. "He usually keeps his calendar in here."

"He left my room about twenty minutes after he introduced me to Lyra." I inched along the sofa, worry overtaking any concern that I was alone with five well-trained, highly dangerous, agitated vamps.

Everyone but Sergi turned to me.

"Let's save that for another time." Sergi turned back to his tablet.

"Where's his tablet?" I had to ask, though they probably covered that before I arrived.

"We haven't located his phone or tablet." Lucas seemed more troubled than the others. "Taking his phone makes sense, but he doesn't always take his tablet." He jumped up and moved to the espresso machine. Though no one had asked, he started making drinks. "It was my turn to watch Ginger, and I left before six."

Simone continued her search in a drawer to her left. "I was at Oasis until Sergi called this morning. The last time I spoke to Devon was a couple of days ago."

Eyes turned to Bella and Jacques, and though I expected Bella to respond it was Jacques instead. "We had the day off and had gone down to the city." Which meant San Fransisco, which was a couple of hours drive south of Santiga Bay. We got back around two a.m. Instead of staying at the mansion, we continued on to the safe house."

"The sedan was pulling out of the driveway when we drove past." Bella finished the story. "We both thought it was Sergi."

Lucas dropped cups of espresso in front of Simone and Sergi, then picked up the phone. He whispered something into it, waited a moment, and hung up before moving back to the coffee bar. "The sedan is still gone. According to Mateo, Devon didn't say anything about where he was going or how long he'd be gone. He was polite, but there was an edge to his tone." He shrugged. "That could be Devon on any given day."

"I assume everyone checked their messages?" My question sounded lame. Of course they would do that, but sometimes in the heat of the moment, the simplest of things were overlooked. I reached for my back pocket, a reflexive habit, then remembered I'd left my phone in my overnight bag after checking for messages. There hadn't been any.

No one seemed to think the question stupid because they all nodded.

"Ah, here it is." Simone closed the drawer to the right. "That's unusual." Her blank expression didn't falter. She never let her emotions show when she was working, but I caught the glance she gave Sergi, and the pit in my gut turned into a hole the size of a meteor. A large meteor. Like apartment sized. I could only assume by her earlier statement that Devon never left his calendar in that drawer. Was that a message in itself or just a sign of being distracted?

She flipped through the pages until settling on one which would either reflect yesterday or the entire week. I couldn't see the pages, so it might have been a monthly calendar. I found it odd that he would use a paper calendar rather than his tablet. Perhaps he kept two calendars for some reason, then I remembered him writing letters with a fountain pen and linen paper. A man caught between two worlds—the old and the new.

"He doesn't have any specific meeting listed for last night or this morning." Sergi stood behind her, reading over her shoulder. He pointed to something. "What's that mark?"

Simone frowned. "He left a message. This is strange. He hasn't used symbols for some time."

"Symbols." Sergi moved back to his tablet. "I'm not sure I still have the legend to decipher it."

Bella moved to lean over the desk. "Don't bother. I recognize it."

Sergi's brows rose. "You weren't even around when we used symbols as messages." He didn't appear to think she was lying, he was just curious. A ding from his tablet distracted him.

"Devon asked Jacques and I to use the old system when we started trailing Venizi. He didn't want anything traceable." She jutted her chin toward the calendar. "That symbol means he's taking a secret meeting with someone who isn't a friendly."

"Is there a message drop to know who he was meeting with?"

"Sometimes. But usually not until we know the information is good."

"I don't think we have to guess anymore." When Sergi looked up, his face was one I never hoped to see again. It was a strange combination of fear, anger, and disbelief. "Councilmember Boretsky was found dead this morning. His throat had been ripped out. Devon's sedan is in the parking lot."

He stared at Simone. "They found a vial of Magic Poppy in the front console."

Thank you for Reading

Don't miss out on the release of *Addicted in Blood*, Of Blood & Dreams, Book 3

Coming Spring 2023

IN THE MEANTIME, consider downloading a **free prequel** to the Of Blood and Dreams series - *Lyra*. This novella is set one-hundred years before the start of the series.

Lyra
The catalyst. The victim. The bridge.

The Roaring Twenties. The time of flappers and Prohibition.

For Lyra, a young vampire and aspiring painter, the world is her canvas.

When she meets Hamilton, a sculptor and her family's gardener, time stops. He understands her like no one else.

But he's a human. And he's not the only one who's drawn to her. An ancient and powerful vampire has declared his desire to seduce her.

A perfect storm that sets the stage for all that is to come.

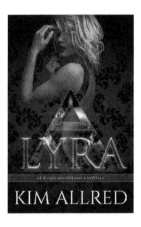

MAKE sure you never miss a new release!

Follow me at Amazon, Goodreads, or BookBub

Join my newsletter or FB Readers Group - Kim Allred's Heart Racing Romance

If you can't wait and want to get more information on my other series, check out my website.

About the Author

Kim Allred lives in an old timber town in the Pacific Northwest where she raises alpacas, llamas and an undetermined number of free-range chickens. Just like most of her characters, she loves sharing stories while sipping a glass of fine wine or slurping a strong cup of brew.

Her spirit of adventure has taken her on many journeys including a ten-day dogsledding trip in northern Alaska and sleeping under the stars on the savannas of eastern Africa.

Kim is currently working on the final books for the Mórdha

Stone Chronicles series and the next books in her paranormal romance series — Of Blood and Dreams. The first book in her new time travel romance series - Time Renegades - is on the horizon.

For more books and updates:
www.kimallred.com